M.J.,

MW00789464

YOURS
ALWAYS

It was such an
honor meeting you at BWAE'17.
I'm so glad you enjoyed
Sletcher's story!

RHONDA R. DENNIS

All the Best,

Rhonda Dennis

Yours Always

Copyright © 2014 RHONDA R. DENNIS

This is a work of fiction. Names, characters, places, and incidents are either the product of the author's imagination or are used fictitiously, and any resemblance to actual persons, living or dead, business establishments, events or locales is entirely coincidental.

ISBN: 0991386833
ISBN-13: 978-0-9913868-3-3

DEDICATION

To all who struggle with personal demons. May you
find help, comfort, and peace.

ACKNOWLEDGMENTS

Big thanks to Donette Freeman for helping me once again!
Thank you to Lindsay of Cover Sparkle Designs for the
spectacular cover! You're both amazing.

one

"Thank you for calling Pole Co. My name is Savannah. Are you calling to report a power outage or an emergency situation?"

"Who's this?" a frail geriatric voice calls through the speaker of my headset.

"You've reached the Power of Louisiana Electric Company's customer assistance line—Pole Co. Are you having issues with your power, sir?"

"No. Can't say that I am," the shaky voice answers. "Maebelle! Are we having issues with our power?" He yells so loudly that I want to bat the headphones off of my ears.

"You're supposed to be calling the water company, Stanley. Why are you bugging the nice people at Pole Co. when our problem is a water leak?" I hear a click on the line and then another geriatric voice, female this time, begins to speak to me. "Hello? Yes, Pole Co.? I'm sorry to have wasted your time. I used to be able to trust Stanley with these things, but his mind's gone to crap since he started on the new meds. He can't seem to keep anything straight anymore."

"I'm still on the line," a disgruntled Stanley mumbles.

"Hang up the phone, Stanley," Maebelle demands.

"You can't tell me what to do. I'm still the man of this house."

"Save the 'I'm the man' crap for when you're capable of wiping your own ass."

"Woman! Don't you make me get out of this chair!"

"Are you married?" Maebelle asks me, and I stumble over my words.

"Uh… No, ma'am. I'm not. Is there anything power related that I can help you with today?" I inquire while frantically searching for a way out of the conversation.

"We've been married for sixty-eight years. You know what I've learned in those sixty-eight years?" Maebelle questions. I hear Stanley's heavy breathing over the other connection.

"Ma'am?" I'm uncertain I want to hear the answer.

"Marriage sucks," she answers matter-of-factly. "Men want you to be their mommas, their nurses, their chefs, their secretaries, their housekeepers, and a host of other things that make their lives all nice and comfy…"

"Thank you for the advice, ma'am," I interrupt, desperate to take another call—any call.

"Now don't be in such a hurry. Take a second to listen to me, young lady. There's something that sucks worse than marriage," Maebelle asserts.

Stanley is still huffing into the phone. Lizzy, my one and only friend, sits in the cubicle across from me pretending to blow her brains out with her thumb and forefinger. I point to my headset while nodding and mouthing the words, "Me, too."

"Yes, ma'am. Something worse than marriage. Are you sure you have no power issues that you'd like to report?"

"I understand that you big city folks are all busy and don't have much time to waste on us old people, so I'll let you go shortly. Just listen to this one thing I'm gonna tell ya."

It's been a write up free couple of months, and I need my record to remain intact if I want a chance at the fifty dollar gift card the company will draw for at the end of the quarter. It's time for me to do some damage control before she calls in a complaint. "Ma'am, I'm very sorry if it came across as though I'm not interested in what you have to say. My intention was to assure that there were no life-threatening issues that needed to be immediately addressed." Lizzy, who has finally disconnected from her call, shoots me two thumbs up for the excellent recovery. She pulls the wire that connects her earpiece to her desk then still sitting in her chair, she rolls over to my cubicle to plug into my extra port so she can hear both sides of the conversation.

"Well, isn't that nice of you. Isn't that nice of her, Stanley? She wanted to make sure we were safe."

"Who are we talking to, Maebelle? Is it Jonut?"

"No, Stanley. It's not Jonut. You go ahead and hang up now okay?" Maebelle insists.

"Tell Jonut I love her when you talk to her,"

3

Stanley says before clicking off of the line.

Maebelle resumes our conversation. "Jonut is a nickname we have for our daughter, Josephine. We don't see her much, and sometimes Stanley gets confused. Anyway, as I was saying, marriage sucks. It sucks the life and soul out of you. There are days I want to kill him, and there are days I want to torture him before I kill him." Lizzy is working so hard at containing her laughter that she almost falls out of her chair. "There are days I wish he'd never been born. There are days I wish I'd never been born. But, listen to this carefully. They are just thoughts. Random fleeting thoughts that cross my mind when I'm upset about accidentally burning supper. Did he make me burn supper? No, he didn't, but I heaped that blame on him. Or when I forgot about a load of his underpants in the washer and they soured. He bore the brunt of that blame, too. What about the abuse he got when I gave birth to our child? Twelve hours of non-stop name calling during labor, and that man took every last bit of it and fed me words of love and encouragement to boot!"

Lizzy and I are now captivated by her speech.

"When and if you get married, those thoughts will come to you. You're going to fight. You're going to have resentful moments. You're going to wonder if it's worth it all. My Stanley is eighty-six years old, and he was diagnosed with terminal cancer four weeks ago. If we're lucky, I might have another couple of months with him the doctors say. All that complaining I did earlier… all that truth I gave you… you'd think I regretted marrying him, wouldn't you? Well, I don't. I'd give anything to have sixty-eight more years with him.

"You can complain about every dropped sock, every dirty dish left behind, every piece of dirt tracked through the house, or you can deal with it and spend that time you would've spent complaining giving him a kiss. Or maybe a tight hug. Or even jotting down a little note for him to find. So here's the truth—marriage sucks because one day it will end. It's inevitable. The beginning is usually a fairy tale; the end hurts more than you could ever comprehend. It's what you do with the middle that's the most important. Make the most of it. Now I'm going to walk up front to give Stanley a kiss before I get on the phone with the water company." *Click.*

Lizzy looks at me, tears welled in her eyes. "Best. Call. Ever," she says with a sigh. I'm still rendered speechless. "Oh, crap! My board is lighting up. Signal me if you get another call like that!" She rolls away to plug her headset back into the appropriate slot on her desk, then gives me a sort of point/wave to signal that I have a call waiting, too.

Rapidly shaking my head does nothing to help me clear my thoughts. "Pole Co. What do you want?" I blurt, desperately wishing I could suck my words back in, but there's no way that's happening. I also want to bang my forehead against my desk. That's not going to happen either.

"The list is pretty long. Are you sure you have the time to listen to all of it?" An amused male voice comes through the line.

Embarrassment socks me hard in the stomach. There goes my chance at that gift card I want so badly. "Sir, I sincerely apologize for my lack of professionalism. If it's okay with you, may I please start again?"

"Totally unnecessary," the smooth voice replies with a hint of playfulness.

"It would make me feel so much better," I insist, my gut slowly unclenching.

"If it'll make you feel better… *Bring, Bring,*" he loudly calls into the receiver.

It's the last thing I'm expecting to hear, and I cup my hand over my mouth to contain the snort that's trying to break free. "What in the world is that supposed to be?"

"Isn't it obvious?"

"Not really," I tease.

"It's a ringing phone. You remember when phones used to ring, don't you?"

"Of course I do, but I don't remember them sounding like that."

"How about you quit busting my chops and answer the phone? I said b*ring, bring.*"

Still trying to keep my laughter bottled inside, I take a shaky breath before answering him. "Thank you for calling Pole Co. My name is Savannah. How can I assist you, Mr. …?"

"Reilly. Fletcher Reilly. Now that I have you on the line, why don't you tell me what flustered you so much that you forgot how to answer the phone?"

Another response I wasn't prepared for. "I…I really don't think I can, Mr. Reilly. It's nothing, really. Just an unusual call," I awkwardly answer while stumbling over my words.

"Ah, come on. It's got to be good. You know what they say about bottling things up, right? You know you want to talk about it," he coaxes.

A broad smile crosses my face as I lightly tap an ink pen on the scratchpad in front of me.

"Come on. Feed my curiosity. You can't leave me hanging." Something about his voice intrigues me. It's comforting, confident, and relaxed. I silently scold myself for my lack of professionalism, but the daring side of me kind of wants the conversation to continue. In a split- second decision, I decide to play his game.

"So what you're telling me is that, in your opinion, discussing a work related phone call with a complete stranger is actually good for my mental health?"

"Absolutely."

I smile. "I have a question for you, Mr. Reilly. When you initially called, did you hear the recording that stated the calls to this center may be monitored?"

"I did. Are we being monitored?"

"No," I admit.

"Then I fail to see the problem. So, what's up?"

I put my forehead in my palms. "Oh, this is so gonna get me fired," I mumble into the headset.

"Or, it could get you promoted. The recording asked if I'd be willing to take a brief survey after the call. Maybe my glowing review will help you to rise through the ranks."

"Yeah, I doubt that," I scoff.

"How old are you?" he asks.

"How old are you?" I fire back.

"Twenty-nine," he answers without hesitation.

"Twenty-seven."

"So, what are you wearing?" he asks, his voice dripping with sexiness.

Oh great! He goes from charming to pervert in seconds flat. Time to get out of this conversation.

"Uh, look I… uh…"

He laughs. "Wait! Wait! Don't get flustered! I was just picking. I wanted to break the ice a little more. That's all. I swear it was only a joke."

"Fletcher. I mean, Mr. Reilly, do you have a power related issue that I can help you with?"

"Ah, and I get shot down. I guess I went too far. My most humble apologies, Savannah. I didn't mean to offend you."

"You didn't offend me, but I do suddenly have a queue of calls that are waiting to be answered. I'm sorry, Mr. Reilly, but I really must tend to your problem, and then move on."

"I understand. Okay, my problem is that I can't find my bill, so I'm unsure how much I owe for this month," he explains.

"That's no problem at all, Mr. Reilly. Will you please verify your address for me?"

"You want my address? Does that mean you might come by for a visit one day?" he questions in a playful tone.

"I sincerely doubt that."

"You're breaking my heart, Savannah. 4617 Fulton Road, apartment 2."

"I'm sorry about your broken your heart, Mr. Reilly, and thank you for verifying your address. It shows that the balance owed is $187.39. Is there anything else I can help you with today, sir?" I ask in my most professional tone.

"Will you send me a friend request now that you have my personal information? You do use social media, don't you?"

"That would be an unethical invasion of your privacy and a huge violation of company policy, Mr.

Reilly."

"So you're telling me that if I, Fletcher D. Reilly, who resides on Fulton Road in Lafayette, Louisiana, would like for you to find me on social media so that I can offer my services as listener extraordinaire in order for you to preserve your precious mental health by letting you discuss your day with me, that would be a violation?"

"Yes. Very much so."

"That's it. I must speak to a supervisor. That policy is antiquated and a hazard to all involved. It must be amended immediately. I'll hold while you connect me," he jokes.

He's hooked me again. "Mr. Reilly…"

"Call me Fletcher."

"Fletcher, I need to move on to the next caller," I say with a smile.

"Will you find me? Come on. It's an internet friendship, not marriage. You can delete me, block me, whatever if you don't like me, but at least give me a chance."

I'm silent for a beat before conceding. "Okay, I'll find you."

"You're not married are you?" he asks.

"Shouldn't you have asked that first?" I scold.

"Maybe. Are you?"

"No," I say with a laugh.

"Okay, that's good. I don't need some guy showing up with a baseball bat or something. I mean, you do have my address and all," he teases.

"No need to worry about that, Fletcher. It was nice speaking with you. Is there anything else I can assist you with today?"

"Did you write my name down?"

9

I playfully roll my eyes. "I don't have to. Trust me, I'll remember."

"Goodbye, Savannah."

"Goodbye, Fletcher. Have a nice day." I disconnect from the call and toss my headset to the side. The queue has emptied, so I signal to Lizzy that I'm going for a break. She gives me a wink and the "okay" gesture, so I bolt from the call center to the closest restroom.

"What in the hell just happened?" I ask the perplexed reflection looking back at me. Staring into the mirror isn't going to help me to decipher anything, so I smooth my dark shoulder length hair, dab at the corners of my hazel eyes with a tissue, and take a deep breath before stepping into the hall. I still have thirteen minutes before I'm due back to my desk, so I step through the large double glass doors that lead into a courtyard just outside the building. Lizzy, with her phone to her ear, paces frantically while chewing on her thumbnail. She looks up when she hears the door clicking shut.

"There you are! Where were you? Oh, my gosh! What is going on today? First, your call with the married couple, and then the call I just took. Ugh! The woman was so freaking mean to me. You won't believe what… Hey. Are you okay?" She ends her rant long enough to snap her fingers in my direction.

"Huh? Oh, yeah. Rude lady. That's terrible."

"No, what's terrible is the way you're acting. Did that call really throw you off that badly? I know her words were pretty powerful, and believe me, I appreciated hearing them, but you're acting way funny. What's wrong?" She twirls a strand of her honey blonde hair around her finger while batting her mascara-laden lashes at me. Eyes the color of peridot shamelessly demand an answer.

"I guess it's the combination of that call and the one I took right after it. Some guy named Fletcher Reilly wants me to send him a friend request."

"Was he a freak? Did he make you feel icky?"

"No, and I think that is what's bothering me the most. He was funny and charming, very charismatic. And his voice! Lizzy, I could've listened to him go on for days about nothing."

She gives me an odd look before she whips out her phone and madly swipes at the screen with her finger. "It's finally happened! A man has grabbed your attention! Is he hot?"

"No, he didn't necessarily grab my attention, and I don't know if he's hot. I didn't check his profile."

"Why in the hell not?" Lizzy snaps.

"Because I haven't had a chance!" I shoot back before I can stop myself.

"So you admit that you intended to search him out? Whoa, momma! Holy hell! Fletcher Reilly, you stay right where you are because this dirty girl is coming for you!" Lizzy says to her phone.

"Now wait a minute! Let *me* see!" I demand while making a mad grab for her phone. She pulls it just out of my reach.

"Are you sure you want to see this? I'm not sure you can handle this level of hotness, Savannah. We know that your interaction with members of the opposite sex is extremely limited."

"Shut up and show me. We only have five minutes before we go back to work."

She acts as though she's going to give me the

phone then pulls it away several times before I'm able to snatch her wrist. My breath catches when I see Fletcher's profile picture. Donning full desert battle dress and holding his helmet toward the camera, he smiles broadly while entering the doorway of a Blackhawk helicopter. His eyes are hidden behind a dark pair of wrap-around sunglasses, but even so, he is by far the most handsome man I've ever seen. His hair is dark, clean cut, but not super short. It's clear that his lips, though taut from his smile, are full and just begging to be kissed. His nose is straight and perfect for his face. I can't seem to pull my eyes away from the screen.

Lizzy tries stealing it back from me, but since I'm holding it with a death grip, she settles for peering over my shoulder. "Tom Freaking Hardy wants to get to know you, and he's never even seen you! Why couldn't his call have been sent to my desk?" she asks with a pathetic sigh.

"He does look like Tom Hardy, doesn't he?" I say with a silly grin.

"Uh, yeah. Totally could be his twin."

Reality comes crashing. "Wait! First, how do we know that this is actually him? Maybe it's a friend, or his brother, or some random stranger's picture he threw up as his profile photo. Second, this is absolutely insane. I answered a question for him, and he wants to get to know me better? That's insane, isn't it? Like isn't it borderline creepy?" I ask before nervously gnawing on my lower lip.

"Or," Lizzy says melodramatically, "is it the most romantic thing ever? Imagine retelling the story ten years from now as you're flanked by five kids and celebrating your eighth wedding anniversary."

I squint at Lizzy. "Seriously, you already have us married with five kids? Have you forgotten who you're talking to?"

"Not at all! It's time for you to lighten the hell up. Did I forget to mention that I'll be celebrating too, but I'll be with his slightly younger, but equally handsome brother?" She lets out an obnoxious squeal.

Shaking my head, I throw my hands up, smiling as I walk to the glass doors. "Break's over. Let's finish out this shift. I can't wait to get home."

Lizzy is right on my tail. "Why are you in such a hurry to get home? So you can pick up where you left off with Fletcher?"

"No, Lizzy. Will you give it a rest? It's been a long day. I'm ready to pour myself a huge glass of wine, sink into a nice, warm bubble bath, and forget about the millions of problems rolling around in my mind right now."

She stops in the middle of the gray carpeted hallway; her face is solemn. "I'm so sorry, Savannah. I wasn't thinking. How's your grandpa doing? Any change?"

Tears threaten to fall, but I refuse to let them. "I'll fill you in later." Swallowing the ball of emotion that was once heavy in my throat, I take solace in the fact that it's now packed away deep in my gut, right where I like to keep all of my emotions.

Lizzy gives me a quick hug before tugging on the door to the call center. "Of course, but if anymore calls from hot strangers who want to hook up come through, transfer them to my desk."

I smile. "Deal."

two

Later that night, after a nice long bath, I'm stretched out on the sofa while finishing a bottle of moscato. All is quiet except for the *Friends* episode playing in the background, and even though I love the gang dearly, even tales of Chandler's nubbin fail to keep me entertained. It's Friday. I'm single. The world is mine to conquer, yet my butt remains glued to the couch cushion. I toss the soup spoon I used to shovel a pint of turtle ice cream inside of the empty carton, and then sigh. This routine is becoming too comfortable, and though I scold myself, the larger part of me simply doesn't care.

Too lazy to walk to the kitchen, I stretch as far as I can to place the empty container onto the coffee table, knocking off my laptop in the process. "Ugh! Really?" I snap, finally giving up. I roll off the sofa and trudge to the kitchen. "Might as well pour myself another glass of wine while I'm here," I mumble.

There's just enough to fill the goblet to the brim, and I even go so far as shaking the bottle to encourage those last few drops to join the party. I open all the food cabinets and even stare into the fridge for a while—not because I'm hungry, but because I'm just THAT bored. A bag of pretzels calls to me from a basket on the counter, so I snatch it up with my free hand. I'm almost back in the living room when I come to my senses and give the bag an over handed toss back onto the countertop.

I stare at the laptop while I drain the wine glass. An internal war wages in my mind over whether or not I should visit Fletcher's page. *What if he's a murderer? What if he's the most wonderful man who ever existed and it's divine intervention pushing me to him? What are the odds of that happening? Is he really as good looking in person as he is in his pic? If so, he's way out of my league. Is that HIM in the picture? Oh, that voice. Maybe I can agree to be his friend and we'll never actually meet, but we can just talk on the phone. Sounds reasonable, right? No! Of course he'll want to meet. Well, one thing I can do without him even knowing is enjoy the hell out of that profile picture.* I smirk as I open the laptop.

The picture has changed, but it's definitely the same Tom Hardy doppelganger. This time he's straddling a motorcycle and wearing a black t-shirt, jeans, and the same dark wrap-around sunglasses. The scruffy beard he sports adds to his sex appeal, as well as the few tattoos that peep out from under the sleeves of his shirt. I catch myself moaning out loud.

"This is stupid." My hand rests on top of the screen, and I'm just about to slam the lid closed when something in the picture catches my eye. I immediately message him.

Me: I hope you were serious about me contacting you when you mentioned it this afternoon.

Fletcher: Hi, Savannah. Yes, I was serious. Wow, you're gorgeous. How are you?

Me: Thank you. I'm fine. Question...

Fletcher: Yes?

Me: The bike in your profile picture—is it yours?

Fletcher: Yes. Why? Do you like to ride?

Me: I used to, but I haven't been in a while. I recognize the bike. It was my dad's.

Fletcher: What? Really?

Me: The paint job is custom. I lost my parents a few years ago, and they had a lot of debt, so I had to sell off their belongings. That bike was his pride and joy. I'm glad to see that you've taken such good care of it.

Fletcher: I have taken good care of it, but I have to admit that this new information makes me feel a little awkward.

Me: More awkward than asking a stranger from the electric company to befriend you via social media?

Fletcher: Lol. Yes, more awkward than that.

Me: I'm sorry. Well, I'll let you go. I just wanted to ask you about the bike.

Fletcher: Wait! Do you have to go? The awkwardness is fading. Lol. I'd like to talk a little more, if that's okay.

Friends is still on the television, I'm out of wine, and I'm in a robe. What can it hurt?

Me: Yes, that's fine. No plans for you on a Friday night, either?

Fletcher: Nah, I'm more of a homebody. What about you? You're absolutely beautiful. Why aren't you out there being wined and dined? (Yes, I just scrolled through more of your pics. Simply stunning.)

Me: Lol! You sure are a sweet talker, Fletcher. You know, I could ask the same of you. (I'm scrolling your pics, too, and you're not so bad, yourself.) Are you with or without the beard right now?

Fletcher: With.

I waggle my eyebrows and smile broadly.

Me: Nice!

Fletcher: Do you like facial hair?

Me: I'm okay with it.

Fletcher: What else do you like? (Asked with ZERO sexual innuendo.)

Me: Not a whole lot.

I look around the room.

Me: Moscato, ice cream, and reruns.

Might as well be upfront and honest from the start.

Fletcher: Same going on here, but I have beer instead of moscato and pizza rolls instead of ice cream. Reruns are on the TV.

Me: *Friends?*

Fletcher: *Everybody Loves Raymond.*

Me: Really?

Fletcher: Yeah. Is that hard to believe?

Me: Maybe a little.

Fletcher: Why?

Me: Because I figured you'd be watching

some UFC match or something, I guess.

Fletcher: Nah, not tonight anyway. Look, this might be presumptuous, but I'm really not a fan of typing. Do you think we could talk on the phone?

What do I do? Think! Okay, if I agree, worst case scenario, he has my cell phone number, calls me a hundred times a day, and I have to change the number. Is there anything else that can go wrong? No, not that I can think of anyway. Plus, I get to hear his voice again. That alone is worth the risk of him being a possible psycho stalker.

Fletcher: It's okay if you'd rather not, I just thought…

Me: No, it's fine. My number is 555-5248.

I nervously chew on my thumbnail while staring at the phone. It rings within a minute. "Hello."

"I want you to know that I don't usually do this," he remarks.

Oh, my gosh! His voice is sexier than I remember! "Do what? Call girls?" I tease.

His laugh is hearty. "Yeah, that too, but what I meant is you should know that I don't make a habit of calling utility companies with the hopes of befriending the call taker."

"That's good to know," I mention. "What made today different?"

"I liked talking to you."

"That's it?" I ask.

"Should there be more?" he returns.

"I guess not." The silence that lasts for several seconds is abruptly ended when we both speak at the same time. "I'm sorry, you go ahead," I insist.

"No, you go."

"I was going to ask you about the bike. I remember the man I sold it to, and you most certainly aren't him. How did you end up with it?"

"I won it in a card game."

"What! Really?"

"No, but that would make a great story wouldn't it?"

I realize that I'm smiling, something that before communicating with Fletcher Reilly, I didn't do very often. Generally, I'm pretty comfortable living in a state of semi-melancholia. Disappointment doesn't hurt so much if you're expecting it.

"I bought it from some guy when I returned home from my first tour."

"Oh, yeah. Lizzy and I saw the picture of you wearing a uniform when we…" Oh, my gosh! I just completely told on myself, and he knows it because I hear him chuckling in the background.

"When *we* what? When *we* went on over to Fletcher's profile to sneak a peek at him?"

"Talking about yourself in third person is very unbecoming," I say, desperate to change the subject.

"Fletcher is offended by your statement."

"Fletcher best get over it."

"Fletcher thinks that Savannah is probably a beautiful shade of red right now, and he's sorry that he can't enjoy it. Or, maybe he can. Do you have webcam?"

"Oh, no! We're not going there, so don't even think about it."

"A man can try, can't he?"

"He can try; doesn't mean he'll succeed."

"You're a feisty one, Savannah Mason. I might be falling in love."

"Guess I'll have to waste my Saturday getting a restraining order."

"Against?"

"You!"

"I should've guessed that I'd be too much man for you. Just as well we discover this now."

"You are so full of yourself!"

"Fletcher prefers the term self-assured."

I roll my eyes. "Fletcher would."

"Tell me some interesting facts about you."

"I'd love to, but I can't."

"You can't or won't?" Fletcher asks.

"Can't. For me to do that, I'd have to be interesting."

"Being evasive. Okay, let's start small. What's your favorite movie?"

I suppose there's no harm in answering a few questions he can get the answer to just by looking at my profile.

"*Gone With the Wind.* Yours?"

"Not *Gone With the Wind.*"

"Who's being evasive now?" I query.

"*The Godfather.*"

"Never saw it."

I hear exaggerated coughing in the background. "Never saw it! How is that possible?"

"I guess I make a better lover than a fighter."

Fletcher's teasing tone instantly stops, and

there is dead silence on the line. After a second or so I hear, "Hey, now. I'm trying to keep this conversation in the **G** to **PG** range. We'll be having none of that." He mockingly sighs. "What is it with women and their constant sex, sex, sex attitudes?"

It isn't until he mentions it that I realize what I'd said. Clamping my hand over my mouth, I try to hold in my chuckle, but it comes out as an obnoxious snort. That's what I get for being so out of practice in the humor department. I really should laugh more often.

"What was that?" he teases. "Did that sound come out of you? You snorted didn't you? You did!"

The struggle to stay composed leaves tears welling in my eyes, and I pull my hand away from my mouth long enough to eke out a "No."

"Deny it if you must; I know the truth."

"Whatever," I retort once I get my breathing back under control.

"Can we meet in person?"

"Huh? I…"

"I know it's weird how all of this is going down, and I promise that I have no agendas, expectations, or felonies, for that matter. It's just that I haven't laughed this hard or felt this talkative in a very long time. How about we meet for pizza? You can bring a bodyguard if you'd like."

"I don't have a bodyguard, per se. I have a Lizzy."

"Ah, you have a Lizzy. Well, I have a Ben. How about we meet at Giovanni's at seven tomorrow night?"

"I don't know. I'd have to check with Lizzy, and her weekends are usually full…"

"Just text me when you decide, and there's no pressure. I'd really like to meet you, but only if the feeling's mutual."

"Okay. I'll check with Lizzy, and I'll get back to you. Goodnight, Fletcher."

"Goodnight, Savannah. Sweet dreams."

When the call ends, the faint taste of blood alerts me that I'm chewing my lower lip again. After a quick mental scolding, I allow myself a few seconds to replay the conversation with Fletcher before calling Lizzy.

three

"What's wrong?" Lizzy hurriedly shouts into the phone.

"What? Nothing. What's with the drama?"

"Savannah, you *never* call this late. It's as if the phone lines cease to work past ten o'clock as far as you're concerned."

"It's only…" I steal a glance to the clock above the TV, "…midnight! Oh, my gosh! Lizzy, I'm so sorry. I had no idea it was so late! We were talking, and I guess I just lost track of time."

"Who was talking?"

"I was talking to Fletcher."

"Fletcher! The Fletcher from this afternoon?"

"How many Fletchers do you know?"

"That's beside the point. Tell me everything!"

"He wants to meet me in person."

"Really!" she squeals. "Are you going to do it?"

"I'm thinking we should."

"We? We who?"

"We, me and you. And he has a Ben."

"A Ben for whom?" Lizzy asks.

"For you. We're meeting them tomorrow night at Giovanni's Pizza."

25

"We are?"

"Aren't we?"

"We are! Time?"

"Seven."

"I'll come over after lunch. I'm doing your hair and makeup."

"No, you aren't. See you tomorrow at six."

"Fine. Whatever. See you tomorrow. Night."

"Night."

I love how Lizzy and I can communicate with minimal words. Don't get me wrong, we can be very long winded at times, but as far as the basics go, one or two words are plenty.

All is quiet again, and as I lie in bed waiting for sleep to overcome me, I think back to Dad's motorcycle and my teen years. My dad was often gone for weeks, and sometimes months, at a time. When he flew in from offshore, he'd swing by the school and surprise me with a ride home on the back of his motorcycle. It truly was his pride and joy: garage kept, polished daily, custom painted to look like python skin. Dad was a large, burly man, and one of his trademark requests was for people to check out the monster "pythons" he sported. His strenuous and demanding work on an offshore oil platform earned him huge biceps, which in addition to showing them off, won him many an arm wrestling competition.

When Dad was gone, so was Mom. We weren't close, and frankly, I think she resented having me. It was okay though; I was happy to be alone. Alone was far better than the awkward and forced interactions that happened when she was home.

Don't get the wrong idea. I had guidance and support when Mom disappeared, but it came from her father, Grampy. He's currently battling the debilitating effects of a nearly lifelong addiction to unfiltered cigarettes. I've been using the money left from Mom and Dad's estate to see that he has the best possible care in a local assisted living facility. There was supposed to be lots and lots of money, but between the double funeral and the secret credit card bills Mom had run up, most of it went as quickly as I received it. Thank goodness Dad made sure the house was paid off. I stuck every penny from the sale into a special account, and that's what I've been using for Grampy's care.

I mentally chastise myself for letting so much of my past seep into my present, and before I can wrangle up another issue to internally debate, I pop a sleeping pill and go out.

"What was I thinking? Too much wine. That's it! I was drunk. There's no way in hell we're going tonight, so don't even think about trying to persuade me."

"Why are you freaking out on me?" Lizzy asks, her long luscious lashes batting hard to show her annoyance.

"Lizzy, I accepted a double blind date from a customer. That's completely unacceptable!"

"Why?"

"Because!"

"Will you quit yelling, and for goodness sakes, quit pacing. I'm getting motion sickness watching you."

"You call him. Tell him I'm sick. Tell him I'm missing. Tell him I…"

Lizzy grabs my shoulders and forces me to face her. "Stop. Breathe. Relax. We're only meeting for pizza. You're totally blowing this out of proportion. Look, I know it's been forever since you've had a date, and this must be super frightening for you, but you have to calm down. Honestly, you're scaring me. I've never seen you like this."

I close my eyes, and while pinching the bridge of my nose, I release a pent up breath. "You're right. I need to calm down. If I'm uncomfortable, or if things go awry, we'll leave. Right?"

"Yes, we'll leave."

"But what if you're having fun with your guy and Fletcher turns out…."

"Did we switch roles or something?" she asks, mockingly touching her face as she turns to look in the mirror. "I'm supposed to be the ditzy neurotic one, while you're supposed to be the wise and mature one—even if you are emotionally distant. I think you get docked a few maturity points for indifference."

"Oh, hush! Yes, that's right. I'm SO mature, just not where men are involved, obviously."

"You do have a history of… hmmm, how do I put it nicely? Finding the most rottenly craptastic men to start relationships with, but this one is different. I just know it."

"You're just saying that because you want to meet Ben."

"Pretty much."

"You're such a witch."

"But you love me anyway. Please tell me

you're not wearing that tonight."

"What's wrong with this?" I ask, hands on my hips as I tap a sneakered foot against the floor.

"Nothing, if you're about to play softball."

"There is nothing wrong with this!" I say while checking my reflection. "A t-shirt and jeans are classic."

She sighs. "Whatever. Let's get going." She shoos me out of the door and pushes me towards her car. Oh, her car! My frustration with Lizzy's vehicle is best understood if I explain a few things.

For as long as I've known Lizzy, her sense of style has been quite unique. Her dresses are generally retro fifties housewife, complete with the short strand of pearls and perfectly styled coif. When she isn't channeling her inner Donna Reed, she dresses in clothes too cutesy for doing anything of substance. For instance, the day she helped me to clean out my parents' house so I could put it on the market she wore a nautical themed outfit. Her ensemble consisted of white, high-waisted shorts adorned with four plastic knot buttons, a tucked in navy blue sailor's shirt with white trim and anchor patches, as well as cherry red patent leather heels and the lips to match. Her heart was in the right place, but her mind? I often wondered about her.

So, back to Lizzy's car. It's green. Seafoam green. With gigantic white polka dots, eyelashes above the headlights, a pair of pursed pink lips on the front bumper, and a huge pink bow fastened to the roof. The car's rims are white daisies with yellow centers, and the luggage rack in the back is adorned with a customized sign that says *Luvsy Wuvsy My Little Bugsy. Beetle Power!* Did I mention how much

I DESPISE riding in that thing?

Regardless, I suck up my reluctance and let Lizzy take the lead in this situation. We arrive at the pizza place, and I tell Lizzy to bring me home. She refuses. We get out of the car. I tell Lizzy to bring me home. She still refuses. We make it to the door of the establishment, and before I can say it, she snatches the back of my shirt with some sort of superhuman strength. She smiles politely at the family standing behind us.

"Hi. Please go ahead of us. Enjoy your evening. Your children are adorable." As soon as the door closes behind them, the smile is gone and she's pushing me aside. "Listen to me, and listen well. I've had enough of this childish behavior. If you want to go, then go. My goodness!" She stops snapping at me long enough to smooth her dress.

"Me? Childish? You have a pink bow on top of your car!"

"Leave my car out of this! Seriously, I'm not going to spend my evening running after you. If you want to go, then go."

I give my feet a shameful glance. "We really have switched roles, haven't we?"

Lizzy's face softens. "It certainly seems so tonight. Are you in, or are you out?"

After a brief pause, I relent. "I'm in, and I promise to pull myself together."

"That's my girl!" She hugs me tightly, then swats me squarely on the behind when I turn to walk inside. This earns her a scowl, but it doesn't faze her in the least. Instead, she hops up and down in the entryway, squealing while happily clapping her hands together. The entire restaurant stops and stares our way, and I want nothing more than for the floor to open up and swallow me whole.

"Lizzy Lou? No way! Is it really you?" A tall, clean cut man with a strong, chiseled jaw and the most amazing hazel colored eyes quickly moves towards my friend.

"Mercedes Benz! Oh, my gosh! I had no clue that YOU were the Ben Thibodaux I'd be meeting with tonight. This is so amazing! I've always wondered what happened to you."

He smiles down at her while taking one of her hands in his. "I haven't been called Mercedes Benz in years. You look amazing, Lizzy. How long has it been?"

"We moved from Baton Rouge my eighth grade year, so… TOO LONG!" Another squeal rocks the restaurant. The manager peeks from behind a semi-closed door, shakes his head, and loudly pulls it closed.

"Lizzy, I'm sorry to interrupt, but maybe you should.."

"Ben, you have to meet my friend, Savannah! Savannah, this is Ben."

"Very nice to meet you, Savannah," he says, barely stealing a glance my way. Lizzy Lou and her perfect appearance clearly dominate his attention. I look past Ben, and there he is, staring our way with a confused look on his face. *How is it possible for him to look even better in person than in the pictures?* My heart starts racing, my palms get sweaty, and my breathing turns a little erratic. Nerves clench in my stomach, and I fight the urge to bolt. He smiles as his large hands leave the back of the chair he pulls from under the table to gesture that I should join him.

This can't be. It can't. People as beautiful as he is don't go on blind dates at pizza parlors. Something's wrong. Something's very, very wrong. I try to stop the negative thoughts by smiling as I go around Lizzy and Ben and make my way to the table. "Hi, you must be Fletcher. It's so nice to meet you." That's what I intended to say when I reached the table. What poured out of my mouth was a mix between a nervous giggle and, "Pizza. Yum."

Fletcher's brows furrow, but only briefly. It's long enough to make me want to smack my head against the table repeatedly. "Yeah, pizza's one of my favorites."

"I like hamburgers, too," I mumble. *SHUT UP! Oh, my God! Why won't my brain freaking work? Run! Just cut your losses and run!*

Fletcher gives me the old "bless her heart" look. "That's two things we have in common," he replies.

I shake my head from side to side. "I'm sorry. This isn't me at all. I'm so embarrassed." Taking the seat he's offered, I extend my hand to him once he sits across from me. "Hi, Fletcher. It's nice to meet you."

He accepts my outstretched hand and squeezes with a firm, but far from bone-crushing, grip. "I'm glad you accepted my invitation. Please, don't apologize. Truth be known, I'm nervous, too. I'm pretty much a homebody, but Ben keeps pushing me to get out more. I finally take his advice, and this happens." He points towards Lizzy and Ben who are still fawning all over each other. "I swear he knows everyone."

I let out a chuckle. "Yes, Lizzy is quite the social butterfly herself. I've been hearing the same things from her. 'Let's go dancing, Savannah. We should go to a ball game. Ball games are full of men, Savannah. You'll never find your perfect match if you refuse to leave your apartment.' I've heard them all."

"So what's your issue? Why don't you venture out much?" Fletcher inquires.

"What?" I ask, slightly taken aback.

"Why do you choose to be a homebody?" he clarifies.

"Can't it just be because I like staying home?"

He shakes his head. "Not likely."

"Damn, straight to the intense stuff. Okay, I don't like venturing out much because I work a lot. I'm usually wiped out when quitting time rolls around, and on my limited days off, I visit with my grandfather. It doesn't leave much time for club hopping and such."

"I never was into that scene. I've always been a simple country boy. I'd rather be in a tree stand than on a dance floor any day."

"So you're a hunter?"

"I don't get to as much as I used to, but I manage to make a trip every once in a while."

"Then tell me, what's *your* issue?"

Fletcher lets out a deep laugh. "My own words come back to bite me." He sighs. "It's kind of a long story, and Ben and your friend are heading this way. Can we talk about it later?"

"Sure, as long as it's not something malicious you're keeping from me."

"Malicious? Me? No way," he says with a grin.

With her arm laced through Ben's, Lizzy

storms the table with gusto. "Sorry about that. I'm still in such shock that the Benz here is your friend!"

"Who'd a thunk?" Fletcher replies in what I immediately pick up on as sarcasm, but Lizzy remains clueless. Ben shoots him a warning glance. None the wiser, Lizzy continues to ramble about their childhood until the waitress comes by to take our order. She takes a breath long enough to order a sweet tea, and the rambling immediately commences. Ben listens to each of her words intently, but Fletcher and I were over the conversation the moment it started.

At first, Fletcher's gestures were simple and barely noticeable, but as soon as I realized what he was doing, I join in. Before long, we are secretly trying to outdo one another. He very casually starts out with a yawn/stretch combo, and as soon as he's sure they aren't looking, he gestures as though he's hanging himself with an imaginary rope. I cover my mouth to conceal my smile then slowly roll my hand to the side of my head to make a gun gesture with my fingers. Before I can "pull the trigger," Lizzy turns to ask me a question. Smiling, I quickly redirect my finger to my ear and pretend to scratch an itch. Fletcher quickly looks away to hide his grin from the clueless two.

"Am I missing something?" Lizzy asks looking between me and Fletcher.

"I don't think so. Savannah, is Lizzy missing something?"

"Lizzy, my love, the only thing you're missing is a mute button," I toss out, and Fletcher nearly hits the floor from laughter.

Lizzy squints at me while smirking playfully, and slowly, her lips erupt into a full, lopsided smile.

"So, I'm talking too much? Okay, you asked for it. I'm zipping it the rest of the night. All future conversation is on you, and you alone. Good luck with that," she asserts while pantomiming zipping and buttoning her mouth shut before haughtily crossing her arms over her chest.

"What's that mean?" Ben asks, looking confused.

"It means that she knows that I'm not much of a conversationalist, and instead of picking on my dear sweet friend for her incessant chatting, I should thank her for jumping in and taking some of the pressure off me," I answer. Lizzy smugly raises an eyebrow while a smirk crosses her lips.

"I have an idea," Fletcher offers. All eyes are now on him. "It's obvious that Lizzy and Ben have a lot of catching up to do, so why don't you guys do that? Savannah, if you're okay with it, why don't we get our own table and let these two do their thing?"

Lizzy's eyes light up. "Actually, I'm not really in the mood for pizza." I shoot her a nasty look because I know what's coming.

"I was just thinking that, too," Ben volunteers. "I'm more of a steak kinda guy. What about you, Lizzy Lou? In the mood for a steak?"

"Why yes I am!" she giggles while abruptly standing. "Savannah, if you need a ride home, just call and I'll swing by to pick you up. Unless..." she flashes a pearly white smile in Fletcher's direction.

"I have the bike outside. I don't mind bringing you home," Fletcher says, catching the tail end of the non-verbal, gesture-laden scolding I'm giving to Lizzy for abandoning me with a man who is practically a stranger. "Unless you're uncomfortable

35

with me bringing you home."

Lizzy replies, "If it's an issue, I'll just ride with Ben and leave my car for you, Savannah."

"Uh, no. I'd rather take my chances with Fletcher," I retort.

"Chances?" Fletcher says with a laugh.

Lizzy's hands are on her hips. "There is nothing wrong with my car, Savannah Rose Mason."

"Your car is wearing mascara, lipstick, and a hair bow, Elizabeth Jordan Cole."

"No way! I've got to see this!" Ben exclaims, dashing to the parking lot.

"Wait for me!" Fletcher says, tossing a twenty onto the table to cover the drinks we'd ordered. I'm right behind them, and everyone is laughing and cackling once we get outside. Well, everyone but Lizzy.

"My car is cute!" she defensively calls after us. "Don't pick on her! You'll hurt her feelings."

The guys stop mid-stride when they spot the bug. All is quiet for a few beats before one of the men lets out a loud belly laugh. He is quickly joined by the other, and before long, peals of laughter resonate throughout the parking lot.

"I thought you were joking," Fletcher directs to me.

"Nope."

"She's a beaut," Ben offers. "Don't expect me to go riding around town in her, though."

"No one asked you to," Lizzy says with a pout. "She's my baby, and I love her no matter what you meanies have to say about it!"

"It's a great car, Lizzy. I'm sorry I laughed, but I really thought that Savannah was exaggerating.

It caught me off guard, that's all. I'm sorry if I hurt your feelings," Fletcher remarks.

"Yeah, me too," Ben affirms once he stops laughing.

"Me, three," I say, pulling Lizzy close with a one-armed hug.

"What?" Fletcher says, looking in Ben's direction. "I think that's a great idea!" Ben gives him a confused look. "Ben just whispered to me that he's going to let you drive to the steak restaurant as a way of saying he's sorry."

"Wha…" Ben barely has time to stammer before Lizzy excitedly bounces up and down.

"Yay! Beetle power! Get in!" she squeals after unlocking the doors and climbing into the driver's seat. Ben shoots Fletcher a seething glare as he climbs into the passenger seat of the seafoam green automobile. Fletcher pulls out his phone and steadily snaps picture after picture as the duo drives away. His laughter is heavy as he reviews them, and I join in when he holds the screen so I can see them, too.

"This is some serious blackmail material!" Fletcher says before tucking his phone back into his pocket. Our laughter fades, and it's just the two of us in the dark parking lot near the pizza house. "Should we go back inside?" Fletcher asks.

I shake my head. "I'm not really in the mood for pizza anymore. You said you have the bike, right? Can we go for a ride?"

"Of course," he says, leading me to the far end of the lot. There it is, and it's exactly as Dad left it. My emotions threaten to mutiny, but my brain overrides them. With all that I've had to overcome in my life, I've gotten really good at swallowing down my emotions and keeping a perfect poker face—at least until it was time to meet Fletcher this evening. I still don't know what that was all about! Stuttering, stammering, and talking gibberish: those are Lizzy traits, not Savannah traits. Regardless, I've regained my composure, and no matter how sexy, good-looking, or amazing this man may be, I'm in complete control of my actions and emotions.

He offers me a helmet. "Where to? Do you have any suggestions?"

"Not really," I answer while fastening the chin strap.

"I have an idea," he says as he straddles the bike.

"Care to share?" I ask, taking the seat behind him.

"Nah, I'll let it be a surprise," he says, revving the engine. He kicks it into gear, and we're off on our adventure.

four

"What in the world?" I ask, removing my helmet. While doing a slow one-eighty degree turn in the parking lot, flashing lights, roaring rides, screaming kids, and sinfully delectable aromas bombard my senses. Suddenly, my mind is screaming for funnel cake, and my gurgling stomach seconds the demand. "A carnival? Why are we here?"

"Would you rather go somewhere else?"

"I was six years old the last time I went to one of these things. It doesn't really look as though they've changed all that much."

"Six? Wow, why so long?"

I shake my head. "Too long of a story. Do you think they still sell funnel cakes at these things?"

"I have it on high authority that they do. Come on," he says. Taking my hand in his, he begins to lead the way to the concession area. Uncomfortable with what I consider an unwanted act intimacy, my body stiffens, and he feels it. "I'm sorry. I shouldn't have…"

I hold up my hand to stop him. "Don't apologize, Fletcher. I should probably tell you a little more about me, and I guess now is as good a time as

39

any." He remains quiet as his eyes search mine for a hint of what's to come. "There are some things about me, things that happened in the course of my life, that make me different from other people. I only have one friend, and I like it that way. My last remaining relative is knocking on death's door, and I'm not really all that freaked out about it. Don't get me wrong, my grandfather is one of the most spectacular men to grace the earth, but I know that once he's gone my life will continue. I don't need to be touched, to be held, or to be fawned over. I'm very self-sufficient, and if I find myself in a mess, I find my way out of it. I trust very few people, I work hard, and I'm telling you this mostly so you'll fully comprehend how absolutely uncharacteristic it was for me to accept your invitation to meet, much less for me to be here with you right now. A lot of people mistake my forwardness and lack of social interaction for bitchiness. I'm not a bitch, I don't think I'm better than anyone, and I certainly don't have a stick up my butt. I'm just a loner, always have been, and probably always will be. Anyway, I thought you should know."

"What made you say yes?"

"Excuse me?"

"If everything is as you want it, why did you say yes to me when I asked to meet you in person?"

"I've repeatedly asked myself that very question."

He smiles. "I know why you said yes."

"Oh, really? Care to enlighten me, wise one?"

"You say you're okay with your life, but you aren't. Your cynicism is a defense mechanism, and I know this because you and I are very much alike. I've been hurt more times than I care to acknowledge, so

I'm not even going to go there, but I learned something over the years: the journey through life isn't meant to be a solo trip."

"Who says?" I counter.

"Everyone."

"Everyone? Really? Everyone told you that?"

Fletcher lets out a laugh. "Yep."

I smirk while shaking my head. "You're such a nerd. Come help me find a funnel cake." I feel a little foolish for overreacting to his hand holding by assuming it was an act of intimacy. The man was simply guiding me toward the concession stand, and I freaked. To rectify the situation, and by rectify I mean to save face, I take his hand in mine and practically drag him towards the action. Fletcher doesn't say anything as he takes large strides to keep up with my fleeting pace. Once we arrive at the brightly lit food trailer, I look over and catch him snickering.

"What's so funny?" I ask, taking my place in line.

"I bet you were the bossy kid growing up, weren't you?" he quips.

I ball up my fist and hold it in his line of vision. "Yep, and I was the kid who went around giving fat lips, too."

"I absolutely believe that," Fletcher remarks.

I plant the same fist steadfastly on my hip. "Really?" I ask, incredulously.

Fletcher feigns fright. "Oh, no! Are you going to hit me right here in front of all these people?" One of the women in line turns to give me a nasty glare.

"No, I'm going to save that for our second

date," I retort.

"Ah, so you've committed to a second date with me."

"I did no such thing. That was a joke reply."

"Joke reply. *Pffft.* If ever there were a Freudian slip that was surely it. You want to date me. Admit it."

"I'll do no such thing, and if you don't cut it out, our first date is as good as over."

He squints his eyes at me. "I call idle threat on that one. You're having far too good of a time to leave."

"I don't make idle threats, and the jury's still out on the good time. I'm here because of a sweets craving."

"Which you got because of...."

"You. I'll give you that one," I hold up my index finger, "but that's it."

Fletcher chuckles. "Victory never tasted so good."

I'm next in line, but before I can order, I'm stopped by a cacophony of pre-pubescent giggles. "Uncle Fletcher, you came!" a young girl with dark curly hair and sky blue eyes exclaims as she throws herself into his arms. The trio of preteens with her say in unison, "Hi, Uncle Fletcher," before shamelessly resuming the giggle fest.

"Of course I couldn't miss your carnival night fundraiser, Molls. Have you been having fun?" he asks, placing her on the ground.

"Lots! I dunked mean old Principal Collins with my first pitch!"

"Atta girl! See, Uncle Fletcher's pitching practice pays off."

"I wish you'd teach me how to pitch," one of the trio requests. Two more requests and another round of giggles follow.

"Is she with you," the dark headed girl asks loudly enough for me to overhear. Fletcher nods, and before he can speak, she's thrust her hand toward me. "Hi! I'm Molly. Did you know that my uncle is a hero? He's even got the medals to prove it."

"That's enough, Molly. She's not interested in all of that," Fletcher says, suddenly red with embarrassment.

I arch a brow. "Hero, huh?"

Fletcher vehemently shakes his head. "Far from it. Veteran, yes. Hero, no."

"Molly! What did I tell you about wandering... Oh, Fletcher. I didn't expect to see you here." A woman who looks like she'd just finished sucking a bag of lemons approaches. It's a shame that she wore such a deep scowl; otherwise, she'd be a beautiful woman. Her hair is golden brown and falls to her shoulder blades, while her eyes are the same shade as Molly's. Though she has pale skin, it's becoming on her, not wan looking.

"Julia." Fletcher's greeting matches her icy tone. "Molly asked me to come, so here I am."

Julia shoots daggers in Molly's direction, but once she realizes that Fletcher isn't alone, she thaws a touch. "I'm Julia Halsey, Fletcher's sister. And you are?"

"Savannah Mason. It's nice to meet you."

"Likewise," Julia dryly replies.

Fletcher pulls a couple of twenty dollar bills from his pocket and passes them to Molly. "Here, share some of this with your friends. Go have some fun." Before a word can be uttered the group is gone.

Julia sighs heavily. "I was trying to get her to leave. Now she'll be on the rides for at least another hour."

"Would you mind getting those funnel cakes for us, Savannah?" Fletcher asks, passing me a bill before he shoves the wad back into his pocket.

"No, not at all," I answer, overjoyed to have an excuse to get away from the palpable tension.

Though they aren't loud, I can tell from their body language that the conversation isn't lightening up any since my departure. They're still at it once I have the funnel cakes in hand, so I make my way to one of the picnic tables and slowly begin picking at the pastry. It's even better tasting than I remembered, and I allow myself to get lost in the sweet memory that accompanies it.

"Daddy, can I have funnel cake every day?" I ask. Powdered sugar dusts the entire front of my lemon yellow sun dress.

"You could, but you'd have no teeth before long. Look at all of that sugar. I think you got more on you than in you." He playfully tugs at one of my pig tails.

"I already lost four of them," I say, smiling broadly to show the newly vacated spaces.

"I know. Don't remind me. You're growing up way too fast. I'll blink, and the next thing I know, you'll be graduating."

I giggle heartily. "No way, Daddy. I'm going to be your little girl forever."

He stoops down to my level. "You won't always be little, but you'll always be my girl." He tweaks the tip of my nose and wraps me into his overly large arms as he showers me with kisses. "Sugar kisses!" *I burst into peals of laughter. His last kiss lands on my forehead.* "I know I'm gone a lot, but you know I love you right?"

"Yep!" *my tiny voice squeaks out.*

"How much do I love you?" *he asks.*

My eyes roll around as I recite the poem he made up for me. "You love me more than crawfish stew. You love me more than the roogarou. You love me more than a mosquitoless night. You'll love me forever with all your might."

"That's my girl! What do you want to ride now?" *he asks, tossing the empty paper plate into a nearby garbage can.*

"The Ferris wheel!" *I shout.*

"Oh, really? That looks awfully high to me. You sure you want to ride that?"

"Yes! Yes! I want to ride it, Daddy!"

He chuckles. "Alright, we'll ride the Ferris wheel." *A car stops in front of us, and the attendant helps us into our seat. The wheel jerks mightily as it moves to load the next rider and my stomach begins to do nervous flips. By the time the attendant loads four more carts, my heart is pounding.*

"Daddy, I don't want to ride anymore. I'm scared." *I dig my face into his side.*

"What are you scared of, sweetheart?"

"It's so high. What if we fall?"

"Daddy will never let you fall."

"You let me fall when you were teaching me to ride my bike and when you taught me to skate." *He gently rubs my arm.*

"True, but those times were different. Daddy will only let you fall if it's to teach you a valuable

45

lesson. There's a big difference between letting you get a scuffed knee so you'll be able to ride with your friends and letting you splat off a Ferris wheel, right?"

"Daddy! That's gross!" I say with a giggle.

"You've got nothing to be scared of. Daddy's got you. Look, I think I see our house from up here, but I'm not sure. Look out that way the next time we come around, and you tell me what you think."

I became so busy searching for our house that I forgot to be scared. Dad taught me to divert my attention when I became afraid, and that technique still gets me through many tough times.

"Hey, you okay?" Fletcher asks, taking a seat on the bench across from me.

"Yeah, I'm fine," I answer, shaking off the last few remnants of the memory I'd recently been lost in.

"I'm sorry for the way my sister acted. She's a bitter old hag sometimes. I usually just ignore her when I can."

"You don't have to apologize for her. It's fine."

"Eh, still…" He lets his sentence dangle as he bites into his funnel cake. "You looked like you were in deep thought. What's running through your mind?"

"Oh, not much. Just remembering my last visit to a carnival is all."

"From when you were six?"

"Yeah. My dad brought me."

"Did you have fun?"

I give a slight smile. "I did."

"If you don't mind me asking, what happened to him?"

"He died," I icily reply.

"Yeah, I know that, but... never mind. Do you know that you have powdered sugar here?" He pantomimes rubbing his entire chest, and I look down with horror. Sure enough, I'm completely dusted. A white cloud poofs around me as I brush the sugary mess from the front of my shirt.

"Well, that's embarrassing," I mumble under my breath.

"It's cute," Fletcher counters. I give him an eye roll.

"Any on my face?" I ask.

"Just a little," he answers, gently brushing my nose, both cheeks, and my chin with his fingertips.

"Oh, my gosh! Really! Evidently, I eat like a pig."

Fletcher laughs. "Stop being so negative. Do you want to go on a ride? Play some games? What's your pleasure?"

I give it a little thought before answering. Rides sound fun, but all the ones I'm seeing intimidate me. "Games." Without another word, we venture towards the Ping-Pong ball toss. I'm relieved to see little trinkets nestled away safely in water-tight baggies instead of the bloated, semi-alive goldfish that are generally regarded as the grand prize in this activity.

"Awww, no fish?" Fletcher asks.

"Too many parents complained, so no fish," a gravelly voiced septuagenarian with a vapor cigarette tucked behind her ear rasps in explanation. "Got plenty of other crap for you to win, though."

A young female with not a hair out of place softly chastises the cantankerous woman with a very simple, "Mrs. Velma, remember our talk?"

"Oh, yeah. We have plenty of other garbage for you to win."

The young woman rushes over. "Mrs. Velma, I think it's time for your break." As soon as Mrs. Velma shuffles out of ear shot, she leans over the railing of the carnival booth and apologizes to us, "She's been the school's bookkeeper since the sixties, and she refuses to retire. I'm Lollie Evans, history teacher. That's Lollie, as in Lollipop." She coyly extends her hand in Fletcher's direction, but her eyes are burning with lust.

People like her annoy the hell out of me because they're so predictable and fake. I figure she'll be using the old "whoops, I dropped something" tactic soon, and I'm not disappointed. A basket full of Ping-Pong balls conveniently tumbles over, each ball making a distinctive *plink* as it hits off the edges of the glass bowls. I laugh because Fletcher, completely unaware of the show she's setting up to give him, asks me if I'd like to try the dunking booth. I nod, letting out a brief snort when I glance back to see Lollipop's derriere provocatively shifting in the air as she retrieves the balls. She snaps upright and is disappointed to find that her show was pretty much in vain because her only audience is a hormonally challenged group of teenage boys. The look on her face as she scans the crowd while shooing the boys away makes the entire event worthwhile. Yeah, karma's going to get me good for enjoying it so much.

We're standing in line at the dunking booth when Fletcher looks my way. "Tell me more about yourself, Savannah. What deep, dark secrets do you harbor?"

"None. You pretty much know all there is to

know about me. What about you?"

"Same here. Pretty boring for the most part." We fall silent again. I've inched two places forward in the line when Fletcher speaks. "Look, I'm just going to say it. It's obvious that we both have pasts that we're not ready or willing to share. Let's just agree that as far as we're concerned, the only past we have is the one we've created together."

"Agreed," I say, extending my hand out to seal the deal with a shake. We grow quiet again.

After a couple of minutes, Fletcher asks, "Hey, do you remember that time we went to the pizza parlor with Lizzy and Ben?"

I laugh so loudly that I quickly cup my hand over my mouth as I get odd stares from the people around us. Fletcher grins broadly. "I got you to laugh again!" he says, eagerly pointing an accusatory index finger in my direction.

"You did," I admit once I remove my hand. "Consider yourself very lucky because it's pretty rare for someone to get a laugh out of me."

"Why? Are you depressed?" Fletcher blatantly asks. I'm uncertain if he's joking or serious.

"Nah, I'm just dull," I answer.

He leans in closely like he wants to whisper something to me. "I just think you haven't been hanging around the right people."

"Perhaps," I agree with a shrug as we're suddenly bombarded by the giggly trio.

"Will you dunk her, Uncle Fletcher? She's my mean science teacher, Mrs. Gibbons. I kept missing, and she laughed at me," Molly says with a pout.

"I'll do my best," he promises, tossing one of the softballs up and catching it in his palm. He does it again, but this time, I snatch the ball mid-air and rocket it squarely in the bull's-eye before anyone has time to react. Molly is stunned, Fletcher is impressed, and the mean science teacher is letting everyone within a two block radius know exactly how cold the water is.

"I want YOU to teach me how to pitch, Miss Savannah," Molly excitedly requests.

"Maybe one day," I say, launching another ball as soon as the teacher sits on the bench. She plunges back into the tank, and when she comes up this time, she shoots an evil glare in my direction. I figure I'd best slack off, lest Molly end up with perpetual homework. I hand the remaining softballs to the girls. "Okay, let's see what you've got, ladies. Oh, and Molly, you don't have to call me Miss Savannah. Just Savannah is fine."

"Not according to my momma. She'd be so mad if she found out I called an adult by her first name," Molly explains.

"I understand because I grew up the same way. It's a Southern thing. I don't want you getting in trouble with your momma, so Miss Savannah is fine. Now, show me your best pitch."

They each lob their balls, and they fall way short of the target. The shivering science teacher looks relieved as we move away from the booth. "We're gonna ride the bumper cars. See ya later, Uncle Fletcher!" And as quickly as they had arrived, the trio disappears into the crowd.

"What would you like to do next?" Fletcher asks.

I steal a glance at my watch and realize that it's nearly nine-thirty. Though it's early for most, it's the equivalent of an all-nighter for me. "I think I'd like to go home now," I answer.

"Is it the company?"

"No," I say with a smile. "This is late for me. I should be in bed nodding off to the sound of the TV."

"It's inexcusable for someone your age to publicly admit that. Okay, I'll bring you home, but first, how about dinner and a movie tomorrow night? And I'm not talking about the early feature, unless it's a deal breaker. Then we can have lunch and a movie."

"I'm not sure…"

"Come on. You know you want to."

"Okay, we can do dinner and a movie, but the movie can't be one of those super sappy love fests, nor can it be a shoot 'em-up-guts-all-over-the-place movie. Also, there are no guarantees that I'll actually watch the entire movie; I might sleep through it."

"Okay, got it. Anything else I need to know? " Fletcher asks as we make our way to the parking lot.

"I loathe sushi."

Fletcher laughs. "Okay, no sushi." Almost as an aside, he mutters, "But you like hamburgers and pizza."

I give him evil eyes. "I can't believe you have the audacity to pick on me! I'm sorry I was a little frazzled when we first met, but…"

In a tone much too sexy for any sane woman to ignore, Fletcher asks, "Why were you frazzled?"

I swallow hard before softly answering, "It's Lizzy's fault. She made me ride to the pizza place in that car of hers."

His smoldering eyes call my bluff. "Oh, I see."

With a smirk on his face, he fastens his helmet and straddles the bike before gently patting the backseat. "So, where do you live?"

I give him my address, and fifteen minutes later he drops me off at my door. Once I'm inside my apartment, I dread checking the answering machine. Without a doubt, there will be hundreds of messages from Lizzy asking about the evening. Just as quickly as I finish that thought, I realize I haven't received a single message, text, or communication from her the entire night. I check my phone to make sure it's operational, and it is. With a huff, I plop onto the sofa and snuggle one of the pillows tightly. My mind drifts, but I don't like any of the scenarios playing out, so I shut it down and finally manage to get some sleep.

five

Boom! Boom! Boom! Boom! I slowly wipe the accumulated drool from the corner of my mouth before groaning. My stiff neck and puffy eyes are reminders why I hate sleeping on the sofa. Stumbling to the door, I wipe the sleep from my eyes and find Lizzy standing in the hall. I unlatch the chain to let her in, but before I can finish she's already bursting through the door.

"Tell me everything!" she exclaims, far too perkily for my taste.

"Everything?" I blandly say, taking the cup of coffee she's thrusting in my face.

"You know what I mean," she scolds.

"There's not much to tell." I wrap a blanket around myself before reclaiming a spot on the sofa. "We went to a carnival. It was okay."

Lizzy's eyes shine with disbelief. "Okay? Just okay? Why do I have a hard time believing that?"

"Because you think every story has to have a fairytale ending. Sorry Lizzy, but that's not always the case. Sometimes things suck, and sometimes they're just meh."

"'Fletcher' and 'meh' are two words that can never be used in the same sentence."

"If you say so. What happened to you last night?"

"Love. That's what happened to me last night. I fell head over heels in love," she squeals while clasping her hands together tightly.

"Overnight? Can you remember the precise time? Was it 11:32, or maybe 11:34?" I sarcastically ask while shrugging my shoulders.

"Tease if you must, but it happened."

"Congratulations," I say dryly.

"And… I'M GETTING MARRIED!" Lizzy squeals.

"Hunh?" I ask, shaking my head from side to side with disbelief. "Married? You met the guy last night."

"No, I met the guy in middle school; we reconnected last night."

"Oh, that makes it so much better," I say, rolling my eyes.

Lizzy crosses her arms over her chest. "I have to say, I thought you'd be a little happier for me."

I sigh. "I'm sorry, but I worry about you. You and Grampy are all I have left in my life, and now you rush in here professing love and wanting to get married to someone you haven't seen in years. It's ridiculous."

Lizzy sits beside me. "Is that the problem? Are you worried that you're going to lose me as a friend?"

"No, I'm worried about your judgment."

"I'm a grown woman, Savannah."

"Your car has lips and a hair bow."

"My car is precious."

"Cars aren't meant to be precious; they're meant to get you from point A to point B."

Lizzy glares as she impatiently taps her foot. "You're jealous."

"Jealous? Jealous of what?"

"My happiness. You can't stand it when other people enjoy themselves. No, with Savannah it's all about self-loathing and depression."

"Excuse me! Walk a mile in my shoes and then tell me why I should believe in the fairytales."

"I was with you through most of it, Savannah. I know full well what you've been through, but what's the point of surviving all of it if you refuse to live your life? Moping around your apartment and answering calls at work is not living. Life is out there!" she yells, throwing open the curtains and pointing out of the window. The bright beams of sunlight have me scattering away like a vampire. "You have to let go of the darkness, Savannah."

"I don't hold onto it; I've made peace with it. I don't strive to be anything but okay, and then it doesn't attack me anymore."

"What? Do you hear yourself? It's not a person hell bent on revenge! Who's the immature person now? You refuse to be happy because you're scared it'll be taken from you. That's a terrible way to go through life."

"Don't you see? It's not about living; it's about surviving. Just surviving is enough to make me happy."

"Darling, you need to look up the definition of happy because your version of it's very distorted."

"I need to get dressed. I told Grampy I'd visit

today," I say, rising from the sofa. Lizzy pushes me back down.

"None of it was your fault. You shouldn't feel guilty, Savannah."

"I don't want to talk about it," I say, trying to push past her.

"Savannah, don't ignore me. Listen to me. You. Bear. No. Guilt."

"Stop it," I say, covering my ears, "I don't want to talk about it."

"Get it out. You'll feel better. You're bottling things up again."

"Would you shut up! Why won't you leave me alone? Just leave me alone," I say, swallowing hard so that the tears that threaten to spill will remain trapped.

Lizzy softens her tone, "I know you better than anyone. Ever since Grampy took a turn for the worse, you've been even more reclusive than usual, and I'm not just talking about your holing up in this place. I'm talking about emotionally, as well as physically. You're right; you're a survivor and the strongest person I know. I envy your strength, but with every tragedy, a little piece of you dies. I see it. My fear is that eventually there'll only be a shell of you left behind, and that would be the most tragic of all. I love you, Savannah, and I don't ever want to lose you."

"You're right," I admit with downcast eyes, "I have been shutting down. Grampy's about to die, and besides you, he's all I have left in my life. Can you even begin to fathom how much that's going to hurt? Of course I'm going to do what I have to so I can protect myself from that pain."

Lizzy pushes the hair off of my shoulder and offers me a slight smile. "Of course you are. Just don't go too far with it. You're on the cusp. What kind of friend would I be if I didn't warn you about it?"

"A better liked one, that's for sure."

"Ha, ha. You can tell me all about last night while you get dressed," Lizzy requests while shooing me towards the bedroom.

"Wait. Are you really getting married?" I ask.

"I am." She grins broadly.

"When?"

"Next month."

"Are you serious? Next month! That's...," Lizzy cuts me off with an arched brow, "...amazing news. I'm happy for you."

"Thank you," she beams, "There's not a doubt in my mind that Ben is my soul mate. We are one hundred percent meant to be together forever."

"One hundred? Not sixty-forty? Seventy-thirty?"

"One hundred," Lizzy asserts. I shrug.

"What do your parents have to say about it?" I ask.

Lizzy and her parents don't have the best of relationships. They are extremely wealthy and spared no expense entering Lizzy into every pageant they could find. Along with those pageants came endless hours of classes and practice sessions, dress fittings and elocution lessons. Visiting my house was like a vacation for Lizzy. With Mom and Dad always gone, we pretty much did whatever we wanted, whenever we wanted, and however we wanted. Unfortunately for her, she always had to return to that lifestyle she secretly resented. This went on until college graduation, after which, Lizzy proclaimed herself emancipated. She exchanged the BMW convertible, the designer wardrobe, and the luxury apartment her parents had furnished for her freedom. They speak to each other occasionally, and she'll also get a check from her mother every now and again, but that's about the extent of their current relationship.

She picks up a bottle of perfume, pops the top, and gives it a sniff. "I haven't told them. You're the first to know."

"When are you going to tell them?"

"I'm not sure I'm going to."

"What! Lizzy, you can't get married without telling your parents."

"Why not? Mother will try to swoop in and take over everything. Father will insist on the best of everything, and before I know it, Ben and I will be getting married on a paddleboat in the middle of the Mississippi River with every magnolia from here to Shreveport adorning anything that will sit still. The cake will be a ten tier monstrosity, and the guests will be five hundred people I don't even know. Trust me, it's better they not know."

"They'll never forgive you."

She sighs. "No, they won't." Lizzy grasps my shoulders. "Please promise me that you won't let them take over my wedding. Promise," she says with desperation.

I look her in the eye. "I promise that I'll try my best to keep your parents from taking over your day."

"And you'll try your hardest to keep them away from Ben?"

"That, too."

"Thank you." She bear hugs me.

"So if you aren't getting married on a paddle boat, then where are you getting married?"

"His vacation house on Lake Martin."

"You're getting married at a vacation house? What would Donna Reed say about that?" I quip.

"You just shush. It's going to be gorgeous."

"You're sure about this? You don't want to take a week or two to ponder this major, life-altering decision?"

"Nope."

"You're kooky, but you're far from stupid. If this is what you want then you have my full support."

"You're the best!" She excitedly jumps up and down a few times before bear hugging me again. "Okay, I'll let you go, but first, on a scale of one to ten, how was last night?"

"Seven."

"Sounds promising. Are you going to see him again?"

"We're supposed to go to dinner and a movie tonight."

Lizzy works to contain her squeal. "I want to hear all about it! I don't care what time it is when you get back..." she chortles. "I forgot who I was talking to. I'll be expecting your call around ten."

"You know me so well."

"Give Grampy my best."

"I'll do that. Congratulations."

Lizzy smiles broadly. "Thank you," she says while leaving the room. I hear the front door latch as she lets herself out.

My heart is in my throat as I approach the door to Grampy's room. The nurse warned me that his condition had deteriorated quickly, and that they were doing all in their power to keep him comfortable. Frankly, I'm terrified of what I'll find inside. I've seen death. Lots of terrible, tragic deaths, however, I've never been around someone who knows it's coming.

I sneak into the room, and still devoid of the courage to confront my anxiety, I hang out by door.

"Savannah?" Grampy's weak voice calls.

"Yes, sir. It's me," I say, finally coming into his line of sight. He doesn't look nearly as frail as I'd expected. His appearance is weak and tired, but still every bit my Grampy. I pull a chair close to the rail of the bed and take his hand in mine.

"How ya doin', Old Fart?" I ask, trying to keep the mood as light as possible.

He pulls on his oxygen mask and lowers it slightly so I can hear him. "Better now that you're here, moonshine."

My odd nickname goes way back. Grampy sang the song "You Are My Sunshine" to me when I was younger. Ever the cynic, once he finished singing I told him that I was nobody's sunshine, because sunshiny people are bright, happy, and cheery. I wasn't any of those. His reply was, "Savannah, even if darkness surrounds you, you still shine plenty bright. Problem is you don't realize it. Think about it, even if it's hidden, the moon still shines brightly in the darkest of night skies. If you won't be my sunshine, then from now on, you'll be my little moonshine."

A stabbing pain grips my heart when I notice

how hard he has to struggle to get those few words out. I pray my poker face is resolute because Grampy doesn't need to know how heartbroken I am seeing him in this precarious state.

"Can I get you anything?" I ask, softly stroking his hair.

"Nope, I'm good now that you're here," he rasps.

I manage a smile.

"I waited for you," he continues.

"You waited for me?"

He nods, and with a shaky hand, he reaches for my cheek. "You're the thing I love most in the world. Remember that, moonshine."

"Grampy...," I manage to stammer after swallowing the huge lump that forms in my throat.

"Shhhh. Listen. Forgive yourself and find happiness. Do it for me. I'll be checking in on you, and I want to see you happy. Lucas...."

"No, Grampy. Don't."

"Shhh. I'll see him. I know it. I'll take care of him. We'll go fishing together, even though I hate it. There has to be fishing in heaven, don't you think?"

His words are killing me, and I struggle to maintain my composure.

"Forgive yourself, Savannah," he says.

"Grampy, please..."

"Shhh. Your parents will be there, too. I'll let them know you're okay. Don't make a liar out of me. Find your happiness."

Every inch of me is ready to bolt from the room, but I know I can't leave. My stomach is on fire, my heart feels as if it is squeezed in a vice, and I

61

feel as though I have a soccer ball lodged in my throat. Every word Grampy says makes the pain even more intense, and I have no idea how to make it better except to beg him to stop.

"No, this is important. You will listen. You've beat yourself up since you were a child. Enough. End it. Happy. I want you happy. Promise me."

"Grampy, I can't promise that, but I can promise that I'll try."

"That's good enough for me. But, it has to be a real attempt. Nothing half-assed."

I manage a semi-smile. "Yes, sir."

"Good. I'm glad we got that out of the way. Now we wait." He visibly relaxes.

"Grampy…"

"Oh, hush child. I'm not scared. I'm ready. My only regret is not being able to see you like I usually do."

"Are you sure I can't get you anything?"

"I'm sure. I'm tired. I'm gonna close my eyes for a few minutes."

"Okay, Grampy. I'll be right here," I say, continuing to stroke his soft, snow white hair. And that's how I remained until the room slowly filled with darkness. A soft rap at the door startles me. Fully expecting a nurse, I'm shocked to see Fletcher enter the room.

Very softly, he whispers, "I'm sorry to intrude, but I was worried about you because you didn't answer the door when I showed up for our date. I called Ben, who passed the phone to Lizzy, and she told me where to find you. I brought you some supper, some snacks, magazines…," he says, shuffling some bags around in his hands.

I'm completely in awe of his thoughtful and kind gesture. I gently remove my hand from Grampy's so I can rise to greet him. My legs are wobbly from sitting for so long, and immediately the pins-and-needles feeling starts from my knees to the tips of my toes.

"It feels good to walk around a bit," I say, accepting Fletcher's offering, "Please, come in."

"Are you sure?"

"Yes, I'm sure," I say, unpacking the bag with the food. Inside is the biggest burger I've ever seen, along with a vat of fries. I arch an eyebrow in Fletcher's direction.

"I wasn't sure what you'd like, so I ordered the first thing on the menu."

"This is way more than I'll ever eat. Will you share it with me?"

"What? Okay, you just lost cool points," Fletcher whispers.

"How so?" I ask, cutting the burger in half and pouring half of the fries onto an opened napkin. I push the hospital cart that I'm using as a table next to Fletcher, and I take a seat beside him on the sofa.

"Do you know how impressive it would be for you to finish that entire burger?"

"Seriously, that's what you find impressive?" I ask.

"That's not all that I find impressive, but yes, I think it would be pretty kick ass."

Grinning as I shake my head, I give him a look before devouring my portion of the meal. I look down at the empty containers.

"I didn't realize how hungry I was. Thank you

for all of this."

"I'm glad I could help. Is there anything else you need?"

"No, I'm good. I'm going to hang around here with Grampy. He's been sleeping since this morning," I sigh.

"Rest is good."

"Yeah."

"Well, I guess I should get going," Fletcher says, lightly resting his palms against his thighs.

Internally, I struggle with asking him to stay. I really don't want to be alone, but asking for help is not something that comes naturally to me. "Uhm, it would... I would..."

Fletcher looks confused for a second before he figures out what I'm unsuccessfully trying to request. "I could stay a little longer if you'd like."

A sigh of relief escapes, "Yes. Thank you."

He shifts to find a more comfortable position on the sofa, one where he gets a better view of me. "Tell me about your grandfather."

I get into a similar position. "Where do I start? Let's see. He grew up in Cameron Parish, started working at the age of thirteen, and besides my dad, is pretty much the only positive male role model in my life. My dad was gone a lot because of his work, and Grampy was there whenever I needed him. After my parents died, I moved in with him for a while, but his condition deteriorated to the point that I was no longer able to leave him alone."

"What did he do for a living?"

"He worked as a contractor."

Fletcher nods his head. "I used to work for a contractor before I went into the army."

"How long have you been out? Uh, discharged? Whatever you call it."

"Six years, and I had a medical discharge."

"Medical discharge?"

"Yeah, it's a really long story best told on another day."

"I understand. Thanks for serving."

Fletcher grins, "You're welcome."

"Moonshine?" Grampy's frail voice calls. I'm at his bedside in an instant.

"Yes, Grampy. I'm still here." Fletcher looks confused. "It's a nickname," I quickly explain.

"Who's visiting?" Grampy inquires.

"This is my friend, Fletcher. He brought me some supper and stayed behind to keep me company. Did we wake you?"

"No. Send him over."

"What?" I ask, uncertain of what I heard.

"Send him over," Grampy repeats.

"Uhm, okay. Fletcher, my grandfather would like to talk to you," I say, shaking my head and shrugging my shoulders. Grampy shoos me away when Fletcher reaches his bedside, so I stand in the corner of the room, gnawing away at my fingernails while I desperately try to overhear their hushed conversation.

"You have my word, sir," Fletcher says, lifting the elderly man's hand and placing it in his own. After he finishes the handshake, he gently replaces Grampy's hand on his chest and joins me in the corner. "He wants to talk to you."

I'm instantly at his bedside.

"Will you help me sit up more? I'm too flat."

"Sure, Grampy." I push the button, and he

smiles when the head of the bed is finally in a position he likes.

"Good," he says through his mask, "I think I'm going to take another nap."

"Okay, Grampy. Rest well. I'm right here if you need anything," I say, placing a soft kiss on his forehead.

He squeezes my hand, "I know, my girl. You've always been there for me. I love you."

"I love you, too. Always."

He smiles while gently nodding his head, and his hand goes lax in mine. I bury the emotions I'm feeling before rejoining Fletcher on the sofa. Grampy's new position offers us a better view of him, and I find myself mesmerized with his oxygen mask. Condensation builds, then instantly disappears with each full respiratory cycle. Over and over again, I watch as the mask fogs up, and then goes clear. Fogs up, goes clear. Fogs up, goes clear...

SIX

"Miss Mason, excuse me. I'm sorry to wake you. Miss Mason?"

A nurse in rose colored scrubs stands before me. Disoriented, I open my eyes wider to get my bearings. The sun is just rising because the room is coated with a pinkish-orange glow. I must've fallen asleep on Fletcher's shoulder. He jerks awake as soon as I move, and I slowly turn my neck to work out the horrible kink.

"Yes?" I ask, "Is everything okay?"

"Miss Mason, I'm so sorry, but your grandfather has passed away. I checked in on him about twenty minutes ago, and there was no change in his condition. I was making another set of rounds, and... I'm very sorry for your loss."

I will the nurse to stay where she is. She's blocking the sight of my lifeless grandfather with her body, and I'm not ready to see him. My amazing grandfather is gone, and all that remains is the shell that he carried himself around in for his eighty-two years on earth. His zeal, his compassion, his caring, his life—gone. That damned vice grips my heart again, and the pain is virtually unbearable. I purposely zone out in an effort to make it easier to deal with the situation.

Fletcher pulls me into his arms and hugs me tightly. I'm glad I'm facing toward the window and not toward Grampy. I'm so emotionally detached that I don't even reprimand him for holding me; I just go with it. The trees are gently swaying in the breeze outside. Cars travel up and down the streets. People bustle from one sidewalk to another. Life goes on, but not for my Grampy.

It takes me a little while, but a level of detachment that makes functioning possible finally occurs. I push free from Fletcher's arms and stand to look the nurse squarely in the face. "What now?" I ask.

"We'll give you as much time as you need to spend with him. After you've paid your last respects, we'll be in touch with the funeral home of your choice, and they will take over from there."

"His wishes were for Kincaide Funeral Home to handle his final arrangements. He worked out something with them... I don't know what it is. He just told me to use Kincaide."

"Very well. I'll contact them shortly." She stays in the room just a bit longer, doing something by Grampy's bed. I still won't look. I hear the door shut, and Fletcher's shuffling stops behind me. His hand's upon my shoulder, and I close my eyes.

"I'm fine. I don't want to do the whole touchy-feely-cry-and-talk-it-out thing. Okay? I just want to handle this my way."

"He's smiling," Fletcher says quietly.

"What?"

"Your grandfather. He died smiling."

Slowly, I pivot around, my gaze fixed

downward. Once I'm lined up with the foot of the bed, I gingerly will my eyes to move upwards until I see him. The nurse had removed the oxygen mask from his face, and it now rests on the table beside him. His hands are carefully crossed over his upper abdomen, and he's still in the same semi-reclined position he'd asked to be put in a few hours before. Despite my original hunch that Fletcher said such a thing in an earnest effort to provide comfort, I learn that my guess is wrong. Indeed, a very peaceful looking Grampy, head positioned towards the sofa Fletcher and I recently vacated, has a soft smile upon his face.

"It's a relief that his death wasn't agonizing. I have to go now," I say.

Fletcher reaches out for me, and I firmly snatch my hand away from his. He holds his hands up and takes a slight step back.

"I'm sorry," I mumble, "I just need to be away from here. Now."

My palm rests on the door handle when Fletcher asks me to stop. He's so close that I swear his warm breath is brushing across the nape of my neck. Flipping around to confront him, I'm about to tear into him when he gestures for me to hear him out. Rolling my eyes upwards, I stay, but I make sure he knows it's under duress.

"Would you like some time with him— alone?"

"No. I was here when he needed me. He's gone, and so am I." Yanking the door open, I dash down the hall and nearly tackle an elderly woman using a walker. I offer her a half-assed apology before barreling into the parking lot. Fumbling for my keys, my heart sinks when I realize they aren't in my pocket. In my haste, I'd forgotten everything behind—my purse, my keys, the magazines and books that Fletcher brought, as well as Grampy's personal items. Inhaling deeply, I push aside the gut-wrenching pain and growing discomfort.

Suck it up, buttercup. If you want to leave, you'll have to march back inside and claim your things. I do just that and meet a confused Fletcher in the hallway.

"I forgot my purse," I explain.

"Yeah, I was on my way to find you," he says, holding several bags.

"What's all of that?" I ask.

"Your things, your grandfather's things, and some stuff the nurse brought in after you left. Come on. I'll walk you to your car."

I nod, grateful that I don't have to face Grampy again, yet I'm reluctant to share that gratitude with Fletcher. Instead, head held high and shoulders back, I lead the way to the parking lot. My trunk opens once I push the button, and Fletcher places the bags inside for me.

"I'm sure you want to be alone, but promise me that you'll call if you need anything."

"I will," I answer curtly.

"Are you sure you're okay to drive? I don't mind bringing you home."

"I'm absolutely fine. Thanks again for staying with me last night," I say, ducking into the driver's seat.

"You're welcome. Drive safely."

I close the door, and I'm out of the parking lot before Fletcher makes it to his bike.

Though I'm utterly exhausted, I can't go home. Not yet. Damn this constant internal struggle! My body wants me to feel, to mourn, but my mind won't let me. It's not the first time I've been in this position. Patience is what I need to get through it. It might take a little time, but the sadness will eventually disappear into the indifference that I consider status quo.

I make one stop at a nearby strip mall before continuing on to the cemetery. The route is so familiar that it's as though the car's on autopilot. Enter the second gate, pass three cross streets, slight curve to the right, fourth oak tree, and there it is. I pull the blue teddy bear from the bag and lower myself to place it next to the marble cross that adorns the tiny grave.

"Lucas, it's Momma," I say out loud before falling to my knees. "Baby, I miss you more than you could ever know. Grampy promised me that he'll take you fishing, so I need you to keep an eye out for him. I love you and Grampy so very much, and one day I'll be there with you, my love. When that day comes, I'm going to hold you in my arms and never let you go. I'm so mad at myself for failing you, and I'm sorry that I wasn't a better mother. Lucas, my sweet precious boy, please forgive me." I curl into a ball, and hugging the marker of my son's final resting place, I begin to sob.

The sobs give way to shaky breaths. The sound of crunching gravel makes me lurch to attention. Quickly dashing the remnants of tears, I turn to see Fletcher standing nearby.

"I... I'm sorry. I was worried about you, so...," he stumbles over his words.

"I told you I was fine," I snap.

"You don't look fine," he says softly as he closes the gap between us.

"It's nothing," I say, repositioning the teddy bear before walking away.

"Lucas Calloway," he reads. "Who's Lucas?"

I stop cold. Every bit of me wants to yell, "He's nobody you need to concern yourself about!" However, my heart won't let it happen. Lucas was incredibly special, and I'd never do anything to put negative energy around his resting place. Lucas had too much of that when he was alive; no way would I chance plaguing him with that now.

I walk to a cement bench under a tree about three rows down, and Fletcher follows. We're silent for a while, and I'm appreciative of that.

"Please understand that this isn't something I typically discuss. My past is so…," I sigh heavily. "My dad was a great man, but he was gone all of the time. My mom wasn't a great person, and she disappeared whenever he left, so I basically raised myself. Except for Grampy. Grampy kept an eye on me, but he wasn't able to fill the void left by my parents' absence. I was lonely, bored, young, and impressionable. When I turned seventeen, this loser disguised as Prince Charming wriggled his way into my life. He made big promises about our future together, but they were lies to get me to sleep with him. I fell for it, and a month later I found out I was pregnant.

"I was overjoyed; he wasn't. His parents demanded a DNA test, and once it came back that Lucas was his son, they forced him to marry me. I was so delusional that I thought I could make him love me and the baby. Instead, Lucas and I only served as mementos of the life we stole from him. He despised us, and he made sure I knew it.

"He refused to better himself. He dropped out of college, called in sick nearly every day at work, and eventually he quit working all together. I did everything I could to take the pressure off him: cooked, kept the apartment clean, never bothered him with the baby, waited on him hand and foot. Nothing worked.

"One day we were out of food, and when I asked him for a few dollars to get the baby something to eat, he told me to go out and earn it. What was I supposed to do? My baby was hungry, we had no money, my dad was offshore, my mom was God knows where, Lizzy was at college, and Grampy was on vacation. I had no one to call for help. There was no choice but to have Paul watch Lucas while I scrounged for money. The only place that would hire me immediately and give me some daily take home money was a little café a few blocks from our apartment. Being that our car was repossessed, it was what I considered the best option."

I stand, crossing my arms over my chest as I turn away from Fletcher. "Lucas devoured the food I brought home for him the first night. Paul got upset that I didn't bring something home for him too, and even though I explained that I only had enough money to buy for the baby, he got mad and stormed out of the house.

"I ignored it. I went back to work the next day, but this time I made enough in tips that I was able to bring him some food from the restaurant, too. It wasn't what he wanted to eat, so he threw the plate against the wall and then left it for me to clean up. I got up the next day and did it all over again. It killed me leaving Lucas behind because I missed him so much while I worked, but I knew if I didn't work, he wouldn't be able to eat."

Putting the story into words hurts so much that I take a few seconds to compose myself before going on.

"After my fourth day of work, I came home to find Paul passed out on the sofa. I was scared to wake him, so I tiptoed into Lucas' room so I could snuggle with my baby boy. I knew something was wrong as soon as I entered the room, and my worst nightmare came to life when I peered into the crib. I called for an ambulance, and they tried everything they could to save him, but he was pronounced dead at the hospital. Paul was nowhere to be found, and I wouldn't see him again until his trial.

"He killed our baby. He was tired of hearing Lucas' cries for me, so he drugged him." I bite my lower lip to keep it from trembling. "He told the judge that he never intended to kill him, only to sedate him enough to stop the crying. It was a ploy to get a reduced sentence. After he was found guilty, and sentenced to twenty-five years in prison, he yelled to the courtroom audience that he was happy the little shit was gone and he hoped that I'd be next.

"My dad had friends who know people, and I've been assured that even to this day Paul gets regular visits from those sympathetic to my situation. He spends more time in the prison infirmary than his cell. They've shifted him to protective custody, solitary, even different facilities, but somehow the word always gets out about what he did.

"I suppose I should take some solace in knowing that he's living in a personal hell, but you know what? My hell is so much worse than his. Black eyes fade, broken bones heal, lacerations mend; my heart will be shattered forever.

"So, anyway, that's Lucas' story. He's my son, and I miss him so much that I can barely breathe sometimes."

All is silent, so I look over to see if Fletcher is still there. His face shows utter shock mixed with intense sympathy.

"Fletcher, when I say that my life has been filled with tragedy, I mean it. You still don't know the half of it. You should run away as quickly as you can and thank God that you dodged a bullet when it came to getting to know me better."

"I don't want to run. I want to hold you."

"I'm not the type who likes or needs to be held. We discussed this the first day we met."

"Clearly, the problem is that you haven't been held enough. I want to change that. I want to help you to heal, Savannah."

I let out a huff, "I'm beyond help."

"As long as you're breathing, you're not beyond help. Look, I'm not a therapist, but I do know some things about healing from traumas. You're not the only one with a rotten past. Let me show you how much better life can be with someone who supports you. You shouldn't be alone right now. If you don't want me, then at least let me call Lizzy."

"No. Not Lizzy. I love her, but I'm not ready for her sunshine and rainbows. I want to mope, and be sad, and wallow in self-pity for at least a day before she comes around."

"Then you'll need me as a barrier. Let me stay with you."

I give him a look to show that I mean business. "You won't try to cheer me up?"

"Not a chance," he affirms.

"I don't want any mock therapy sessions."

"Understood."

"I might not even talk to you at all."

"That's absolutely your prerogative."

"Fine, you can come over later. I need a few hours to be alone."

"Is six okay?"

I nod as I walk away from him. I blow one final kiss in Lucas' direction, say a silent hello to my dad as I pass his headstone, and make my way to my car. Once again, I drive away before Fletcher, so I catch a quick glimpse of him in the rearview. He's kneeling beside a grave a few sections away from Lucas' and my parents'.

I hope to rest the few hours before Fletcher's arrival, but of course, it doesn't happen. Staring at the stark white walls, I will myself to drift into semi-consciousness, but instead mental images of Grampy holding eighteen-month old Lucas in his arms flit in and out of my mind. These images should make me feel comfort and relief, but jealousy rages deep inside of me. I want to be the one holding my baby! My teetering faith allows me to see these images, but that tiny bit of faith that I cling to isn't enough to diminish the pain and loneliness.

I contemplated suicide after Lucas died, and now I find myself entertaining the same thoughts.

What's left for me to live for? I have a sucky job, no family, one friend, bills that I'll never pay off... However, the same thing that saved me before saves me again—I'm not a quitter. Never have been, and obviously, I never will be. Perhaps a glutton for punishment is the more accurate term for me? Regardless, I'm bound to continue my arduous journey, except now I'll be even more alone.

Not a single tear has been shed since visiting the cemetery, and I feel a little guilty about it. Shouldn't I be a huge sobbing mess right now? I just lost my grandfather—my only living relative. My advocate. My savior. I want to cry so badly, but the tears refuse to surface. All of them are reserved for the days I visit my son.

Tired of moping in bed, I shower, then rummage through my drawers for a tank top and a pair of shorts. I'm running a comb through my damp hair when Fletcher knocks on the front door. I don't even offer a "hello" before jumping straight to the point.

"I'm fine. I really don't need a babysitter."

Fletcher scratches his beard. "Oh, so I should just leave, right?"

"Yep. I'm good."

Fletcher nods, but remains in the doorway. "So, you have plenty of food to eat?"

My eyes roll up in my head as I do a quick mental inventory of what's in my fridge. Zilch. "I'll have something delivered."

He purses his lips and shifts them to the side. "Do you have movies to watch, books to read... things like that to help distract you some?"

"I have cable, and I have plenty of magazines thanks to you."

77

His tone changes to one more serious, "You shouldn't be alone."

"I'm usually alone. It's not something that's new to me."

"That needs to change," he says, propping his arm against the door jamb.

"Why? It's worked just fine all of these years."

"Because you're missing out on a lot, Savannah."

"Like what? Some big, strong, handsome guy hugging me and telling me that everything is going to be okay? I already know that everything is going to be okay. I've almost died twice, lost a child, survived an abusive relationship, buried both of my parents, and now I'll be burying my grandfather. It sucks, but I know that when it's all said and done, it's just another day. I'll wake up tomorrow, I'll go to work, and I'll continue to function, just like I've always done—until the day that I don't. And I refuse worry about that day until it comes. It might be sixty years from now, or it might be five years down the road. Who knows? So, I'm definitely okay to stay in my apartment by myself."

"Wow, I don't know what to say."

"You don't have to say anything. I appreciate that you stopped by. Goodnight."

He shoves his hand against the door. "Wait. Savannah, every bit of me is saying that I shouldn't leave you alone tonight."

"Hoping for bereavement sex?"

Fletcher flushes. "What? No! I assure you, I'm not that guy."

"Then what do you want from me? You don't

even know me."

"That's just it. I don't want anything *from* you. I just want to be there *for* you."

I open the door fully so he can enter. "I don't get it. Why?"

"Just because," he says with a hint of frustration, "I can't put it into words. It's a feeling."

"I hope you don't expect me to entertain you. I'm not feeling very sociable right now."

"I'm not," he affirms.

"Fine. Have a seat. What would you like for dinner, pizza or Chinese?"

"Chinese," Fletcher volunteers. I dig around the kitchen junk drawer until I find the menu I'm searching for. "I don't need that," he says when I try handing it to him. "Hunan shrimp, extra spicy."

Give him a perplexed stare.

"What?" he self-consciously asks.

"Have you been talking to Lizzy?"

"Only to find out where you were last night. Why?"

I let out a *hhmmmph*. "That's what I usually order. Spring rolls or egg rolls?"

"Spring," he answers without hesitation.

"Sweet and sour or duck sauce?"

"Sweet and sour."

"Egg drop soup or wonton soup?"

"Egg drop. Is this some sort of test?" he asks with a chuckle.

"Are you sure you haven't talked to Lizzy?"

"About Chinese food? No, I assure you, I haven't."

"I guess it's just coincidental that you like all the same things that I like?"

"Obviously it is."

I shrug my shoulders before dialing the number. It's almost embarrassing that they don't even ask for my name or address anymore; however, it's somewhat entertaining to hear the surprise in the order taker's voice when I ask for two of everything.

"Okay, food will be here in about twenty minutes," I say, taking a seat next to Fletcher. I stare ahead silently as thousands of questions come to mind, but not one of them has me curious enough to actually verbalize it. Through my peripheral vision, I know that Fletcher is looking in my direction, and after a while, I give in to the urge to face him.

"What?" I ask, raising my eyebrows to make him aware of my observation.

"I just... you kind of let it slip earlier that you almost died twice, and I can't help but notice the scars on your legs..."

Dammit! I'm so used to being by myself or with Lizzy that I completely messed up and put on shorts. Pants or jeans keep the questions at bay.

"How is it that I've managed to avoid discussing my personal life with anyone for as long as I can remember, yet you pop into my life and all of my secrets suddenly surface?"

"When is the last time you socialized with someone other than Lizzy or your grandfather?"

"I socialize daily, thank you very much," I assert.

"Random calls from Pole Co. customers do not count."

I look to the floor. "Oh, well then I don't know."

"Sounds to me like it's long overdue."

I rise from the sofa. "Well, no one asked you."

Fletcher laughs, and I'm miffed because it's not the reaction I want. He needs to get angry, hurt, or upset, then storm off into the night never to be heard from again. *Ah, who am I kidding? What is it that makes him so different from everyone else? Why do I feel drawn to him? Compelled to confide in him? Unable to speak clearly when he's near? I really don't want him to go, but it's against my nature to relent.*

"No, I wasn't asked, but it needed to be said."

I spin around to face Fletcher. Ever the cynic, I blatantly interrogate him. "What do you get out of this? What's your motive for trying to wriggle your way into my life? I'm broke. Every penny I had went to help Grampy. I'm boring. As you well know, I'm not a social butterfly. I'm not easy. I can't even remember the last time I had sex. So what? What is it? Why is it so important for you to be here with me?"

His eyes darken, and his face softens somewhat. He slowly closes the distance between us, and I start to back away. When he reaches to touch my cheek, I instinctively jerk my head to the side, but it doesn't stop him. He gently moves his hand so that I'm forced to look into his eyes. "I want to make this perfectly clear. My only motive is to be able to spend time with you. I hate that you've been hurt so much. You're a beautiful woman who has so much to offer, and I'm not talking about money, entertainment, or sex. You've cocooned yourself away for so long that you don't even realize you're already a butterfly. I see it plain as day. I want to be around you because you're intriguing, and frankly, being around you makes me happy. Look, I know where you are because I was there not long ago. Let me show you something."

He slowly raises the hem of his shirt to expose a wondrous six pack and a hard, chiseled chest. I have no clue where he's going with it until he turns around. His broad shoulders are just as rock solid as the rest of him, but they are heavily scarred from what must have been a horrific injury. The thickened tissue, colors ranging from brilliant white to near maroon, trail down his back, and disappear beneath his waist band.

Sucking in deeply, I bite my lower lip to stop the gasp that wants to come. "Fletcher, I…"

"You want to know what happened, right?" he asks, slowly pulling the shirt down.

"Yes, I do," I shyly admit.

"The same way I want to know about your scars. I think we can help each other out, Savannah."

"But, I don't need help? I'm okay with my life. Why do people keep telling me that okay is bad?"

"Okay is just that—okay. It isn't extraordinary or spectacular. Life should never be described as simply okay."

"If you say so. Are you going to tell me what happened, or are you going to continue with the impromptu therapy session you promised we wouldn't have?" I demand in a bit bitchier tone than I intend.

Fletcher raises his hands. "You're right." He takes a moment before he begins, "It happened when I was overseas, and I'm not going to draw out all of the gory details. Long story short, an IED explosion ignited our patrol vehicle, and I was trapped inside."

"I'm sorry you had to go through that. The pain must've been excruciating."

"You have no idea," he mumbles under his breath.

I'm uncertain of how to respond, so a twinge of relief courses through me when the delivery man knocks at the door. Fletcher is on his feet, and before I can protest, he's paid for the food and tipped the driver. He sends him on his way.

"You didn't have to do that," I say.

"No, I didn't. I'm starved; let's eat."

"That's it?" I ask.

Fletcher gives me a strange look. "What more do you want?"

"I figured there would be some long lecture about how my allowing you to pay for dinner equates to me overcoming my control issues, or something equally ridiculous."

Fletcher holds his chopsticks like drumsticks. "I'm offended by your assumption, but intrigued by your hypothesis. Perhaps it's a step in the right direction?"

"Perhaps you should start filling your mouth with food instead of observations."

"Ooooo, feisty. Nice."

I crack a smile. "Thanks for dinner." He returns the smile then hungrily digs into his carton of Hunan shrimp. I place my carton on the coffee table.

"Is something wrong with your food?" Fletcher inquires.

"No, the food is great. It was stupid."

"What was stupid?" he asks, swallowing his mouthful.

"The way I got the scars on my legs."

"Why don't you let me judge that for myself?"

I shrug my shoulders. "I was stupid and naïve as a kid."

Fletcher shakes his hand, so I pause my story. "Isn't that what kids are supposed to be? Well, not stupid, but naïve and carefree?"

"Probably, but raising yourself kind of makes you grow up pretty quickly. You know that my mom started leaving me alone at an early age, so I used to cry the entire time she was gone. I was terrified being alone in that huge house; I was barely in preschool, and the threat of the boogeyman or ghosts coming to get me haunted my every thought. The first few times she came home to find me a cried out, sobbing mess, she gave me butt whippings, but that didn't work. My fear was so intense that it outweighed the physical pain of her punishment.

"Once she realized this, she tried a different strategy—lying and manipulation. She told me that it was another one of our special secrets, and I couldn't share with anyone, not even Dad." I stop long enough to sigh. "If only I'd confessed everything to him way back when... Anyway, Mom came up with this elaborate story about how she and I were actually superheroes, and how she couldn't use her powers since she got married, but I still had mine. Supposedly, I needed to figure out which powers I was given because she wasn't even sure what they were. That said, she *did* know for certain that *courage* and *bravery* were two main traits I'd carry," I say in an exaggerated superhero voice.

Fletcher remains quiet even though his body language indicates that he wants to interrupt the story.

"I was still scared, but it did get easier. The boredom was replaced with me trying everything I could to get my superpowers to work. One day I tried to fly, and I did just that. I flew off of our sofa and belly flopped right onto our glass coffee table."

Fletcher lets out a wince, and I nod.

"Yeah, it wasn't pretty. Luckily, I waited until just before she got home to take flight. If not, I'd have likely bled to death. She stayed home with me for about a week after I was released from the hospital, but she was so mean and cantankerous that I couldn't wait to be alone again. Anyway, that's the story behind the scars. Stupid, huh?"

"The only thing stupid about that story is the fact that you were abandoned, lied to, and unjustly punished. My God, Savannah, how old were you?"

"Four or five. Somewhere in that range."

"Why didn't you tell someone? I can't even fathom being in that situation."

"I grew up learning that I shouldn't bother Daddy with anything because he worked so much. I was told doing so would preoccupy his mind and that he could get hurt or killed because of it. I was supposed to keep the bad stuff to myself and only tell Daddy the good things."

Fletcher slowly shakes his head. "Whoa. I... I don't know what to say."

"Don't say anything. It's all in the past, and I've turned out okay. See, I'm still here. I'm a survivor."

"But you're still not living a real life, and now I know why. You probably don't have a clue what normal is."

"Hey!" I snap, "I'm introverted, not a freak."

"I didn't mean it like that," Fletcher insists.

"Then what did you mean?" I ask, upset with myself because I broke my nondisclosure rule.

"I mean that you didn't grow up traditionally."

I cock my eyebrow in his direction. "If you consider being raised traditionally as having a mom and dad who constantly dote over you and such, then no, I didn't grow up traditionally. And you know what? Neither did the majority of the people who inhabit this vast planet. It happened. It sucked. I don't dwell on it. I don't roll around in self pity begging others to feel sorry for me or give me things just because I had it tough once upon a time. Those incidents were simply events that occurred. I got over them, and I moved on. Why is that so hard for you to comprehend?"

"How did you do it? How did you continue to function after going through losing your parents—your child?"

I shrug. "What's the alternative? Shrivel up in a ball and become a burden on society? Kill myself to end it all? Don't think I haven't thought about those options, but only briefly. No matter how small, I always find something that pushes me forward. For instance, I just lost my grandfather. I'm heartbroken over losing him, and rightfully so being that he was my only living relative. My job is to keep his memory alive, so his life and death won't be in vain. Same with Lucas. It felt like I couldn't breathe for months after he died, but if I give up, his memory will be lost. I live for them. I live to protect their memories."

"But you don't live for yourself, Savannah. If you keep being so isolated, who will be there to preserve your memory or to keep the memories alive once you're gone?"

I should be upset with his constant challenging. Instead I smile. "That's what I have Lizzy for."

Fletcher smiles. "Touche. But seriously, you trust your life story in the hands of a woman who dresses up her car?"

"Absolutely," I say, pulling my carton of Hunan shrimp closer as I kick my heels up onto the coffee table.

Fletcher laughs. "You two certainly qualify as the odd couple."

"You think?" I ask, casting a coy look in his direction. "What about you and Ben? What are your thoughts on the upcoming nuptials?"

"I'm not sure what to think, but I know that Ben is one of the most level-headed people around. If he thinks this is right then it must be."

"Lizzy said they're supposed to be getting married at his lake house? That in itself has me uncertain about all of this. Lizzy is not the outdoorsy, roughing it type of person."

"Maybe she's found her inner adventurer?"

I shrug. "Maybe. Tell me about Ben."

"We met while playing high school football and have been best friends ever since. When I joined the army, he went to culinary school. Ben gained a lot of experience working in several different kitchens, and now he owns his own restaurant here in town. He's looking to expand in the near future."

"I'm impressed," I say. "Maybe I've been there. What's it called?"

"Triceratops."

"Home of the Bronto Burger," we say

together.

"I love their food! That's Ben's place!"

"Yep," Fletcher answers with a smile.

"I've always wondered how they came up with the dinosaur concept. You have to be in the know. Spill."

"I know all about it. Remember how I said we met while playing high school football?"

I nod.

"There were actually three of us who, for lack of a better term, ruled the school."

"So you were *that* guy?"

Fletcher laughs. "Yeah, I guess I was. Ben, Brody, and I were beasts on the football field, so as an inside joke, we started calling ourselves the triceratops. Yes, I know that it wasn't the best nickname, but at the time, we sure thought it was. I'm not sure how, but it spread, and before long, everyone referred to our trio as the triceratops. Fast forward a bunch of years, and Ben decided he could use it as a marketing scheme for his new restaurant. It worked better than anyone ever imagined."

"I'd say. The place is packed every time I visit."

"Yeah, he's a natural when it comes to that kind of stuff. What about Lizzy? Tell me about her."

"We also met in school. It started simply enough. We shared a couple of classes, and she'd ask me all of these random questions the entire class period. I ignored most of them, but she still kept at it, day after day. Then she started sitting with me at lunch. I told her that I wasn't the friendly type, and that she needed to sit somewhere else, but she didn't care. Nothing I did would stop her from seeking me out so she could bombard me with her cheer and enthusiasm."

"Obviously, she wore you down."

"Eventually."

"How long did it take?"

"About three months and a black eye."

Fletcher laughs. "Which of you had the shiner?"

"Both of us."

"What?"

"I was walking home from school, and of course, Lizzy was right on my heels yapping about some boy she liked or something. I'd finally had enough, so I popped her in the eye."

"What did she do?"

"She hit me back. I invited her inside for a cold pack, and as we sat there icing down our faces, we became friends."

"Did you ever ask her why she was so persistent? It seems to me like a lot of others would've given up way before she did."

"I did. She said it was because she knew I needed her. It was a strong feeling she had whenever she was around me."

"Was she right?"

I contemplate it for a few seconds. "I suppose she was."

Fletcher nods. "She sounds like she's a perfect match for Ben."

"I hope it works out for them."

"Yeah, me too."

I start to pick up the empty cartons around us, and Fletcher follows me into the kitchen with the ones I couldn't carry. After everything is put in its place, I glance at the microwave clock, and I'm shocked to see that it's nearly eleven o'clock. Time always seems to fly when Fletcher's around.

"I suppose I should let you get some rest," he announces, taking his cue from my yawn.

"Yeah, I'm pretty worn out. Uh… I want to… Uhm…"

"No thanks necessary," Fletcher says with a grin.

"Fletcher?" I ask, my arm propped against the open door frame leading into the hallway.

"Yeah?"

"I've been meaning to ask this since yesterday, what did my Grampy say when he called you over to his bedside?"

Fletcher runs his hand over his beard. "I was going to talk about that tomorrow. He said you should expect a letter, and he wanted me to make sure that you read it. He told me that you'd likely toss it to the side, so my job is to make sure that doesn't happen."

My face scrunches. "A letter? Did he mention anything else?"

"Nope. That was it. He said what he had to say, and then he thanked me for being there. That's it."

"Okay, I guess I'll keep an eye out for this mysterious letter. Thanks again. Good night, Fletcher. Be careful going home."

"I will. Good night, Savannah. I'll be in touch."

I give a slight wave while closing the door. After making sure the apartment is locked up tightly, I head to the bedroom. I briefly touch base with Lizzy via text before cuddling with my pillow and going to sleep.

RHONDA R. DENNIS

seven

My legs nervously pulse in rapid fire succession as I wait in the plush office of the funeral home director. Lizzy wanted to come along, but I assured her that I could handle it, and that I was sure it would go well. I should've taken her up on her offer because I'm completely creeping myself out.

I think the part that's most bothersome is my knowing that Grampy is in the building. Is he behind the wall I'm facing? Down the hallway? Across from the kitchenette? Is it like the TV shows where his bloated, cyanotic corpse, draped in nothing but a simple white towel across his groin, is stiffly lying on some ice cold steel table? Or worse, maybe he's tucked in the refrigeration unit, his body being preserved like a hunk of meat until it finds its final resting place.

A deep shiver runs through me, and I'm seriously about to bolt from the room when an extremely thin, balding man with a hook nose and glasses three times too big for his face enters the room. "Are you okay?" he asks. I hate that damn question so much! It's almost certain that according to the asker, you do NOT look okay in the least, so why ask the obvious? Why not just come out with what he or she really wants to know, "What's wrong with you?"

"I'm fine," I lie, praying that the panic I'm feeling doesn't turn into a full blown attack. *Oh, my God! Please hurry this along. Please, please, hurry this along.*

Almost as if he's read my mind, he says, "I won't keep you long," while pulling out the massive brown leather chair behind his desk so he can take a seat. Albeit a small one, a wave of relief washes over me. "Can I get you some coffee? A soft drink? Water?"

I shake my head. *You can get this over with so I can get the hell out of here.*

"Very well. First, let me offer my deepest sympathy for your loss." His hands are clasped in front of him in that professional I'm-going-to-pretend-to-give-a-crap-because-it's-my- job-and-I-have-to pose.

"Thank you." *Yeah, I'm sure you're absolutely heartbroken that my Grampy died. Do you think I suddenly forgot how you make your money? Wow, this guy looks just like the nasty old man from* The Simpsons. *What was his name? Oh, jeez! Any other time I'd know it! Come on. I can hear his voice, see his character... Mr. Burns! That's it! This guy looks just like Mr. Burns.*

"...so moving on to the other issue."

What other issue? Oh, what was the first issue? Pay attention, Savannah! "I'm sorry. I was slightly distracted. Would you mind repeating what you just said?"

He works to clone a sincere smile. "Of course. Your grandfather has taken care of all the arrangements. He asked that there be no service of any kind and that his remains be cremated. He specified that you're the only remaining family member, and it was very important to him that you not be burdened with any decisions related to his final arrangements."

I nod.

"The second issue that I was referring to is this." He opens the top desk drawer to hand me a thick envelope. *Ah, here it comes. The bill. I wonder how much this is going to cost me? Good thing I didn't ask for a cup of coffee. I'll bet it would have been tacked on for sure.*

I take the envelope from his outstretched hand. "Do you make payment arrangements?" I ask.

"We do, but it's not necessary here. Your grandfather has already paid for everything."

"He did?" I say with more surprise than I intend. *I've been paying for everything that his retirement and his social security didn't cover. Where in the hell did he get the money to pay for his cremation?*

"Yes, ma'am, he did. He also paid for the custom urn that holds his ashes."

"Custom urn?"

He picks up the headset of his phone, pushes a button, and softly speaks, "Melanie, we're ready for Mr. Bernard, please."

My heart thuds in my chest. Grampy is here, but he's nothing but a pile of ashes. When I arrived, I honestly thought I'd be picking out coffins and hymns today, not actually taking Grampy home with me.

I tuck the envelope into my purse while waiting for Melanie, and an awkward silence ensues. Mr. Burns and I fake smile at each other, as he gently rocks back and forth in his chair. I'm just about to fake a coughing spell just to break the stare down we have going on when Melanie finally enters the room with a bronze fishing pole in one hand, and a large bronze bass in the other. A thin metal line attaches the two.

"What's that?" I ask.

"That's your grandfather's urn."

"No, urns are ceramic and vase-like. That's a fishing pole, and my Grampy hated fishing. If this is a joke, it's not very funny."

"It's a custom urn. He designed it himself."

"I don't understand. Where exactly is my grandfather? It's just a figurine. A statue. A knick-knack."

"He's inside the fish. There's a little opening in the mouth. See? If you ever want to open it, you just twist here…"

"No! That's quite alright. Thank you," I say, jumping out of my seat. "Is that all?"

"Yes, ma'am. That is all."

"Thank you," I say, awkwardly taking the pole and fish from Melanie and rushing to my car. I sit in the parking lot a good five minutes just staring at Grampy's remains sitting on the seat next to me. I break the trance and debate stopping by Lizzy's. I mentally veto that idea and continue on to my apartment. I'd no sooner pulled into my parking spot when the familiar python-skinned bike rolls up next to my car. I crack the door.

"Hi, Fletcher," I say as he removes his helmet.

"Hi. I thought I'd check in on you. Are you doing okay?"

"Yeah, I'm fine." I go to the passenger side and wrestle the fishing pole out of the car.

"What's that?" Fletcher queries.

"Grampy," I say, giving one final tug to free the pole from the door frame.

"Excuse me?"

"You see this?" I ask, holding the piece out so he can get a better look. "This is what happens when funeral home attendants let senile old men make their own final arrangements."

"I don't follow. You said it's your Grampy…"

"He's inside the fish," I explain. Fletcher takes a couple of steps back, but slowly, a smile crosses his lips.

"You got me. Seriously, how did it go today?"

I give him a look that says I'm not joking.

"Do you want me to carry it for you?" he asks, obviously uncomfortable with the situation.

"Sure," I say, pushing the pole and fish into his hands then winding the metal line between his fingers so it won't drag on the ground.

"Uh, okay." He awkwardly juggles the assortment while I fumble for my keys. "Where do you want this?" he asks once we're inside the apartment.

"The coffee table for now, I guess." After tossing my purse onto the sofa, I kick off the heels I'm wearing and slowly unbutton the black suit jacket that covers the matching dress I have underneath. "I'll just be a second. I'm going to change. Help yourself to anything in the fridge."

"Thanks," Fletcher says, shaking his head as he tries to arrange the urn in a way that allows all of the elements to remain on top of the coffee table.

I debate the whole pants versus shorts issue before I decide that since the cat's already out of the bag about the scars, I may as well get comfortable. Shorts and a t-shirt have me feeling much more relaxed by the time I find Fletcher on the sofa staring at the new addition I'd acquired. I plop down next to him and do the same.

"So, your Grampy liked to fish?" Fletcher asks.

"I always thought he hated it. He used to tell me that he got bored waiting for the fish to bite, so he preferred crawfishing and crabbing, those kinds of things."

"Then why did he…"

"I have no clue," I interrupt.

"Wow."

"Yeah."

"Did you read it yet?" Fletcher asks, nodding his head toward the thick envelope that hangs halfway out of the purse I'd tossed onto the sofa.

"Nope."

"You know I promised…"

"Yes, I know. I'll do it now," I say with a huff.

"Don't get indignant about it," Fletcher says with a playful smile. "I'm only following orders."

I return his playful grin before tearing into the envelope. The first thing I notice is an odd shaped key that tumbles out of the folds of the letter to land on the floor. I dip to retrieve it before settling in to read the note.

"No, no, no…," I say as I peruse the page.

"What's wrong?"

I drop the note to my lap, lean my head back, and run my hands over my face. "A misunderstanding. A huge, stinking misunderstanding is the reason my Grampy is spending his eternity inside of a bronze bass."

"What?" Fletcher asks with a semi-laugh he tries hard to conceal.

I sigh heavily. "I remember this day well. Oh, my goodness! I can't believe he was awake. Okay, the facility called to say that Grampy wasn't feeling so well, and that he was running a fever. Lizzy and I went over to check on him, but he was sleeping when we got there. We quietly talked in the sitting area until he woke up, but evidently, we weren't that quiet."

Fletcher looks confused, and I can't say that I blame him.

"Lizzy was always trying to set me up with a date, and she said that we both needed big fish. She was sure she was close to catching hers because all she'd caught so far were minnows that needed to be thrown back. I told her that minnows were too much fish for me, and that a big fish was not on my agenda. She kept arguing back and forth, so to shut her up I finally agreed that I, too, wanted a big fish."

A smile crosses Fletcher's face as he finally realizes where this is going.

"According to the letter, Grampy had a secret cash stash that he told no one about, and he used part of it to buy a boat. For me. A person who knows zero about boating. A person who has no vehicle capable of towing said boat. Oh wait! Here, he's provided for that, too," I say, pointing to the spot on the letter that says I've inherited his pickup truck. "Too bad I sold the truck to pay for his cable bills at the facility. Seriously, how do you buy a freaking boat while living in an assisted living facility?"

"The internet?" Fletcher offers.

I toss my hand out in a shooing motion before I continue reading. "If I never catch that big fish myself, all I have to do is look at Grampy's statue and know that I've caught a whopper of a fish, 'because that's where I am, and you caught my heart the day you were born.'"

The room is silent as I let Grampy's words sink in. Picking up the letter, I scroll through until I reach the end, then I fold it and tuck it back inside the envelope. Still inside is a stack of bills, which is what is left of Grampy's secret stash--$1,500 for me to spend on something that will make me happy.

Resting back on the sofa, I toss the envelope, and it lands next to Grampy, the old man with a heart of gold, forced to spend eternity trapped in the stomach of a bass because of Lizzy's burning desire to find a partner. I start to giggle, and the giggle turns into a chuckle, and finally, the chuckle into a full blown laugh. Though the action feels somewhat foreign because I never belly laugh, it feels good. Fletcher soon joins in, and before long, we're both wiping tears from the corners of our eyes.

"You wanna see my boat?" I ask, reaching for a tissue.

"Sure. Where's it supposed to be?"

"At some marine store off Johnston. Here's the card of the salesman that Grampy used." I hand it over to Fletcher.

"Want to take your car or the bike?"

"Can we take the bike?"

"Of course." Fletcher smiles.

"Let me put on some pants…"

"Why? It's not that far away. Plus, it's like a hundred degrees out there."

"My scars…"

"…are not as noticeable as you think they are. And so what if they are. You know how they say that women dig scars on men?"

"Yeah," I answer, remembering the ones splayed across his broad back.

"Well, men dig scars on women, too."

"What? No way. Guys dig big boobs, tiny waists, bubble butts, and a pretty face."

"That's what guys dig before their hormones level off. Once they catch up with our brains, we realize that while all of that might be nice to look at, it's not necessarily what you want to come home to each night."

"Really?"

"Honest."

"Are you at risk of losing your man card for divulging all of these dark secrets to me?"

Fletcher laughs. "No, but don't spread it around, okay?"

"So what about the middle aged guys who hang out at the restaurants with the scantily clad waitresses? Shouldn't their hormones have leveled out?"

"They crave the attention, and it's cheaper than a strip club."

I laugh again. "Thank you for enlightening

me."

"Anytime," Fletcher says with a wink while handing me a helmet. He straddles the bike then holds out his hand to help me onto the back. He fires up the engine, and I tightly wrap my arms around his waist as we head off in search of the marine store.

Nothing goes the way I anticipate once we arrive at the boat place. First, Terry Kent, the salesperson, isn't the gentle, older man I'd pictured in my head. Instead, he's a pimply turd of a teenager dripping with attitude and a false sense of empowerment because he knows he has me between a rock and a hard place. I want a refund on the purchase, but according to Terry, it isn't an option. Adding insult to injury, I'm threatened with additional charges if the boat isn't removed from their property by the close of the business day. I plead, argue, and fight to no avail. Asking to speak to the manager is a joke because Terry IS the manager. Asking to speak to the owner is even worse because Terry's dad owns the joint. Defeated, I ask to see my boat.

Terry tosses down the cell phone he's been paying attention to instead of me, and begins an attitude-laden walk outside a double door that leads into a lot full of boats. He's practically sprinting, but I drag my feet as he impatiently stops and stands next to a brand new bass boat. Fletcher reaches him before I do, and I don't know what exactly is said, but he's much nicer when I finally catch up.

"*This* is the boat my grandfather bought?" I ask with disbelief. "How much?"

"I'm supposed to say that the cost doesn't

matter, it's taken care of," Terry says in absolute monotone.

"Fletcher?" I say, nodding him aside, "How much do you think a boat like this runs?"

"At least twenty-five grand."

I close my eyes and sigh. "That's more than I thought." I amplify my voice, "How did he pay for this?" I ask Terry.

"It was a cash sale. No returns."

"Yeah, I know. You made that perfectly clear while inside, Terry." My tone drips with disdain. "How am I going to get this home?" I ask Fletcher.

"We'll go to my place and pick up my truck. Then we'll come here, get the boat, and bring it to Ben's camp. He's got plenty of room out there to store it."

"I'm really not used to this. I always do things on my own, but I honestly see no way for me to handle this one by myself."

"Hey, don't get all weird about this. It's not that big of a deal."

"It is to me," I argue.

"It is to you *only*."

I give a half smile before telling Terry that we'd be back shortly for the boat. He couldn't care less, and he hurriedly makes his way back into the air conditioned show room.

Back on Fletcher's bike we go, and suddenly I'm a little nervous and excited because this will be my first time seeing where Fletcher lives. We leave the congestion of the city and end up at a really nice apartment complex nestled deep down a tree-laden path. He stops in front of the garage door of one of the townhouses closest to the road, and once the door is fully opened, he parks the bike next to a huge black pickup truck.

"I didn't know this complex existed. These are so nice and quiet compared to where I'm at."

"Yeah, ideally, I'd have my own place in the middle of nowhere, but this does okay."

I hand him the helmet I'd been wearing, and he puts it on the seat of his bike. "Nice truck," I say, running my hand down the side of the spotless vehicle.

"Thanks. I guess it's pretty obvious that I don't use it all that often. This is pretty much where it stays."

"I'm sorry you have to break it out for me."

"I'm not. Did you want something from inside before we go? A drink? Snack?"

Curiosity gets the best of me, so I ask for some water just so I can check out his place. The first thing I notice is how impressively neat the townhouse is. Everything has a place, and there's not so much as a magazine thrown on the floor or haphazardly tossed onto the coffee table. The second thing I notice is that everything is pretty generic. Neutral colors dominate the furniture, walls, and fixtures. The only splash of brightness comes from the few pictures he has on the walls.

He walks straight to the refrigerator, pulls out two bottles of water, and hands one to me. As I drink, I slowly walk in front of the line of pictures on the fireplace mantel. I recognize Fletcher in the same military picture as the one posted on his page. Further down is a pic of Ben, Fletcher, and another guy, all casually dressed and laughing candidly near the waterfront. More pics of them camping, swimming, fishing, riding ATVs—all at various ages ranging from pre-teen to adult. I recognize Julia in a few of the pictures, and even Molly in some of the ones that seem to be more recent. Though she's not much more than a toddler in most of them, her striking eyes give her away.

"You all look close," I mention as a turn away to face Fletcher.

"We are," he says.

"Who's this guy? I haven't met him yet."

"Remember the story about the triceratops? He was our third, Brody."

"Was? Is he?"

Fletcher's face confirms that Brody wasn't part of the group any longer.

"I'm sorry," I say, quickly trying to think of a way to change the subject.

"It's okay. He died six years ago, and he was Molly's dad."

Suddenly, it clicks. They look so much alike in their photos that I can't believe I didn't put the connection together. "So he and Julia..."

"Yeah, he teased and tormented her when we were growing up, then his focus changed sometime during high school. I wasn't very happy with the arrangement, but there wasn't a thing I could do to stop it. They married the summer after our senior year. Molly came along a few years after. She was six when he died, and I hate that she has to grow up without him. He was a great friend, husband, and dad."

"At least she's old enough to remember him, right?" I ask.

"She remembers bits and pieces."

"A few good memories are better than a lifetime of bad ones."

"True," Fletcher agrees. I hand my empty water bottle to him, and he tosses it into the kitchen garbage can. "Ready?" he asks, dangling his keys in the air.

"Yes. Thanks again for helping me with this mess. I can't believe my grandfather, who obviously hoarded money, spent it on buying me a boat. There are a million other things I can think to do with that money, and I'm stuck with a stinking boat I can't use."

"You can always sell it. You might not make back the full purchase amount, but you'll probably get pretty close to it."

"True." I shake a finger in the air. "Grampy, you got me good with this one." I picture him laughing his butt off at me.

Terry is just as thrilled to see us as he was the first time we arrived, and by thrilled I mean obnoxiously playing games on his cell phone. Fletcher backs up the truck, hitches the trailer, and I'm sure to thank Terry for doing absolutely nothing as we drive away. I'm pretty sure he flips me the bird, but I let it go.

It's a nice, quiet ride to Lake Martin from the boat store, and I enjoy taking in the scenery of the cypress trees, marshy bogs, and vacation houses. Before Fletcher can finish backing the boat and trailer into the side yard at Ben's, Ben and Lizzy are joining us. I spot Lizzy before Ben, only because she's impatiently jumping up and down while happily squealing. She's all over me when I get out of the truck.

"Boat for sale. You want it?" I ask while being crushed by Lizzy's bear hug.

"I just might," Ben says, running his hand down the shiny new hull. "What are you asking?"

"What will you give me?"

"Oh, you're one of those people, huh?" Ben says with a laugh. "This is brand new, never been in the water, right?"

"That's right. Straight from the store."

"Hmmmm. I think we should take her out, and see how she handles before I make an offer."

I shrug. "Y'all launch the boat, and we'll be there in a second! Don't leave without us!" Lizzy yells, practically dragging me inside the house.

"What are you doing?" I ask, rubbing my wrist once she releases it.

"You can't go out in a boat dressed like that," she proclaims, shutting the bedroom door.

"It's exactly the same thing the guys are wearing: shorts and a t-shirt."

"Exactly! We're girls. Swimsuits," she sings while emptying onto the bed a duffel that's chock full of Lizzy-wear.

"Oh, no. I don't think so," I say.

"Yes, ma'am." She starts stripping, tossing her clothes aside as she goes. "I'm wearing the red and white polka dot bikini. You can pick anything else from the pile."

"Don't you have a tank top I can borrow?" I anxiously ask.

"Nope. Pick a top."

"I don't even remember the last time I wore a swimsuit."

"It was the Fourth of July party that I dragged

you to three years ago. Pick already."

"How do you remember this stuff?" I ask, shaking my head as I thumb through the suits. I pick up an emerald green, halter style top. Lizzy nods her approval, so I quickly slide it on. As I'm trying to pull my t-shirt over it, Lizzy snatches it clean off of my head.

"No," she fusses. "You look beautiful. Plus, it's a bizzillion degrees outside. There's no need for layers."

"Lizzy," I say with a warning tone.

"I'm letting you wear the shorts, so consider it a compromise."

I roll my eyes before following her outside. She makes a brief stop to grab some towels then we join the guys on the dock. The boat is bobbing lightly in the water when we arrive, and Fletcher helps Lizzy and me into the boat. As soon as we're in, Lizzy sits up front and snuggles with Ben, who knocks it into gear. I'm in the back seat, across from Fletcher, actually enjoying the feel of the warm sun on my exposed flesh. Listening to the hum of the motor, I find it hard to keep my eyes open. I allow them to close and deeply inhale the slightly fishy-smelling air. I'm more relaxed than I've been in a long time, and I have a fleeting thought that maybe I should keep the boat. That thought is quickly cast aside as reality crashes down. The only reason I'm in this boat is because my grandfather died.

Inwardly, I tell myself that he'd want me to be happy. That it's okay to relax and have fun, but as usual, guilt rears its ugly head with each and every positive thought I have. I'm a little startled when I feel Fletcher's body brush up against mine.

Loud enough for me to hear him over the hum of the motor, yet quiet enough that Lizzy and Ben don't overhear, he asks, "What are you doing to yourself, Savannah? I know you're struggling because it's written all over your face. It's okay for you to have a good time. You're riding in the boat that your grandfather bought for you. If you relax and enjoy yourself, it's like you're giving him the gift of gratitude."

"Is it really that apparent? I didn't really think of it like that. I just keep thinking about how rotten I am for being out on the water the day after his death."

Fletcher reaches out to touch me, and instinctively, I flinch. He slowly lets his hand drop.

"I'm sorry," we both say at the same time.

"No, I'm sorry," I say.

"Just have fun, okay?" he asks. I nod. Pushing to scoot back to his original position, I stop him by putting my hand on his knee. He gently takes my hand into his and gives it a slight squeeze. Heeding his advice, I once again close my eyes and deeply inhale the fresh air around me. The ride must've relaxed me so much that I fell asleep because the next thing I know the boat motor powers down, and we're approaching the dock at Ben's house. Fletcher lets go of my hand so he can jump out to tie up the boat. *He held my hand the entire time.* I feel a smile trying to escape, but I work to contain it.

"She runs like a dream. Great boat. Will you take twenty five for her?"

"Uh, twenty five is perfect. Yes," I say, growing excited. I've made back all of Grampy's money, and I didn't have to go through any hassle trying to sell the thing! I figure Fletcher has something to do with it, but I'm not going to harp on it. Life is starting to look up for me, but I know from experience that it's usually pretty short lived. I'm going to suck up as much of the good stuff as I can before the other shoe drops.

"Hey, Lizzy. Got anything stronger than water inside there?" I nod my head towards the lake house.

Lizzy pops her head up from behind the windshield of the boat. "We have beer, and a few bottles of some other stuff. Right, Ben?"

"Yeah, babe. We sure do."

"What about a deck of cards?" I deviously ask.

"Absolutely," Ben answers.

After raising an eyebrow, Fletcher mutters, "Nice."

The card game gives way to a campfire once dusk arrives, and we all sit around discussing Lizzy and Ben's upcoming nuptials. She tells us that it's going to be a small, intimate affair with minimal fuss and hassle. Aside from Fletcher and me, who will serve as attendants, the guest list might make twenty at most. I still can't believe that Lizzy is going along with whole small wedding thing; the girl's been planning her dream wedding since we were kids. Finally, I get the gumption to ask her about it.

"Are you sure you want to do this?" I ask, once we're inside. She's digging around in the fridge to restock our beer supply.

"Am I sure I want to do what?" she asks, her head still bobbing around inside the door.

"Get married here. Have a small wedding. Minimal fuss."

She knocks the door closed with her hip and

sets the bottles that are laced between her fingers onto the kitchen cabinet. She's looking me dead in the eye when she says, "I've never been more sure of anything in my life."

"It's just… I've seen the wedding folder, and Lizzy, this isn't it. In fact, it's the opposite of the wedding folder."

"I know," she says with a smile. "That folder is full of things I thought I wanted, but now I know they're not that important. I'm getting married to the man, who I feel with all my heart, is my soul mate. This marriage is for me and Ben. It's not so we can entertain three hundred guests. He loves me, and I love him, and we want to be together forever. The only people who need to witness that are the ones who are closest to us. The ones who will truly support us, to guide us, and to be there for us."

"Lizzy," I start softly. "What happened to you?"

She laughs heartily. "I grew the hell up! That's what happened."

"Are you sure you're happy, and that this is truly what you want?"

"Do you have any reason to doubt it?"

After pondering the question, I shake my head. "I'm happy for you, and I wish you the best."

Lizzy snatches me in for a bear hug, and I try fighting her off. She just hugs me tighter. "You have to stop this nonsense. Humans crave touch. There's nothing wrong with a hug, or a kiss, or anything else." She starts planting kiss after kiss all over me while making "muah" sounds. If she weren't so much taller than me, I'd have wriggled away faster, but her darned long arms and legs wrap around me like an octopus, and I find myself stuck.

"Cut... it.... out...," I manage to say in between her barrage of kisses. It's not until the guys join us inside that she finally stops. Both of us share the same deer in headlights look, while the men simply look confused. Lizzy unfurls herself from around me, and I start wiping away at my face.

"Do you want to know?" Ben asks Fletcher.

"I'm not sure. Aren't you curious?" Fletcher asks Ben.

Lizzy snatches the bottles off the counter and starts handing them out. "Oh, hush! We were just playing around. I was trying to get Savannah to loosen up some."

"You women get away with some weird stuff, you know that?" Ben asks.

"What do you mean?" Lizzy inquires.

"Imagine two guys playing around like that. Awkward..."

"Are you jealous that you don't get to play around with your guy friends like that?" she teases.

"No, I'll leave that to you girls, babe. Fletch and I, we don't have to go to those extremes. Check it." He moves closer towards Fletcher, points his chin upward, and mumbles, "Sup? You good, bro?"

Fletcher mimics his gesture, and mumbles, "Yeah, man. All good here."

Lizzy plants her hands on her hips. "How in the hell does that cheer him up?"

Ben looks her way. "Oh, if I want to cheer him up I fart, or if I can't bust one out, I just tell a fart joke. Watch." He cocks his leg to the side and a rumble roars from his pants. Lizzy looks mortified, Fletcher is busting a gut, and I find myself amused, as well. It's so cliché, but damn it, it's funny watching Lizzy fan her face once the aroma wafts her way. I give myself permission to belly laugh, and I feel more of my sadness drift away. I could possibly get used to this new sensation—maybe happiness isn't such a bad thing. Well, at least until it's ripped away from you. I fight thoughts like these for most of the night, but ultimately, it turns out to be one of the best days of my life. *Thank you so much for helping me to see the light, Grampy.*

It's another quiet, lonely Saturday afternoon, and I'm halfway through a TV movie when the phone rings.

"Are you busy?" Fletcher asks.

"Not really. Why do you ask?"

"We never had that dinner and movie date that we scheduled."

"I guess we haven't. So?"

"So, I want to take you out tonight."

From habit more than lack of desire, I start making excuses, but Fletcher stops me. "I'm going to pick you up at five. Dress casual." He ends the call before I can argue. Unsure of how I just let that happen, I glance at the clock to check the time. It's four, so I jump from the sofa and into the shower.

I've become less self-conscious about the scars on my legs since Fletcher pointed out that they really aren't that noticeable. I'd worn shorts several times since to places like the grocery store or to run errands, and never even received as much as a sideways glance. I wonder if the scars appear more pronounced to me because I know their history, or if people just truly don't care about them. Either way, it feels good to wear shorts and skirts again, especially in the heat of summer. So, after I dress in my usual wardrobe of shorts, t-shirt, and sneakers, I sit and wait for Fletcher to arrive. He's right on time.

"Are you nervous about this evening?" he asks when I crack the apartment door.

"No, not at all. I'm... Yes," I admit.

He pulls a bouquet of multi-colored daisies from behind his back. "Does this make you less nervous?"

I smile. "Maybe a little."

He reaches to his right and pulls Molly into my field of vision. "I brought a chaperone. Does this make you less nervous?" Molly is nothing but a big toothy smile as her uncle pats her lightly on the head. I can't help but laugh.

"Chaperone, huh? You up for that, Molly?" I ask, opening the door all of the way.

"Yep! Uncle Fletcher said that if I don't mess this one up, there's an extra twenty in it for me," she says with a giggle.

Fletcher feigns disgust, "You just ruined it! Kiss that twenty bucks goodbye, missy." Molly is giggling so hard that she can barely catch her breath. Fletcher shakes his head and points in her direction. "I told her to say that. That's why she's giggling so much." He pulls a bill free from the stack in his pocket. "Here's a ten. Don't mess anything else up tonight, and I'll slip you the other ten."

"Okay, Uncle Fletcher," she says, still giggling.

"Y'all come in while I put these in water," I say, taking the bouquet from Fletcher. Molly looks around the apartment, and she stops in front of Lucas' picture.

"Oh, what a cute baby! What's his name?"

I'm not sure if it's because the question came from someone so young, or if I was finally making breakthroughs in dealing with his loss, but that stabbing knife sensation that normally cripples me when he's brought up didn't happen this time. Instead, it's almost a peaceful sensation that flows through my body. Though his life was short, he's still important, and by letting others know about how special he is to me serves to preserve his memory. Keeping him out of sight and out of mind helps me to ignore the pain, but it in no way provides any justice to Lucas' memory.

Fletcher turns to look where Molly is looking, and I can tell he's about to say something, but I raise my hand to stop him.

"His name is Lucas. He died when he was a year and a half old. He was my little boy."

"Oh! How sad. What happened?" Molly asks. Again, I stop Fletcher before he stops Molly's questions.

"A very bad man gave him some illegal drugs."

"Is that man in jail?"

"Yes, he'll be in prison for a very long time."

117

In an act that leaves me absolutely startled, Molly encircles her arms around my waist and hugs me tightly. "I'm so sorry that your baby died, Miss Savannah."

Stunned, I slowly allow my arms to fall around her, and I gently hug her back. Her hair smells like fresh strawberries, and is soft as silk. *Is this what it's like to have a little girl?* I tighten the embrace.

"Thank you, Molly." Gently kissing the top of her head, I finally release her from the embrace. "So, where are we going tonight?"

"Uncle Fletcher says that I get to pick the movie and you get to pick where we eat. That's the deal we came up with, anyway."

"You two seem to have some pretty interesting conversations," I comment.

"Oh, we do," Molly says, sounding way older than her twelve years.

"What movie are we seeing?" I ask.

"*Buzz Saw Massacre!*" Molly says, excitedly.

"No," Fletcher says.

"*College Dorm Party III?*"

"Nope. Try again."

Molly huffs a sigh. "You know, I'm not a little kid anymore, Uncle Fletcher. I'm practically a teenager."

"Practically, and actually being a teenager are two different things. Plus, even if you were of age, I wouldn't be the person you'd watch those movies with."

"Well, since Uncle Fletcher has fallen a gigantic notch in my cool people rankings, I guess we'll have to see *Secret Princess*."

"Sounds perfect. I've wanted to see that

movie for a while, but I didn't have anyone to go with," I comment.

"Really?"

"Yep, I'm really glad you picked that one." I move closer to whisper in her ear, "Plus, imagine how funny Uncle Fletcher is going to look watching a princess movie with a bunch of girls."

Molly laughs while nodding emphatically, and Fletcher sends me a questioning look. I simply shrug my shoulders and move towards the door. "Ready to go?" I ask.

"Sure, but I'm not really liking the fact that I'm outnumbered here," Fletcher jokes.

"Oh, you'll get over it. How about we get pizza for dinner?" I ask.

"Pizza! Yay! My favorite!" Molly sings.

"Then pizza it is," Fletcher says, shutting the door behind us. "I want to know what you two were whispering about later," he softly mentions as we walk down the hallway together.

"No way. It's a girl thing," I say, picking up my pace to match Molly's. Fletcher's laughter resonates from behind us.

I smile more on this day than I probably have in my entire lifetime. We laugh through dinner, we're amused by the movie, and we spend the ride home discussing our next possible adventure. I don't want it to end, so when Fletcher asks if I'd prefer to be dropped off first or if I'd like to ride with him to Julia's to bring Molly home, I opt to go with him to Julia's. Big mistake.

There are huge smiles on our faces when we arrive at the quaint brick house with a neatly manicured yard. The smiles instantly dissolve when a scowling Julia opens the front door. "You're later than you said you'd be," she fusses, opening the door wide enough for us to pass through.

"We had such a good time, Momma! Uncle Fletcher and Miss Savannah took me to eat pizza, and we saw *Secret Princess*, and then we played games at the arcade. That's why we're a little late. I kept winning!! Uncle Fletcher said I had to stop though, because we had to get home. I really wish I could have stayed longer. Look at all of the stuff I got!" She holds her bag of candy and trinkets high in the air as if she's showcasing the world's finest jewels.

"That's nice, Molly. Go get ready for bed," Julia says in monotone. Fletcher remains stone-faced, while I feel incredibly awkward and out of place.

"Can Uncle Fletcher tuck me in? Please, Momma? Please?"

Julia sighs heavily. "I suppose, Molly. Go on, now."

"I'll be right back," Fletcher says with an uncomfortable smile. I nod, unsure of what to do. *Should I sit in the truck? Just stand here and wait for him?*

"You want some coffee?" Julia asks. It is a general statement thrown out in the air, so I'm unsure if she is speaking to me. When I realize she is, I accept.

"Only, if it's no trouble."

"It's no trouble. Follow me."

We walk down a hallway filled with photographs, some the same as the ones Fletcher displays at his place. Julia jostles a few things around, and once the coffee is brewing, she offers me a seat at the kitchen table. I accept it, and nervously begin twiddling my thumbs.

"I know I come off as cold," Julia starts. "There's a lot of stuff you don't know about, and Fletcher and I… well, let's just say that our relationship as siblings is pretty tense right now."

"Okay," I mutter, unsure of what my response should be.

"Does he talk to you about Brody?"

"He told me they were friends from childhood, and that you eventually married him. He's Molly's dad, and unfortunately he passed away."

Julia nods. "Does Fletcher tell you anything about himself? About his time in the army?"

"I know he has scars all over his back because he was in a vehicle that caught on fire due to an explosion."

"Figures you'd know that part."

"What's that supposed to mean?"

"A big handsome guy like Fletcher. A pretty woman like you looking to score. It's not rocket science."

I put a warning finger in her face. "Look, you don't know me. You know nothing about me. If you want to jump to conclusions about things that, if I'm being honest, don't even involve you, then you do it on your own time. I don't know what your problem is, but I'm not about to sit here and let you imply that I'm loose, a floozy, or anything of the sort. Fletcher has been nothing but a gentleman since the day I met him, and he's so good with your daughter. You should be grateful instead of fussing or scowling at him all of the time."

"There are things about him that you don't know."

"And likewise for me. There are things about me, about my past, that he doesn't know yet. I'm no angel, but I'm not a bad person. Fletcher has done nothing to make me believe that he is anything but an honorable man, and believe me, I speak from experience when I say I know the difference."

"Brody was driving when the bomb detonated. It killed him instantly."

"What?"

"He and Brody enlisted together. They deployed together. They went on that patrol together."

"Is that why you're so mean to him? Do you blame Fletcher for Brody's death?"

"No!" Julia snaps. "Never."

"Then what's the problem?"

"Listen. It's too long of a story to get into, plus, it's technically Fletcher's story to tell. Just promise me that if you truly care for him that you'll be kind to him. Also promise that you'll let me know right away if you start to notice him acting strangely. Please, promise me."

Though I'm a little freaked out, I nod. "I'm not looking for a serious relationship, Julia. Not anytime soon anyway, so you can relax."

"I apologize if I made you feel uncomfortable." She rubs her face with her palms. "I worry too much. I worry about Fletcher. I worry about Molly…"

"I can understand that, but I'm not a bad person with an agenda. I promise."

Julia releases a pent up breath. "How do you take your coffee?"

"Cream and sugar, if you have it."

"Milk okay?"

"Yes, thank you." She stands near the sink getting our mugs ready, and I see her in a different light. She's not a snooty, bitter hag; she's a tired, worried woman with a lot on her mind. I should have picked up on that sooner, but regardless, it's a fresh start now. She places the mug in front of me, and I carefully draw a sip from the brim.

"I know about Fletcher's scars because he showed them to me so I'd be less self-conscious about mine. My legs are full of them from a childhood accident, so I refused to wear shorts in public. He came to check on me after my grandfather died, and I was wearing them. I wanted to keep them covered, but... Anyway, I appreciate that he did that for me."

Julia nods. "Fletcher's a great man, and I wasn't trying to scare you off. I often say things without thinking them through. Your grandfather, he died recently? I'm sorry for your loss."

I nod. "Yeah, he was old and very sick, so it wasn't a shock, but he was my closest family member. Fletcher helped me a lot. He stayed with me at the facility and remained with me until he knew I was okay."

"Sounds like Fletcher," she says with a smile.

"What's going on in here? I heard my name," Fletcher cautiously inquires.

"Nothing. Just drinking some coffee. You want some?" Julia asks.

"No, I'm good. Thanks."

"And I'm finished with mine. Thank you, Julia. It was great." I rise from my seat and place the mug in the kitchen sink.

Julia leaves hers on the table so she can walk

us to the door. "You're welcome, Savannah. Fletcher, thank you for taking Molly tonight. She loves spending time with you."

"Anytime, Julia. I'm here for her, and you, anytime."

Julia gives a half smile as she gently closes the door behind us. "What happened in there?" Fletcher asks once we're in his truck. "Did you put holy water in her coffee?"

"No," I say with a giggle. "She's grumpy because she's tired, and she worries a lot."

"Is that it?" Fletcher asks. I nod. "Well, I think she needs a little vacation. If I send her away for a spa weekend, she'll need us to keep an eye on Molly. You up for it?"

"I like the way you made this into an 'us' thing. And using the kid to help seal the deal? Real smooth, Fletcher."

"What! I did no such thing."

"You absolutely did!"

"Are you telling me you're not interested?"

"I never said that. "

"So you are?"

"Maybe," I say with a grin.

"I hope you know that 'maybe' means 'yes' in my book."

"I hope you know that 'maybe' means 'maybe' in mine."

"Too bad. My surprise, my rules," Fletcher says as he parks in front of my apartment.

"I had a good time tonight. Thank you."

"I had a good time, too. You're welcome." He comes to my side of the truck and opens the door for me, and we silently walk to my apartment. He lingers in the doorway once I get inside.

"Aren't you coming in?" I ask.

"Nah, not tonight. It's late, and I know you're tired."

"It is late. Well, late for me, anyway," I say.

"I know. It was late for you two hours ago," Fletcher quips. "Sweet dreams, Savannah."

"Good night, Fletcher." I'm all smiles as I close the door.

"Fletcher, I don't know about this," Julia says, nervously pacing the length of her car. Her hair is pulled back in a tight ponytail, and sunglasses are perched high on her head.

"Too late to back out. The trip is already paid for. Molly's going to be fine. Molly, tell your mother that you're going to be fine."

"I'm going to be fine, Mom! Uncle Fletcher talked to Miss Savannah, and we're going to have a huge sleepover at her apartment. We're going to go bowling, and rent some movies, and I get to eat all the candy and junk food I can fit into my belly while you're gone!"

"Molly, shhhh," Fletcher teases.

Julia rolls her eyes, and pulls Molly close. "Look at me. You are NOT to eat as much candy and junk food as you can while I'm gone. Understand?"

"You're not even gonna be here, and you're ruining my fun!"

"Be good," Julia says, giving Molly a kiss on the top of her head followed by a tight hug.

"Are you sure about this?" she asks Fletcher and me. We both nod.

"She'll be fine," I say in as assuring a tone as I can muster.

"Call if you need. I'll have my phone with me at all times," Julia says as she climbs into her car.

"Go! Have fun," Fletcher insists.

"I'm going. I'm going," Julia says, closing the door and waving as she drives away.

"What are we going to do first?" Fletcher asks, loading Molly's suitcase into the backseat of my car.

"I'm long overdue for some pampering. My nails look terrible. I think we should get mani-pedis," Molly says, once again sounding far older than her young age.

"Excuse me," Fletcher asks.

"Ask Miss Savannah. Girls love mani-pedis."

"I wouldn't know. I've never had one. I just do my own nails," I admit.

"What! Uncle Fletcher, we have to fix this right away. Let's get to a nail place stat!"

"Stat? What language are you speaking?" Fletcher, who is obviously amused, inquires.

"Don't you watch the medical shows? It means right away. Like now!" Molly answers with her hand on her hip and a "duh" look on her face.

"No, I do not, and I'm not sure that you should be watching them either," he mentions.

"I'm not a baby. I'm almost thirteen, which will officially make me a teenager. That means I'm on the cusp of maturity."

I can't help but laugh at the dialogue going on between Fletcher and Molly. I'm not quite sure if she's wise beyond her years or just a parrot mimicking the things she's been seeing and hearing. Either way, it's pretty funny.

"Cusp of maturity, huh?" Fletcher whispers under his breath. "You up for this mani-pedi thing?" he directs my way.

I shrug. "I guess."

"Okay, tell me where I'm going, Molly." She shoots out rapid fire directions to a little salon in the center of a strip mall. Fletcher wants to wait in the car, but Molly begs and pleads for him to come inside with us.

"Lots of men get this done, Uncle Fletcher! Please! Come on! You'll like it! I promise."

I bite down on my lip to keep from smiling because it's obvious she's chipping away at his resolve. Sure enough, he caves, and his face is priceless when he enters the salon. He turns on his heel, but a steadfast Molly blocks his path.

"We sit over there," she says, pointing to the row of massage chairs.

"She's right. Please, come this way. Sit," a middle aged woman with oversized glasses and silvery blonde hair insists.

"Oh, I don't think so," Fletcher says, nervously eyeing the joint.

"We have a lot of male customers who really enjoy our services," she says in a super sweet and assuring tone.

"I'm sure they do, but…"

"Uncle Fletcher, please. It's so fun."

He rolls his eyes. "Where do I sit?"

Molly giggles while bouncing up and down.

"You can sit anywhere you like. You caught us at a slow time," the woman says.

"I want to sit in the middle!" Molly says, jumping into her chair. "Miss Savannah, you'll sit here, and Uncle Fletcher, you'll sit here." She points to the chairs on either side of her. "Miss Savannah, we need to pick out the color we want. Come on!"

She launches from the chair to grab my hand, and excitedly, she leads me to a wall of nail polish bottles. She selects a neon yellow shade, but I'm left dumbfounded by the vast number of choices. "How about you pick a color for me?" I suggest. Molly happily takes on the assignment, and passes a bottle of flamingo pink to me.

"Don't you even think of bringing any of those my way," Fletcher warns.

"I wasn't, Uncle Fletcher!" Molly says, handing her bottle over to the brunette who will be doing her nails. "Miss Savannah, you give your polish to the lady doing your nails."

I'm slightly embarrassed to look over and find the attendant waiting for me, so I hurry over to the seat, kick off my flip flops, and dunk my feet into the bubbling, warm water. She pushes a button on the chair and the massagers start to knead muscles that have been tense since childhood. But poor Fletcher, he looks absolutely miserable in his chair, and frankly, he looks a little silly with his jeans rolled to his knees. I give him an encouraging smile, but it doesn't help.

"I'm sorry, Molls. You know Uncle Fletcher will do darn near anything for you, but this is where I draw the line." He jumps from the chair as though it's on fire. "I'm going to be right over here," he says, scooping up his socks and shoes as he carefully makes his way to the empty waiting area.

Molly's disappointment is evident, but it's also very brief, as she soon diverts her full attention to me. "Miss Savannah, are you enjoying this? I can't believe that you've never done this before."

"I am enjoying it very much. Do you do this often?"

"Yeah, my mom and I have a girl's day at least once a month. We get our hair fixed in the morning and then we get our fingers and toes done. After that, we have lunch, and if mom has the extra money, sometimes we go shopping, too!"

"That sounds like a lot of fun. You're lucky to have such a caring mother."

"Your mom didn't do things like that with you?" she asks.

I shake my head. "I didn't see my mom much."

"Did she work a lot?" she asks knowingly. I can't help but smile at how grown up she sounds.

"No, it wasn't work. She just wasn't around much."

"Oh. What did you do for fun then?" Molly curiously inquires.

"I used my imagination a lot. I'd dream up these elaborate stories about how my life would all change once I became an adult."

"Like what?"

"Like how I'd travel to Europe, and while touring castles, a prince would find me and we'd instantly fall in love and live happily ever after."

"I like that one! What else?"

"Another one of my favorites was that I'd visit the Australian outback where I'd find my very own Crocodile Dundee."

"Crocodile who?"

I laugh. "Never mind. It's way before your time."

"Oh, okay," she says, shrugging it off. "What else did you do for fun?"

"That was pretty much it. I'd sometimes visit with my grandfather, or my friend, Lizzy, but that's about it."

"Miss Lizzy is going to marry Uncle Ben. He's not really my uncle, but he grew up with Uncle Fletcher and my daddy, so I call him uncle."

"She sure is. Have you met her?"

"Yep! We stopped at Uncle Ben's restaurant for dinner, and she was there. I like her. She's nice, just like you."

"Well, you'll probably have more in common with her than you will with me. Lizzy loves girly stuff."

"Why don't you like girly stuff?"

"I don't have time to like girly stuff. I work a lot."

"You shouldn't do that. It's not good for your health. You need time to relax."

"How old are you again?" I ask.

"Almost thirteen."

"Well, thank you for the advice. I'll be able to cut back on my hours some now that... Well, I won't have to work as much, so I'll try to relax more, okay?"

"Good! I hope that you get to spend some of your extra time with Uncle Fletcher. He really likes you, you know?" I stumble for words, but find none. "I know these things because my Uncle Fletcher never lets me meet his girlfriends, but he let me meet you."

"Uh, Molly, I'm not his girlfriend, sweetie."

She gives me a confused look. "Why not?"

How awkward it is to be interrogated by a

'tween! "Well, I guess it's because we don't... I don't... I'm not..."

"Not ready to commit, huh?"

"Molly!" I snap, and the women doing our toes smile at each other. "Okay, can we talk about things more appropriate for your age?"

"I get fussed at a lot by my mom for putting my nose where it doesn't belong. She says I need to quit hanging around with the grownups and be a kid, but kids my age are so boring."

"You're at a tough age, but listen to your mom. You'll be grown up fast enough, and then you'll wish you could be a kid again. Enjoy it while you can, because you only get this opportunity once."

"What are some things you wish you had done at my age?"

"I wish I'd visited some amusement parks and water parks."

"You can do that as an adult! Uncle Fletcher, can we take Miss Savannah to the water park one day? Please!" she yells across the room, startling all of us.

"Uh, yeah. Sure, if she'd like to go."

"You will love it! Don't worry about the extra tall slides. They're scary, but I'll hold your hand."

"I don't know."

"Oh, please! You said I should do some age appropriate things, and this is totally age appropriate, right?"

"Maybe," I reply.

Her grin is so broad that one would swear she'd recently won the lottery. We finish at the nail salon, and Fletcher seems overjoyed to have a change of scenery. It's quiet for about two blocks before Molly starts chatting again.

"Can we go to the water park tomorrow, Uncle Fletcher? Please?" She's careful to draw out the please. Fletcher takes his eyes off the road long enough to glance in my direction.

"I don't even own a swimsuit," I admit. "You two are welcome to go without me, though."

"We can get you a swimsuit, Miss Savannah. Please! It won't be any fun without you."

"I guess that means we're going shopping?" Fletcher asks.

"I don't..." Before I can actually argue the point, he's changing lanes and heading towards the mall.

Once again, I'm letting a 'tween dictate my decisions, not merely because she's a little on the bossy side, but mostly because I'm clueless. At my age, I don't even know which stores to patronize for a swimsuit. Fletcher rests himself in a comfy chair near the food court.

"I'll wait right here," he insists.

"You aren't coming with us?" I ask, nervously eyeing the endless rows of shops.

"Nope. Y'all have fun," he says, picking up a newspaper someone has left behind.

"Okay, where do we go first, Molly?" I ask.

"Over here, Miss Savannah!" she says, sprinting off towards a store with a very elaborate summer theme in the picture window. Once we're inside, she runs straight to an end display. "This is the one! You have to get it!" she squeals while holding up what looks like metallic dental floss with two tiny triangular pads.

"There is absolutely no way that I'm even going to consider something like that. This is more my style," I say, desperately reaching for a skirted one piece.

"Miss Savannah, you can't wear that."

"Why not?"

"Because! What about this?" She holds up a more modest bikini, but it's still not something I'm very comfortable wearing, especially if I'm going down water slides.

After much back and forth between the pros and cons of certain suits, a final decision is made, and I'm about to take my navy blue one piece to the register when I stop and face Molly.

"Why don't you pick out a new suit for yourself?"

"What? Really?" Molly asks.

I have the extra money thanks to Ben buying Grampy's boat, plus I don't usually have the opportunity to buy for others, so I act on it. "Yes, it's my way of thanking you for helping me to pick out my suit."

"Thanks!" she says, bouncing up and down as she peruses the racks of swimsuits in the junior section. My biological clock sounds a slight alarm. With no nieces, nephews, or friends with children for me to spend time with, I'd pretty much ruled out children. It's an out of sight, out of mind kind of thing. However, spending time with Molly has me yearning for the child who was taken from me. *Lucas would be in school by now. No uniform shopping, no shopping for school supplies, no taking him for a fresh haircut. What I wouldn't give to tousle that beautiful blond hair of his. No pep talk about how he'll have so much fun making new friends.* The feeling is so overwhelming that I can't breathe. *No watching him open Christmas presents. No birthday celebrations. I've been robbed of so much! I used to be able to imagine his scent. Can I even do that now? Oh, my God! I'm losing him all over again.*

"Miss Savannah, are you okay?" Molly rescues me from my thoughts by tugging on my arm.

"Huh? Oh, yeah… Yes, I'm okay," I answer softly.

"Something's wrong. I can tell. Should I get Uncle Fletcher?"

"No!" I say louder than I intended. "No, sweetheart. Everything's fine. I was thinking about my little boy, that's all. I still get sad sometimes. I'm sorry if I worried you."

She rubs my forearm with her palm. "It's okay to be sad sometimes. I still get sad when I think about my daddy, too. Sometimes I cry all night because I miss him so much. Please don't tell my mom that, though. She'll worry about me, and she'll ship me back to the therapist. Crying helps me. I cry, and cry, and cry, and then you know what?"

I shake my head.

"I think my daddy comes to me."

"Really? What makes you think that?"

"Because every time I do it, something happens that reminds me of him. Like once, a teddy bear he gave me fell off my shelf and landed on top of me, like it was giving me a big hug. And I've found things in my school bag that I didn't put in there. Things like that. Also, I dream about him a lot. Not things that have happened before, but new things that we do together."

"That's nice," I say. "I bet it makes you feel good when you get those signs."

"Yep! I'll bet Lucas gives you signs, too. Have you ever had any?"

I shake my head. "No, sweetie. I don't think so."

"Oh," she says, a little forlornly. "Maybe he will someday," she says, perking up a bit.

"Maybe so." I manage a half smile. The panic I was experiencing slowly dissipates as I redirect my thoughts to checking out. Molly takes my hand in hers as we leave the store, and instead of jerking back like I normally would, I give her hand a little squeeze. A broad smile crosses my lips—I'm growing as a person, I'm casting off my demons, and it feels absolutely wonderful!

RHONDA R. DENNIS

nine

I'm seeing the world in a fresh light, and I'm no longer fighting new experiences. I embrace them instead. Take the water park for instance, hands down the best time I've probably ever had. The cool water offers relief from the scorching sun, and the rush felt while barreling down slide after slide has me begging for more. Molly clings to my side while Fletcher hangs back just a bit. I'm not sure if he isn't enjoying it, or if he is simply trying to give us some "girl time." Regardless, it's a day I'll not soon forget.

I reflect on it all as I sit on the sofa, softly stroking Molly's hair while she sleeps soundly. Her head is nestled in my lap while her legs are draped across Fletcher's lap. Poor thing was so exhausted after the day at the water park that she keeled over in the middle of the movie we were watching while huddled on my sofa. Neither Fletcher nor I have the heart to move her, so there we sit next to a relaxed Molly, undoubtedly dreaming of something carefree and happy judging from the smile on her lips.

"How long has she been out?" Fletcher asks, breaking the silence.

"I'm not sure. I think we lost her somewhere around the horseback riding scene."

"You think she's out for the night?"

"Yeah, I think so. She did a lot of walking, swimming, and climbing stairs today."

"We all did," Fletcher remarks, yawning as he raises his hands high above his head to stretch.

"I'll get her pillow and blanket," I whisper, carefully sliding her head off of my lap and onto the sofa cushion. By the time I return from my bedroom, Fletcher has freed himself, as well, and is arranging the air mattress on the floor.

"I forgot to ask you, how is that? Is it terrible? I've never had a reason to use it before."

"It's fine. Much better than sleeping on the floor."

"Maybe we should have accepted Julia's offer to stay at her place?"

"Nah, really, it's okay. Plus, Molly wanted to be here. I think she just wanted to check things out because she's nosy."

I smile. "Well, she's probably disappointed because there's not much to see here."

"I can't speak for Molly, but I happen to like what I see."

It takes me a second to realize he's talking about me, not my apartment, and my cheeks instantly redden. *Do I or don't I?* He's oblivious to my internal struggle as he arranges the sheets on the mattress, so I make a dash for the kitchen to finish thinking it through. After a few deep breaths, I call him.

"Fletcher?"

"Hey, you called me?" he asks poking his head through the doorway.

"Yes, I did. I, uh…"

He comes closer, his eyes searching mine for a

hint of what I might need. "What is it? Is something wrong?" His voice is laden with concern.

He's within inches of me when I finally manage to shake my head. I don't say anything; I reach my hand behind his neck and pull him closer, so close that my lips rest upon his. He's startled at first, but soon his palms rest on the sides of my face and he's kissing me in a way that leaves me weak in the knees.

"You have no idea how many times I've wanted to do this in the weeks we've known each other," he says before kissing me again. "I'll never push you to do anything you're not ready for, and it was absolute torture to see these full, beautiful lips and not be able to worship them properly."

"I…"

"Shhh, don't use words. Show me what you're feeling," he says, lacing his fingers in mine. I gently touch his face with my free hand before offering him my appreciation, my passion, my heart. It's only after our lips part that I realize our faces are damp from my tears.

"You've helped me to feel again. You've brought me to life, Fletcher."

He shakes his head. "You allowed yourself to feel again, Savannah. It's all you, sweetheart."

"I'm still so scared, though." I debate that for a second. "No, scared is an understatement. I'm terrified, Fletcher. I don't know if I can handle anymore heartbreak. It'll surely crush me if it happens again."

"Hey," he says, tipping my chin so I'm forced to look him in the eye. "I'm right here with you. If your heart gets broken, I assure you, it's not going to be because of me. We're in this together, Savannah. I've never felt this way about anyone, and I'm convinced that we're meant to be together. I'm not telling you this to intimidate you, or to rush you into anything. I'll wait forever if need be, but I'm going to be here, anticipating the day that you see it, too."

I slowly nod my head as I brush away the fresh tears. "It might take me a while."

"No rush."

"Thank you. I… I'm pretty tired. I guess I should probably go to bed now. Goodnight, Fletcher," I say, offering him one last kiss before leaving him in the kitchen.

"Goodnight, Savannah. Sweet dreams," Fletcher says with a smile that makes me feel assured that all is right with the world.

The next couple of weeks are a blur of wedding preparations, which I was assured wouldn't be a big fuss, but is turning out to be quite the ordeal. Work and the occasional date with Fletcher also fill my time. I finally get an opportunity to launch Operation Rescue Lizzy from Diva Land and return her to the town of Reality. Things begin to run quite smoothly after our little conversation, and I couldn't be more relieved.

I work fewer hours since I'm no longer supporting Grampy, and I enjoy the free time with Fletcher. I still find myself afraid, but even so, I continue giving the new experiences my all. With each self-imposed obstacle I overcome, I feel more energized and passionate about living each day to the fullest.

One unusually crisp night, Fletcher picks me up for a date, and tells me that our destination is top secret. At first I'm intrigued, but when he drives his truck down a dark, secluded trail, I begin to get a little nervous. He stops the truck once we enter a clearing, and I'm unsure what's going through his mind. He pulls a blanket and two pillows from the back of the cab, and I become so nervous that my stomach quivers.

"Come on. Let's go stargazing."

"What? You drove me out here to look at stars?" I ask, relaxing somewhat while following him to the back of the truck.

"Yep, but we don't have to stay if you're feeling uncomfortable."

"No, it's fine. It's such a beautiful sight. I've never seen so many stars," I say, slowly twirling to take in the massive night sky. He lowers the tailgate and places the bedding in the back of his pick up, then gives me a boost up. We lie there for hours holding hands and talking about anything and everything while admiring the cosmos. We're discussing our desire to travel when Fletcher rolls onto his side and props himself to look down at me.

"Nothing's stopping us. You know that, right? It's just you and me, sweetheart. We're gonna conquer the world, and there's not a thing that can stop us as long as we're together."

I reach up to touch his face. "You promise?"

"Absolutely," he assures me before lying flat on his back and tucking his hands under his head. I roll to snuggle against him, and his hand falls to cup my lower back.

"Where are we going first?"

"Alaska? We could see some glaciers, pet a moose or two…"

I laugh. "I've always wanted to participate in one of those dolphin encounters. I love dolphins so much. My secret dream was to become a trainer."

"Then we'll go to the Bahamas first, and you'll have that dolphin encounter. I want to make all of your dreams come true. What else ya got?"

"I don't know. Some of them are absolutely silly now that I'm a grown woman. Most of my dreams were contrived when I was a kid. Once I reached adulthood, I quit wasting time on silly daydreams because they depressed me too much."

"Come on. Tell me some of them. It doesn't matter if they're from your childhood," Fletcher encourages.

"They're really silly."

"Let me be the judge of that. Come on. Tell me."

"Well, I used to dream of having a princess party where guests would show up in gowns and tiaras. See, I told you they're a waste of time and extremely stupid now that I'm an adult."

"Stop being so negative. I know there are more fantasies. Think back."

I grow serious. "I used to dream that someone would come along, someone like a distant aunt or cousin, who would actually love me and want to raise me. Once I got older, that dream shifted to anyone who would take me away from that house. It's what I wished for the most, and I think that's why I settled with Paul. I saw him as a way to escape my parents' house, but look at what it cost me. I'd have been so much better off by simply staying alone."

"We can't change our pasts, but we can write our own futures. I want your future to include me. What do you think about that?"

I smile. "I think it's a good idea."

"Good or great?" he jokes.

"I guess time will tell," I tease back.

His demeanor turns very serious, and he slowly raises a finger to touch my chin. "Savannah, it's time that you know just how hard I've fallen for you. The day you answered my call, you turned my world upside down, and everything has finally fallen into place for me. You're my angel, and I love you. I'm so madly in love with you that you're all I think about. I want to spend my days making you happy because that's what makes me happy. It's love—one hundred percent unconditional love that I have for you."

"You just said the 'L' word, and you said it a lot," I say with disbelief.

"Yes, I did, and I'm going to say it again. I love you, Savannah. You're the reason I wake up smiling, and the reason I fall asleep with a smile, too. I hope the feeling is mutual, because I hate to tell you this, you're not getting rid of me now."

"Fletcher," I let his name hang in the darkness for a little while. "I...I," I stutter before giving up on saying anything verbally. I decide to show him how I feel instead. Rolling so my body is on top of his, I give my heart permission to open up to him as I softly press my lips against his.

"Oh, Savannah," he whispers into my ear, "please kiss me like that again." He gently pulls against the back of my thighs so my body lies flush against his. He's every bit as passionate with his show of love for me, and before I fully comprehend what is happening, I find myself naked with a man for the first time in years.

"Fletcher, I haven't..."

"Shhhh, unless you're going to tell me to stop, it's not important," he mumbles as he leaves a soft trail of kisses across my collar bone. "I'll go slowly, I promise, but only if you truly want this? You have to want me." His eyes search mine for the tiniest hint of hesitation.

"I do. I want you, Fletcher. I need you," I admit, caving to the carnal desire. With a gentle touch, he slowly acquaints himself with all of the curves and lines of my body. My skin prickles with goose bumps, but inside I'm burning with desire. I've been with other men, but experiencing these intense emotions along with the physical sensations of sex is foreign to me, and it's absolutely incredible. I've missed out on so much all these lonely years. Fletcher makes me feel beautiful, sensual, and most of all, loved.

I want to show him pleasure and make him feel as special as he's making me feel. Under the brightness of the moon, we become one flesh, and I'm carried away to a world that until now has only existed in my deepest fantasies. The sensations: his lips searing against my sensitive flesh, his hands roaming my most intimate places, his manliness filling me to my core, and his passion consuming every bit of the desire that I hold—they're overwhelming and magnificent. I can't hold it in anymore. In the midst of our lovemaking, I cry out into the night, repeatedly professing my love for the man who has awakened my soul. My old life is gone. Fletcher Reilly has captured my heart, and now it's his forever.

The morning of Lizzy and Ben's wedding arrives, and Fletcher picks me up from my apartment bright and early. I'm dressed in the typical shorts and t-shirt combo, but I have my dress, which is tucked away safely in the garment bag slung over my shoulder. I hop into the truck and give Fletcher a quick kiss before buckling my seatbelt.

Even though the affair has limited guests, it's completely abuzz with activity. Caterers unload crates from the back of a black van, a rental company sets up tables and chairs at various spots on the lawn, a huge white tent is being set up to provide shade during the reception, and at the hub of all of the activity is none other than Lizzy's mother, Prissy Cole. Prissy's dressed in white from her wide brimmed hat to down to her strappy sandals. Her ample girth is tucked into layers of spandex, covered by white knit pants, a white sleeveless blouse, and a wispy white over shirt. A thick gold chain wraps around her even thicker neck, while gold hoops peep from behind her puffy platinum hair.

"Oh, Savannah, my darling! Look at you! It's been far too long, my dear. You look amazing, and you're absolutely ravishing! I presume that this very handsome young man is the reason for that?" She flirtatiously smiles at Fletcher. "How nice to meet you. I'm Prissy Cole, Elizabeth's mother. Who might you be?"

"Fletcher Reilly, Ben's best friend, and

145

Savannah's boyfriend. It's nice to meet you, ma'am."

"Ma'am!" she chuckles obnoxiously as she tosses her hand over her heart. "Oh, such manners."

"I guess it's the military in me, ma'am."

"Oh, be still my heart. Which branch, dear?"

"Army, but I was medically discharged quite a few years ago."

"Well, thank you so much for your service. My husband and I contribute to many veterans assistance programs."

"It was an honor to serve, and I thank you for your contributions."

She laces her arm in his, "Now Fletcher, may I borrow you for a little while? There are a couple of things I'd like done, but there's no one here strapping enough to handle …"

Fletcher gives a fleeting look backwards, and all I can manage to do is shrug my shoulders before Prissy has him near the water's edge. I continue into the lake house in search of Lizzy, and smack into Carlton Cole as soon as I open the door.

I drop the garment bag, but Carlton manages to hang onto his scotch on the rocks; not a drop splashes outside the glass.

"Whoa there! Howdy, Savannah. Boy, you sure are a sight for sore eyes. How have you been?" Carlton Cole has salt and pepper hair, but it's mostly salt at this point. He, like Prissy, is dressed completely in white, from the semi-unbuttoned cotton shirt he sports, down to the loafers on his feet.

"Hi, Mr. Cole. It's good to see you, too. How have you been?"

"I've been okay, Savannah. But I'll let you in on a little secret—the day just got a whole lot better since you arrived." He lets out an obnoxious laugh while hugging my shoulders with his free arm. He reeks of alcohol and cigar smoke. "So tell me. Have you run into Prissy? Has the stick popped free from her ass yet? I need to know because Lizzy sent me out here to see if her mother's relaxed any."

"She seems fine to me, Mr. Cole." I say, wriggling out of his grip. "In fact, she's using my boyfriend to help her with some last minute arrangements. She seemed in a very good mood when I spoke to her."

"Good. I plied her with liquor. Let's hope it's enough to get us through this ceremony. So, little Savannah's done grown up and landed her a man? That's great news. Fabulous! Cheers!" He holds up his rocks glass, drains the last of the liquid, and moves into the kitchen for a refill.

"Uh, is Lizzy in the bedroom?" I ask, more than ready to leave the conversation.

"Oh, yeah. She surely is. She's right back there." He points in the general direction of the bedroom.

"Thank you," I say, slinging the garment bag over my shoulder once again.

"Right. You girls have fun playing dress up," he says, stumbling out of the house and pointing towards the men assembling the tents. "Ho, there! Tent person! Lemme show you something."

I jet inside because I have no desire to witness that impending disaster.

"Lizzy?" I ask, softly rapping on the bedroom door. Her arm frantically searches for anything to grab on to, and my shirt is the first thing her fingers make contact with. Once she has a ball of fabric in her hand, she yanks me into the room with her.

"They're driving me crazy, Savannah. I can't handle this. Please, make them go."

"Deep breaths, Lizzy. Take slow deep breaths," I instruct in the most calming tone I can muster.

She nods, while inhaling. "What's my dad doing?"

"Supervising the tent crew."

"Oh great. Cooter Brown is leading the tent erection. Wonderful. Nothing can go wrong there. What about my mom?"

"She's using my boyfriend to do menial chores because she thinks he's hot."

Lizzy's face softens. "Awww, your boyfriend. I love hearing that more than you could ever know. And though I'm sorry about my mother, you should have figured that would happen when she laid eyes upon him. He's is a total hottie, and you know how Prissy simply adores those young strapping men."

I smile while playfully rolling my eyes. "What can I help with?"

"Nothing. I have someone coming over to do our hair and makeup. Ben's in charge of making sure everything is set on his end. Everything is running on schedule, so we're good."

I pretend to check her for fever. "What have you done with my friend? Lizzy? Blink twice if you've been abducted by aliens or something."

Lizzy giggles. "I'm fine. I've learned a lot by being around Ben. What's the most important thing about today?" she asks, plopping onto the bed.

"Your marriage."

"That's right. I'm here. Ben's here. The

priest will be here. This wedding is happening
regardless. It doesn't matter if I'm in a tank and sleep
pants or that beautiful dress hanging over there. I'm
pledging my love to the man I want to spend the rest
of my life with, and that's all it's about. As long as
I'm Lizzy Thibodaux by the end of the night, frankly,
I couldn't care less about what happens in between."
She pauses to hold up an index finger. "However, my
parents wreaking havoc and running amok, that's
something that will grate on my nerves no matter how
calm I am about everything else."

I smile. "It's going to be fine, you'll see. I'll
run as much interference as possible."

"Bless you!" she exclaims, peeping out the
window. She starts to squeal while running in place,
"Andi's here to do our hair and makeup! Will you
show her in?"

"Sure." I open the front door and show the
young woman with spiky blue hair and multiple
piercings to the bedroom. Lizzy waits until Andi sets
down the large cases she's carrying before giving her
a gigantic hug.

"I'm so excited! It's my wedding day," she
sings.

Andi laughs then introduces herself to me.
She looks at my bone structure, touches my hair, and
looks me over while holding her index fingers to her
lips. "Okay, let's make you gorgeous," she says,
snapping one of the cases open.

Andi works her magic on us, and by the time
she leaves, Lizzy and I are absolutely glowing and
radiant. We have our hair secured in the same elegant
twist, but hers holds a beautiful crystal barrette for her
veil. My dress is a very simple sapphire blue strapless

number that falls just above my knees. Her dress is cut much like mine, except hers is white and reaches the floor. Simple, yet elegant. I grip her hand in mine.

"Are you ready?" I ask.

"I've never been more ready for anything. I love him so much, Savannah. I've grown tremendously in the time I've known him, and I can't wait to see what wonderful adventures our life together will take us on." She gets quiet and her face suddenly bears a serious expression. "I was going to wait to tell you this, but I just as well get it over with."

"What's wrong, Lizzy?" I ask, my stomach suddenly in knots.

"Ben's business is booming, so much so that he's opening new restaurants..."

"What great news! Why would you be afraid to tell me that?"

"We're moving to Dallas, Savannah. It won't be for a few months, but the sooner we can get over there the better."

I feel like I've been kicked in the stomach. I never once imagined a life where Lizzy wasn't more than few minutes from me. Blinking heavily to hide the rogue tear that tries to break free, I scramble to find congratulatory words. "That's wonderful, Lizzy. I'm sure you'll love it there."

"Hey, now." She embraces me. "I might not be around the corner, but I'll always be no more than a phone call away. Plus, we'll be traveling back and forth between the restaurants, so we'll be coming to town often. You and Fletcher can come to Dallas whenever you want, too! It'll be fine. Savannah, your friendship will always be one of the most important things to me, so be ready for lots and lots of phone calls."

The shock begins to wear off, and because I'm feeling a little more secure about the news, I nod. "I'm going to miss you so much. Who can I share the strange work calls with now?"

"Duh, you're going to share with me! I might not be across from your cubicle, but I'll still be your vent buddy. You can give me a rundown of every shift if you want to."

Prissy, now dressed in an iridescent sequined pant suit enters the room. "It's time. Ah, what a glorious day. Here I am, celebrating the union of my daughter and my future son in law, and I simply couldn't squeeze another drop of happiness into my cup. Father's on his way in so he can walk you down the aisle. My, don't you both look beautiful! Absolutely breathtaking," she sings. Normally, such words would be welcomed and appreciated. However, Lizzy and I knew the truth behind them. Her mother is only sugary sweet when she's three sheets to the wind. Normally, she's hypercritical and blatantly condescending.

"Thank you, mother," Lizzy says with fake enthusiasm.

While Prissy isn't looking, Lizzy makes the "she's been drinking" sign with her hand. I nod emphatically, and Lizzy rolls her eyes.

"Ah, there's my princess! Come on. Saddle up so we can make an honest woman out of you." He taps on his elbow. "Giddy up now."

"Oh, dear God," Lizzy mumbles under her breath.

"Remember what's important," I whisper to

her as I take my spot at the door. My signal to go is a light knock, so I flash Lizzy a quick smile as I take my simple bouquet of roses and make my way to the altar that has been set up on the dock.

Fletcher looks so debonair in his suit, and I can tell by the way he's looking at me that he's smitten. The attention makes me blush, and as I cast my eyes downward, an appreciative smile crosses my lips.

The service is short and sweet, but the wedding party is asked to stick around for photos. By the time we finish up, I'm absolutely starving. Fletcher and I make our way to the buffet, and then find a secluded table near the outer edge of the tent so we can observe the festivities, yet not be smack dab in the middle of them.

"I can't believe how good this food is," Fletcher says, practically devouring his plate. I can't do anything but nod in agreement because I'm doing the same. He smiles when he notices that I'm shoveling in a forkful of jambalaya.

"What?" I ask, raising my fingers to my mouth because I'm suddenly embarrassed.

He smiles broadly. "Nothing. You know that I love you, right?"

"That's what you tell me, "I say, taking a big swallow from my drink.

"It's the truth. I'll be yours always."

I put down the drink and smile sweetly at him. "And I'll be yours always." We lean in to share a delicate kiss but are interrupted by Lizzy's screeching.

"What are you two doing hiding in the corner? It's party time! Come on, we're about to kick up the music!" She has a champagne glass in one hand and hard lemonade in the other. I'm not anticipating her night to end well if she keeps chugging like she is.

"Have you eaten?" I ask her over the sound of the music that is now blaring. She's not paying attention to me because she's screaming for the DJ to crank it up. I'm behind her frantically giving him the "no" signal. He gives a wink in our direction, and I'm not sure which one of us it was intended for until the music softens to a level less deafening.

"Lizzy, have you eaten anything?"

"No, why? Is the food bad?" she asks while moving her hips and snapping her fingers.

"No, it's delicious, but we both know that you can't hold your liquor when you drink on an empty stomach."

"Pshh. That's an old wives' tale," she says giggling.

"Wives' tale nothing. Trust me on this one, please. Fletcher, would you mind fixing her a plate?"

"Not at all," he says, leaving us so he can toss a little of everything onto a plate.

"I feel wonderful! I don't need no stinkin' food," Lizzy says with a pout.

"Should I just go ahead and start calling you Prissy now or after you're completely smashed?" I ask.

"Ouch! That hurt, Savannah. That really hurt." She's quiet for a minute. I can tell by the way she's squinting that she's trying to focus her vision. "Okay, maybe I'll eat a little bit," she says, sitting across from me.

"There's my beautiful bride! What's going on over here?" Ben asks, finally joining us. He looks just as toasted as Lizzy.

"What is it with you two? You know you need

153

to eat, right?" I ask.

"Oh, yeah. I didn't do that. I'm on it, boss," Ben says, stumbling as he joins Fletcher at the buffet. We manage to get some food into the bride and the groom, and almost instantly, they're acting slightly giddy, but no longer slurring and stumbling like full on lushes.

"I hereby release you two from drunk jail. You're free to go," I say, waving my hands in a shooing motion.

"Thank you so much for intervening. You know me well. I'd already had four, and we know that my clothes usually start coming off somewhere around number six," Lizzy explains.

Ben snaps his head around. "What? How did I not know this?"

"Well, you know now," Lizzy says, taking his loosened tie in her hand so she can drag him to the dance floor that is set up just outside the tent. "Come on, y'all! I'm going to request a slow song, and the DJ has to do what I say because I'm the bride."

Fletcher and I shake our heads as we follow them out.

The sun has set, and the walking paths are lined with beautiful torches, lamps, and luminaries, the soft glows from which help to illuminate the dance floor. I love being in Fletcher's strong arms, slowly swaying back and forth to the rhythm of the music. Dancing is another activity that I generally avoid, and after thinking back, I figure the last time I did it was for a high school dance. Luckily, it's like riding a bike. Plus, Fletcher is a confident and strong lead. It's so relaxing, so unbelievably perfect that I completely lose track of time.

We're interrupted briefly for a few of the traditions: the cutting of the cake, tossing the bouquet, and such, but then we're right back on the dance floor as soon as it's over. I'm gazing into the eyes of the man I love when the shrill feedback from a microphone stops everyone in his or her tracks.

"I need everyone's attention," Carlton Cole slurs each and every word as he captures the undivided attention of the small group of guests. I steal a glance in Lizzy's direction, and she looks semi-mortified. I whisper to Fletcher that I'll be right back before rushing to the front of the small crowd that has conglomerated around him. I give Lizzy a brief nod to let her know that if he makes a fool of himself, I'm going to be all over it. I just hope I'll be strong enough to rip the mic from him if the need arises.

"Our Lizzy. Elizabeth Jordan Cole. Oops. Excuse me, Elizabeth Thibodaux. Lizzy Thibodaux. Your mother and I… Prissy? Where are ya, Prissy? I can't find you without my glasses."

"I'm right here," she says, pushing aside a couple so she can stumble to stand beside him. She's obviously still just as smashed as he is. *Oh great! Will I be able to handle two of them?* Though I don't feel confident in the least, I give Lizzy a fake reassuring smile.

"Oh, good. There you are. This concerns you, too. It's time for the s-u-r… Oh forget about it, it's time for that surprise thing we have for the kids," Carlton slurs.

Prissy takes the microphone away from him. "We adore surprises, so we have a few. First, Elizabeth and Ben, we're sending you on an all expense paid trip to Italy for your honeymoon!"

The crowd claps while Ben and Lizzy look at each other with astonishment. They both quickly mask it with fake plastered smiles. The rest of the crowd might be unaware, but I know that it's because Lizzy and Ben had already arranged to honeymoon in Aruba.

"Our second surprise, and boy this is a good one, is— a brand new car! Your sporty silver Audi SUV will be delivered to you in a few days. They're finishing up with some of the customizations, so we weren't able to get it here before the wedding, but we know you'll love it. Here's hoping you fill the backseat with grandkids!" Carlton says raising his glass, then sloshing back the contents.

I'm just about to make my move when he speaks again. "And lastly, and I have to admit that this one was Prissy's idea… It was a great one, darlin'. No one's going to guess it! Anyone? Anyone want to try?" He raises his empty rocks glass in a mock toast to the crowd. "Well, I don't blame you. Get ready, 'cause I'm not going to spoil this last one for you. I'm going to let you see for yourself. Maestro, cue the music," Carlton says, just before dropping the mic on the ground and stumbling back into the crowd.

The DJ starts to play another slow song, and when nothing unusual or out of the ordinary happens after the first few bars, people begin to go about their business. Fletcher takes me into his arms, and once again, we're slowly swaying back and forth in unison. All is right with the world.

The first pop scares the hell out of me because I don't know if it's a gunshot, a car backfiring, or what that caused it. When the night sky starts to glow pink, then gold, then purple, I figure out that the big surprise is a fireworks display for the newlyweds.

I try to turn away from Fletcher so I can better see the show, but he's got a death grip on me. I can hear his heart thundering in his chest, and as I slowly pry myself from his arms, I notice that he's drenched in sweat.

"Fletcher, what's wrong, sweetie?" It's like he doesn't hear me. His chest rises and falls rapidly as he nervously looks around the grounds. "Fletcher," I say louder. This gets his attention. "Are you okay, sweetie? What's wrong?"

"Huh? What? Oh. Yeah, I'm okay. I think it might be something I ate. I'm not feeling very well all of a sudden."

"Okay, let's get you home then," I say, concerned because of how sudden the onset of his symptoms are. He looks like he wants to collapse, so I don't even bother telling anyone that we're leaving. I don't want him to know it, but I'm scared for him, and I have every intention of getting him to the closest hospital.

I help him inside the passenger seat, and he practically curls into a ball. Ben, coming out of nowhere, looks into the passenger window and pulls open the door as I start up the truck. "Fletcher, look at me buddy. Hey, look at me. Are you okay?"

"Ben, I'm good. I just need to get home. I'm sure it's something I ate."

I nervously wait for Ben to shut the door so I can get Fletcher some help. "Something you ate? Okay Fletcher, get some rest. I'm going to call and check on you in an hour or so to see if you're feeling any better. If you need me before then, I'm right here.

Just a phone call away, buddy. Okay? Look at me."

Fletcher is still sweating profusely, and it appears as though chills have set in. He manages to look Ben's way and to give him a little nod.

"You call me if you need me," Ben says to me. I nod, grateful when Ben finally closes the door so I can leave.

"Which hospital is the closest?" I ask, driving like a bat out of hell.

"No. No hospital," Fletcher weakly insists.

"But you're so sick."

"I need rest; some rest and I'll be fine. It's just a stomach issue. There's not much they can do for me at the hospital anyway. They'd probably tell me to go home and let it run its course."

I reluctantly concede. "Okay, but I'm not bringing you home. You're coming to my place."

"That's fine," Fletcher says. "Just please get me somewhere I can rest."

I make it to my apartment in record time, and thanks to strength I didn't know I possessed, I manage to practically carry Fletcher inside. He flops onto the bed, his pale face dripping with sweat. I loosen his clothing a bit before dashing into the bathroom for a cool cloth. Gently stroking his face with it, I feel like I should be doing more to help him.

"Can you help me get this stuff off?" he asks, his voice shaky because he's trembling so much.

"Yes, of course." Without hesitation or elaboration, I remove his suit jacket, his tie, his shirt, and his pants. All he's left in is an undershirt and a pair of underwear. I take the cloth and run it over as much of his exposed flesh as possible. He doesn't feel warm to me; he feels clammy. I'm walking to the bathroom to freshen up the cloth when Fletcher suddenly jumps from the bed and shoves me away from the bathroom door. I hear him retching and heaving in there, and I'm unsure of what to do. Mostly, I want to check on him, but part of me is hesitant because I'm not sure if it will embarrass him.

Once the noises become less frequent, I carefully peep around the door jamb. "Fletcher?" I softly ask. "Are you okay, sweetie?"

He's still sitting beside the toilet, his elbow resting on his knee. "Yeah, I'm okay," he weakly replies. "I'm sorry about all of this."

I join him in the bathroom. "There's nothing to be sorry about. I just hope I didn't eat whatever it is that did this to you."

Fletcher gives a feeble smile. "I think you'd be sick by now if you did."

"Do you think the vomiting has passed? Should I help you into the bed?"

"Yeah, I think it's over," he says, pushing against the floor with his palms so he can stand. I wedge myself under his arm. He insists on a brief stop by the bathroom sink so he can brush his teeth, and once he's safely under the covers, I leave him long enough to get a glass of lemon lime soda. He closes his eyes after drinking it down, so I carefully and quietly roll off the bed so I don't disturb his rest.

I hear his phone buzzing non-stop in his pants pocket, so I check it to find a slew of text messages and missed calls from Ben. I type a quick message explaining that he's resting comfortably and that I'll give him a call if anything changes. Ben thanks me for responding, and after I tell him that it's no problem, he's off to undoubtedly enjoy the rest of his wedding night.

I look down and realize that I'm still in my full wedding attire. Too tired to go through the process of washing the product from my hair, removing the goop from my face, and searching for something to wear to bed, I strip to my bra and panties and gently slip into bed beside Fletcher. He pulls me tightly into his arms so that my back rests against his chest. I was so scared before, but he appears to be doing much better now. He's no longer clammy, and he's resting well. I fall asleep by counting his breaths as his chest rises and falls against my back.

ten

The next morning I find myself staring over at Fletcher. He's fast asleep, but that's a recent occurrence. I know this because he tossed, turned, moaned, and groaned the entire night, even jerked to sit straight up in bed a few times. I'm worried about him, but I caution myself not to overreact to the situation. I've had stomach bugs before, and though I felt like death warmed over, I sucked it up and dealt with it. It's different when you have to watch someone else go through it. Witnessing his discomfort and pain left me feeling helpless and uncertain, two sensations that I rarely experienced while living on my own. It's serves as another reminder of how absolutely head over heels I am for this man. Being responsible for another person's care is a huge step for me, and I want to make sure I'm doing it right.

After easing out of the bed, I pad to the kitchen for a light breakfast. I also send Ben and Lizzy a text to let them know that Fletcher is doing much better this morning. After watching TV for a couple of hours, I check on Fletcher. He appears to be in that place between sleep and awake.

"Hi. How are you feeling?" I softly ask as I slide next to him.

"Like I was hit by a truck," he groggily answers. "I'm sorry I got sick last night."

"It's okay. You scared me, though."

"Did I? I'm sorry."

"You were really sick. You should've let me bring you to the hospital."

"Oh, there was no need for that. It was just one of those things. I'll rest today, and by tomorrow, things will be much better. You'll see."

"Are you sure?" I ask, running my hand over his face. It's not just a tender gesture, I'm also checking for fever. He feels perfectly normal.

"I'm sure." He takes my hand and kisses my palm.

"Can I get you something to eat or drink?"

"Just some water for now. Thanks, sweetheart."

I leave him long enough to fill the largest vessel I can find, which happens to be an old mug from a local gas station that ran a special on oversized fountain drinks. It takes two hands to carry it back to the room.

"What is that?" Fletcher asks, amused.

"Water."

"But why is it in a bucket?"

"It's a mug, and you'll need to drink a lot to get back the fluids you lost last night."

"I feel like a horse drinking from a trough," Fletcher says, trying to find the right angle to get a sip. I stick a straw in it, and his smile shows his appreciation. "I think I'll save the rest for later." He places the mug on the nightstand. "Did I ruin the wedding? I don't remember too much about what happened after Lizzy's parents made their big announcement."

"No, you didn't ruin anything. Lizzy, Ben, and I were very concerned about you, but everything went on as planned. I brought you here, and that was it."

"Did I say or do anything silly or strange?"

"No. You barfed a lot though."

"Yeah, I'm feeling it today," he says, rubbing his rib cage. "I should get up and walk around."

He makes a few leisurely laps around the apartment before settling onto the sofa. Sharing a blanket, we pretty much spend the day snuggling. By mid-afternoon, Fletcher is ready to find substantial food.

"Let me take you out. You name the place."

Though I repeatedly warn him that he should continue to take it easy, he insists on an answer. I give the name of a quiet little café tucked between two giant strip malls, because even though I have a huge hankering for Mexican food, let's face it, Mexican doesn't usually sit well on a recovering stomach.

We have the same thing, deliciously rich bowls of steaming seafood gumbo, and I happily watch as the color returns to Fletcher's cheeks. I'm only about halfway done with my bowl when he finishes with his.

"I can get this to go if you're ready to leave," I say, when I notice him fidgeting with his napkin.

"No, take your time. It's fine," he says, scanning the restaurant. He's looking out of the window when he starts tapping his spoon against the table.

"Fletcher," I quietly say, looking around the room to see if he's disturbing others with his drum solo. Fortunately, the restaurant is basically empty. "Fletcher," I say a little louder when I get no response.

"Huh?" he asks, turning to look at me.

"The spoon. You're tapping it…"

He looks down at the utensil in his hand as though he has no idea how it got there. He shrugs and casts it into his bowl. "Oh, I'm sorry."

"You're a million miles from here. Come on, let's go," I insist. "See, I told you we should've ordered in." I let out a little gasp as I raise my hand to my mouth. "Oh, my gosh. I just sounded like a nagging wife. I'm so sorry."

Fletcher lets out a little chuckle. "You did, and it's okay. You're right. We should've stayed in."

"Are you coming home with me? If so, I guess we should stop by your apartment to get some things, right?"

"Actually, I think I'm going to stay at my place tonight, but will you come to visit me tomorrow?"

I'm a little stunned because I really thought he'd be with me tonight, but I do my best to cover it up. "Sure! Absolutely. I'll stop by after work tomorrow."

The ride to Fletcher's is pretty quiet. I don't want to admit it, but my feelings are a little hurt. I mentally scold myself for being such a whiny butt. *The man wants a night alone, so what! Get over it. He's on the mend from a terrible stomach bug. You'd probably want to be alone, too.*

He offers a kiss before going inside, which I happily accept. I promise to bring supper with me for my visit. He doesn't know it yet, but I might bring him a couple of other surprises, too. A slow, devious smile creeps across my lips. Maybe it's time to introduce Fletcher to the naughty Savannah.

Work drags and drags and drags some more. It's so different without Lizzy's constant interruptions and distractions. Frankly, I'm not happy here anymore, and I spend my break searching college courses at one of the local universities. I'm making all of these other changes in my life, so why not put some of Grampy's money to good use? So far the main contenders are nursing and elementary education, with nursing edging out by a hair.

After work, I call Fletcher, and he decides that pizza should be on the menu for supper. As I wait for my order to be prepared, I take a few minutes to duck into the clothing store next door. I make a few purchases, and as I'm checking out, my phone buzzes to announce my pizza order is ready for pick up. I cheerfully pay the young woman behind the register, and I practically skip back to my car. *What has Fletcher Reilly done to me?*

Fletcher looks much better when he answers the door. "What's in the bag?" he asks, curiously poking his head around for a better look once he takes the pizza box from me.

"Nothing for you to concern yourself about. Patience please, my good man."

He plops the pizza onto the counter, encircles me in his arms, and pulls me close. "How was work?"

"Boring," I say, wriggling free from his

embrace. He drops his jaw and turns his palms up in a "what?" gesture.

"I'm starving," I say, popping the lid of the box open. I place two slices on a paper plate, grab a beer from the fridge, and make myself comfortable on the sofa.

Fletcher is all smiles when he joins me. "I don't think I could love you anymore than I do at this moment."

"Wha?" I ask, covering my mouthful of pizza.

"You realize that you're the woman of my dreams, don't you?"

"Fletcher, I…" I'm immediately red faced.

"Don't. Don't get flustered. I like that you're relaxed and comfortable around me."

"Consider yourself lucky. The only other person I used to relax around was Lizzy. Now I find myself at ease around lots of other people, like Molly and Julia. Ben, too. I'm not hiding from the world anymore, I'm at a point where I want to stand on the street and yell, 'I'm Savannah Rose Mason, and I'm ready to conquer the world!'"

"Whoa now. We're supposed to do that together."

"You're right. We'll do that together, but I have decided on a life change."

"Really?" Fletcher asks, shifting so he can give me his undivided attention.

"I'm going back to school. I have the money from the boat sale, which I know you were absolutely one hundred percent behind, by the way."

"I don't know what you're talking about," Fletcher says, gesturing feigned ignorance.

"How did Ben come up with the exact number

the boat was worth, and then not haggle once about the price? Hmmmm?"

"Coincidence, I guess."

"Whatever. Regardless, I think I'm going to enroll in an accelerated nursing program."

"You want to be a nurse? I think that's a great idea."

"Thank you," I say, beaming with pride.

He edges closer to me, drops the pitch of his voice, and whispers in my ear, "You're going to look so hot in scrubs." His finger trails down my throat and hooks the edge of my shirt. He gives it a gentle tug so he can sneak a peek. I pull away.

"I have a little surprise for you," I excitedly say, holding the bag from the clothing store in the air while waving it around.

"You do? I'm intrigued. Give it to me."

"Oh, you're going to get it alright. You stay right here," I say, turning off all of the lights in the apartment except for the dim one over the stove. "I'll be right back."

"I can't wait!" he says, eagerly rubbing his hands together.

After shutting the bedroom door, I strip my clothes off and empty the contents of the bag onto the bed: sapphire blue panties and matching balconette bra, an oversized white button up shirt, and a black fedora. After I tuck my hair inside the hat, I stare at myself in the mirror, and I'm pleased with the reflection. The shirt is unbuttoned enough to expose the swell of my breasts and is long enough to stop mid-thigh. I tip the hat forward slightly and decide that I need one final touch. Opening Fletcher's closet I shift clothes around until I find a necktie. His military dress uniform is hanging in there, and I take a second to admire the patches, pins, and ribbons that adorn the jacket.

Snapping out of it, I drape the tie over my shoulders, grateful that it's already in the appropriate knot. Tying a tie is one trick I never learned. One last glance in the mirror, a deep breath for added confidence, and I slowly open the bedroom door to stick one leg through the gap.

"Are you ready for me, Mr. Reilly?" I ask in my most seductive voice as I join him in the living room.

Fletcher is speechless, and his jaw falls slack. He struggles to put a sentence together, which makes me smile. "Hot," he finally manages to eke out. "So hot."

I pull a chair from the dining area and put it in the middle of the room. "Why don't you have a seat?"

I don't even get a chance to finish the sentence before he's ready and waiting for his next command. Scrolling through my phone, I find the song I want, turn the volume to max, and set it on the coffee table. Never once in my life have I done a striptease, and I hope I'm decent at it. I close my eyes and let the beat of the music course through my body. As I catch the rhythm, I slowly begin gyrating my hips in time to the music. The tie is the first to go, and I gently toss it to the sofa after running it seductively through my fingers.

My eyes are still closed as my shoulders begin to move to the music, and I don't open them until my fingers finish the trail down my chest and land on the first closed button. Fletcher's eyes are smoldering with desire, and I can see how much he wants me from his body language. I feel sexy, secure, and wanted, which makes me more confident in my dancing.

The shirt is completely unbuttoned, but before I take it off, I throw the fedora and it lands on the floor. Teasing him, I pull the shirt closed, slowly open it, and snap it closed again before provocatively bending over to pick up the hat from the floor. I run the brim across my lips before lightly sinking my teeth into it then casting it aside onto the sofa. Walking like a runway model, I approach Fletcher and straddle one of his thick, hard thighs. His eager hands try to pull the shirt off of me, but I give him a playful smack while shaking my head.

"You're killing me," he growls against my neck.

"So you like what you see?"

"Oh, I love what I see. I want it. Now."

"Nope. Not yet," I say, slowly sliding down the length of his thigh, then flipping around so I'm facing away from him. Arching my back, I rest the back of my head against his shoulder while running my fingers through his hair. His hands greedily grab for my breasts, and once again, he finds himself reprimanded.

"No hands, mister," I say, rising from his lap and finally casting aside the shirt. I feel the silky cups of the bra and make sure I press my breasts together to better pronounce my cleavage. After running my hands down my waist and upper thighs, I semi-turn and give my rear a hard smack. Fletcher's breath catches, and I notice that he's having difficulties swallowing.

Taking the tie from the sofa, I loosely drape it over the back of his neck, run it down his arms, and smile playfully as I secure his wrists together. I give his neck a playful lick and a suck before doing the same thing to his lips. His desire for me is so intense that he's trembling.

"Savannah."

"Shhhh," I say, kissing him hard. He greedily returns the affection then moans with pleasure when I raise his shirt to lick and kiss his chest and abs. I'm feeling empowered and sexy as hell when I leave his lap to get the white shirt from the sofa. I twirl it a couple of times, and then blindfold Fletcher with it.

I start kissing his neck again, and the music changes to something with an abrasive beat. I don't even remember downloading the song, but I'm so wrapped up in what I'm doing that I disregard it. It's not until I kiss Fletcher on the lips that I realize something is wrong. Very wrong. He's not trembling with desire anymore; he's broken out in a cold sweat again. His breathing isn't sporadic from want, and he seems terrified.

I pull the shirt from his eyes to find them glassed over. Fletcher's body might be with me, but his mind is somewhere else. "Fletcher," I softly say as his breathing gets more labored.

I reach out to stop the music, quickly untie his hands, and grip his face between my palms to make him look at me. My heart is thudding because I don't know what's going on, but I know in the pit of my stomach that whatever it is, it's bad.

"Fletcher, honey. Talk to me. What's wrong?"

His breathing gets so labored that he starts to

make grunting sounds. He rapidly shakes his head from side to side, and I can't hold his face between my hands anymore. Before I can do anything to stop it, he violently lurches from the chair, and my head smacks against the hard floor. He's on top of me, saying "stop" over and over again. He's looking right at me, but he doesn't see me. I'm scared out of my mind, and I have no clue what's going on or what I should do. Before I can stop myself, I begin to cry.

"I'm sorry, Fletcher. I don't know what I did wrong. I'm so sorry," I keep saying over and over again while he pins me to the floor. As I sob, I notice that his grip begins to loosen, and I take the opportunity to wipe my tears.

"Oh, my God. Savannah! Did I hurt you? Oh, baby, please tell me I didn't hurt you. I'm so sorry. I'm so, so sorry, sweetheart. Please tell me you're okay." He's practically sobbing, himself.

I sit up and push myself away from him to rest my back against the sofa. He crawls over to me. "Are you okay? Please tell me that I didn't hurt you. God, please."

"I'm okay," I manage to say before he smothers me with a hug.

"I'm so sorry, sweetheart. Oh, baby, I'm so sorry."

"You scared me, Fletcher. You wouldn't answer me, and the look that was on your face—it gave me chills. What happened?"

He releases me, and with a defeated sigh, he asks me if I'll please join him in the bedroom. I nod my head, and that's when I realize I have a goose egg forming. I touch the tender spot and wince.

"I did hurt you. Shit! Savannah, is it bad?

171

Should I bring you to the hospital? Do you want to call the police? Leave? I'll understand."

"No. Stop and listen to me. I've been the victim of domestic abuse, and what happened here wasn't abuse. Something was definitely wrong, but you weren't out to hurt me. It's like you checked out or something."

He hands me a plastic bag filled with ice that he's wrapped in a dish towel. "Come on. I'll explain everything. I should have done this a long time ago, but I'd been doing so well…"

I follow him into the bedroom, where he lies in bed and pats the spot next to him. I lie in his arms, and he takes it upon himself to keep my ice pack in place.

"This is hard for me, Savannah. Not many people know about my problem."

"You can tell me anything, Fletcher. Remember how hard it was for me to tell you about my issues, and look how freeing it was for me. Maybe that's all you need? There's nothing you can tell me that will make me want to leave you, so tell me everything. Is it drugs?"

"No, nothing like that." He sighs. "Have you heard of Post Traumatic Stress Disorder? Some people call it PTSD for short."

"I've heard of it, but I don't know too much about it."

"First of all, it sucks. Essentially, it's a mental disorder I developed due to a combination of the physical and emotional trauma I experienced while overseas."

"Is it from the explosion?" I ask.

"Partly," he patiently answers. He removes

the ice pack from my head and uses that hand to lightly stroke my arm. "Are you sure you want to hear the story?"

"Yes, I want to know everything there is to know about you. I want to know all of your experiences, everything that's made you happy, sad, afraid—everything."

He nods his head. "If you decide you don't want to hear anymore, just stop me, okay?"

"Okay," I agree. Butterflies flitter in my stomach because I have no idea what's about to come from his mouth. The only thing I know for sure is that whatever it is, I'll continue to love and cherish him.

"So you know that the truck exploded while Brody was driving, and that he was killed instantly, right?"

"Yes."

He's quiet for a few seconds. "I remember most of it: the smells, the high pitched ringing in my ears, the searing heat from the fire. I was pulled from the wreckage and some kind of garment was tossed over me to quash the flames. Once they were out, I was loaded into the back of a pickup truck and driven to a bunker. The reason the scars are so bad is because I didn't get medical attention right away. I was held hostage and tortured for three days before I was rescued."

Gasping, my body tightens as I try to hold back the tears that are brimming. I couldn't even begin to imagine the agony, fright, and anguish he went through.

"I was hooded and strapped to a chair. With the burns on my back, it was excruciating. I repeatedly begged them to kill me, but obviously they wouldn't. I'm not going to retell every event, every act, every detail, because it's too hard. I wish every single day that I could scrub it out of my memory, but I can't. The memories sit there, haunting me when I least expect it. Like tonight. I loved every second of tonight, and I'll be very upset if you won't give me a repeat performance. Everything was fine until you tied my hands. I started to get a little anxious, but I was so wrapped up in the moment that I cast it aside. But once I was blindfolded…"

"I'm so sorry, Fletcher."

"Don't be. You didn't know, sweetheart. How could you know?"

"So as long as I don't tie you up or blindfold you, you're fine?"

"Unfortunately, no. That's not how this works. Remember the food poisoning at the wedding?"

"Yes."

"It wasn't food poisoning, it was the fireworks. The loud popping and the explosions, they triggered a reaction. I was too embarrassed to tell you the truth because I'd been doing so well. I hadn't had an attack in quite a while, and I thought I'd finally been cured. Obviously, I haven't."

"Have you seen a doctor? Is there some kind of help you can get?"

"I was in a hospital for a long time getting treated for it. Remember how cold Julia was when we first ran into her at the carnival?"

I nod.

"It's because she's still mad at me for leaving the treatment facility against medical advice. I was supposed to stay for another four weeks, but I couldn't take it anymore. The panic attacks had stopped, and I didn't want to stay locked in my room any longer… That's how bad I had it, Savannah. I developed agoraphobia, and I wouldn't leave my room. Therapy and the right meds helped me to get past so many of the issues and obstacles I faced. I didn't see the need to stay any longer. I wanted to be home in Louisiana, where I could spend time with Ben, Molly, and Julia. Julia needed me. Molly was young, and Julia had just lost her husband."

"I understand your reasoning, but I also understand why Julia was upset."

"Well, she's over it now, and that's why I need you to promise that we'll keep this to ourselves. Ben obviously knows, but that's it. Julia doesn't need to know about these recent episodes, okay."

I nod. "Okay. Is there anything else I need to know about?"

"I don't think so. Long as I stay away from triggers, I should be okay."

"I'm so sorry this happened to you."

He lightly kisses me on my forehead. "I'm sorry, too. But if everything hadn't happened the way it did, I might not have found you. So, that's my story."

I position myself so I can look him in the eye. "I love you, Fletcher Reilly. I'll always love you, and I want you to know that you can tell me anything."

"Ah, Savannah. Those words melt my heart. I love you, too. I'm yours always."

I rest my head on his chest and listen to the beating of his heart. We're silent for a long time. I'm not sure what's going through his mind, but I'm going over the things he's confided in me. Tortured. He was tortured for three days with severe burns and injuries from an explosion. The fact that he lived is amazing in itself, but to know that the torture still haunts him hurts my heart. That he had to live it once is terrible enough, but to have to relive it over and over and over, when will his torture end?

His breathing is slow and steady, and I think he's fallen asleep until I feel his fingers unclasping the back of my bra. "So you bought this just for me?"

"I sure did," I say with a smile.
"Thank you," he says, and the way he says it alludes to the fact that he's not talking about the new bra and panties. I take his face in my hands and draw him close to me. What I'd started out intending to be hot and heavy sex turned into gentle and tender lovemaking, but I wasn't about to complain. Fletcher showed me how much he loved me, and I decide right then that he's right—we're soul mates. But, when should I let him know that?

eleven

I slip out early the next morning so I can meet with an admissions counselor before going to work. The admissions process is pretty painless, and I walk out of the building as a nursing student. It's funny how timing works, a new semester is starting at the same moment my future career path becomes clear. Not to mention that I'll be graduating in two years instead of four. I'll start with my associate's degree, start working as a nurse, and then decide if I want to continue on with my education. My journey is unfurling before me, and all I have to do is keep moving forward.

After work, I stop at the store to pick up some things to make a huge grilled chicken salad. Enough of the eating out. If I'm changing my life, might as well include my body in that change, too. I make a quick call to Fletcher to see if he's interested in joining me for supper. He is, but he asks me if I'd mind eating at his place. I tell him that it's no problem and head towards his apartment.

I lightly rap on the door, and he opens is almost immediately. I give him a quick peck before pushing past him to get the groceries unloaded. "I have three different kinds of lettuce, carrots, tomatoes, all kinds of stuff. What's your favorite dressing? I was thinking about making a simple vinaigrette, but if you don't like that kind of thing, I bought a couple of bottles of some other stuff."

Realizing that I hadn't even greeted him properly, I rectify the situation in what I hope comes off as smooth. "So, what did you do today? Were you busy?"

"The usual stuff. Nothing I couldn't handle."

I open the fridge to put the perishables inside and notice it's empty. "Babe, we've got to get this place stocked up. There's not even a bottle of water in here. Why didn't you go to the store?"

"I didn't have time today. I'll go tomorrow."

"You literally have nothing, zero, zilch. Do you want to go while I'm fixing supper?"

"No," he says, coming up behind me. He encircles my waist and draws me near. "I want to stay right here and enjoy you." His lips trail kisses down my neck, and I'm wrought with a deep shiver.

"Stop. Not now," I fuss. "I'll surely cut myself if you keep that up."

He takes the knife from my hand, sets it beside the cutting board, and turns me to face him. His lips are upon mine, and I toss the handful of lettuce I'm still gripping onto the counter. He tightly squeezes his arms together around my thighs, and lifts me from the floor. Our lips remain locked as he fumbles his way into the bedroom.

"I've been thinking about this all day long," he

mumbles as he pauses long enough to cast his shirt aside.

"So have I," I admit between kisses. I unbutton my blouse, and it joins Fletcher's on the floor.

Fletcher pins my arms above my head as he teases and torments my body with his lips and tongue. He's not being soft about it, and I find myself turned on by his aggressiveness. It feels primitive, no thought needed. Just two desperate bodies yearning for the release that's sure to come.

"I want you," I whisper against his lips. "Please. Now." The anticipation leaves me trembling. He accepts my plea, and my eyes roll into the back of my head as he fills me.

"Tell me how you want it," he softly requests in my ear.

"I want it rough," I answer.

"Oh, you want rough, huh?" he asks, thrusting deeply inside of me. "Like that?"

I gasp while nodding my head. "Yes, like that. Just like that."

It's probably one of the best sexual encounters we've had since our first time, and we're both exhausted, sweaty, and out of breath once we finish. I want to jump into the shower, but my body isn't ready to let me move yet. Instead, I lie in Fletcher's arms as he softly strokes my hair.

"Savannah?"

"Yeah," I answer.

"I need to tell you something, and I'll completely understand if it changes things with us. It's hard for me to admit this, but I'm not going to lie to you."

I sit up so I can face him. "What's wrong, Fletcher?"

He turns his back to me and puts his face in his hands as he sits on the edge of the bed. "I don't have any food in the fridge because I've been worried about leaving the house again. What if I have another attack while I'm in the store? Or driving? You've seen for yourself how much they debilitate me."

I move to sit behind him and lightly kiss his scarred shoulder. "Baby, you did those things on your own for a long time before these recent attacks. You've had some serious triggers: the fireworks and me tying you up. I'm so sorry about that. I feel terrible."

"You have nothing to feel sorry for, sweetheart. How could you have known? I love that you feel free and uninhibited around me. I know what you've overcome to get to this point, and I consider it a gift. Not the sex, but the trust that you have in me."

"I love you, Fletcher. I love you in a way that I never thought was possible. You make me feel beautiful and wanted, and it feels natural to be open with you. It was strange to me in the beginning, but now it just feels right."

He kisses my palm. "I love you, too."

"How about we blow off the salad, we get dressed, and we go to the grocery store together. We'll find a place close by. I'll be there with you, and if something happens, we'll come straight back to the apartment. Okay?"

He gives my hand a squeeze. "You're too good to be true. You know that, right?"

"I was thinking the same thing about you," I admit.

The trip to the grocery store is uneventful for Fletcher. He does fine, and I see his confidence beginning to build. After we unload the groceries, I ask him if he's up for an outing to a local pub. He says he'd like to give it a try, especially since we'd worked up such a big appetite with our bedroom antics and our shopping trip. I blush slightly.

"Can we take the bike?" I ask, unsure of whether I'm pushing too hard or not.

Fletcher smiles. "Of course."

Again, he does perfectly fine while we're eating out, and again, I see his confidence level grow. I beam with pride because I feel like the luckiest woman in the world. Savannah Mason has overcome, and her prize is the jackpot to end all jackpots. If I had any friends to call, I'd be bragging to all of them. Life absolutely can't get any better. But, then it does.

Fletcher doesn't drive us back to the apartment once we finish supper. Instead, we take a ride through some of the less congested streets and neighborhoods. I love being on the back of the bike, and I smile as pleasant memories of my dad come back to me. I fully believe he's responsible for leading me to Fletcher. Seriously, what are the odds that some random customer would want to meet with me because he likes the way I sound? There is no way in hell I would normally touch something like that, but my gut kept telling me that something was different about this guy. Seeing Dad's bike is what sealed the deal. I'd have never agreed to meet with him if it weren't for that picture. *If it was you, thank you for sending me the sign, Dad.* I feel a little silly at first, but then I remember that Molly believes in signs, too.

Maybe it's something that a lot of people believe in? Oh well, I'm on my way to becoming a believer.

He stops the bike at a beautiful, tree-filled park, and we follow a path around the pond to a large gazebo that overlooks the water. He stands behind me, his arms draped over my shoulders, as we breathe in the fresh night air. It's so peaceful and quiet that we spend the first few minutes soaking it in. "Savannah?" he softly whispers in my ear.

"Hmmmm,"

"Marry me."

I quickly turn around. "What? Fletcher..."

His finger touches my lip. "Shhhh. I don't need an answer today. I know what I want, and I want to spend the rest of my life loving you. I'm not trying to pressure you. We haven't known each other very long, and to others it may seem foolish and rushed, but sometimes things don't have to follow the norm. Sometimes you just know what you know, and you have to jump in with both feet. That's how I feel. You might feel completely different, and I respect that. So, every single day, I'm going to ask you to marry me, and you can say no every single time I do, but one day... one day, you're going to say yes. We're meant to be together, Savannah. I feel it with every ounce of my being."

"You're right because I feel it, too. Fletcher, you don't need to ask me more than once. I want to marry you. This always sounded so corny to me when I heard it in the movies, but I understand it now—you complete me. I'm whole when I'm with you."

"Aww, baby, I love you so much!" He takes my face in his palms and kisses me with passion and fervor. "I love you. I love you. I love you," he whispers over and over again.

Lizzy and Ben are back from their honeymoon, and this payback is going to be so fun! They're still living in Lizzy's apartment, and I have the key. Ben's car is nowhere in sight as I pull into the parking lot. Perfect! I let myself in, like I've done a hundred times before. "Oh, Lizzy Lou! Guess what!" I yell.

"Savannah?" she asks, running from the bedroom wearing only a half closed bath robe.

"Please tell me that Ben isn't here. I'm so sorry if I interrupted something," I ramble.

"No, he's not here. The only thing you interrupted is the shower I'm about to take. Come on, I have the water running. You can keep me company while I'm in there."

"Wait," I insist, "this isn't news I can give to you while you're showering."

"What are you talking about? Is everything okay?"

"Everything is wonderful! Great! Magnificent!"

Lizzy plops onto the sofa. "Oh, dear. It's happened. You've snapped."

I laugh. "No! I haven't snapped. I buried the past, and I'm starting fresh. Life is beautiful, and it's a gift."

Lizzy gives me an uncertain look. "Fletcher Reilly must have one huge..."

"Lizzy!" I snap. "Well, he does, but that's not what this is all about, and I guess you really didn't need to know that either..."

Lizzy smiles broadly. "You've been getting some of the good stuff. Fletcher's got a big wiener. Fletcher's got a big wiener. And he knows how to use it," Lizzy playfully sings.

"Will you cut it out? Listen to me, please."

"Okay, fine," she says, shaking her head and shrugging her shoulders. "Lay it on me."

"I'm going to marry him. He asked me, and I said yes. Lizzy, I'm going to do this. I'm really going to do it."

Lizzy begins to cry. "I'm so happy for you. Savannah, if only you knew how much I worried about you. How sad I was that you weren't allowing yourself to experience happiness. How heartbroken I was that you felt destined to be alone. This is such a relief, and I'm thrilled!"

"There's more."

"More?" she asks, swiping away at her tears.

"I enrolled in nursing school. I start next week."

"What! Are you kidding me? Savannah, I'm so proud of you! You're going to make a great nurse."

"Thank you." I give her a huge hug.

"My shower!" Lizzy squeals, breaking the embrace to dash towards the bathroom. She sticks her hand inside the shower and frowns. "It's cold. Oh well, that means I get to hear more of your story while I'm waiting for it to heat back up. Sit! Do you want some coffee?"

"Sure," I agree while reclaiming my seat on the sofa. Lizzy busies herself with getting out the mugs and such, so I go on with my story.

"So many good things have happened to me

since Fletcher came into my life. I can talk about Lucas without bursting into tears. I've forgiven my mother for her evil ways…"

Lizzy cuts me off. "Forgiven her? Savannah, she's the reason you're without a father. She was a horrid woman who regularly abused you. How can you forgive her?"

"I said that I forgive her, but I'll never forget what she did. I still haven't told Fletcher about that yet."

"You haven't? Frankly, I'm surprised he didn't hear about it with all of the news coverage it received."

"He was probably away during that time. Plus, why would he remember? The case is memorable to those involved, or maybe to a few who actually remember the event. Not many remember the names and details."

Lizzy shrugs her shoulders. "I guess. So when's the wedding?'

"I don't know. We haven't discussed any of that."

"Any chance it might be happening soon? Like before Ben and I leave for Dallas?"

"Lizzy! Just because you and Ben had an overnight engagement doesn't mean everyone else does, too. Some people stay engaged for years before marriage."

"Please don't tell me that you want to wait years," she says, handing me a coffee mug.

"No, I don't," I say giggling.

"You giggled! I still can't get used to that. I love it."

"Stop."

"Seriously, Savannah. You're like a whole different person. Not that the person you were before was terrible or anything, it's just that you were..."

"Boring?"

"Yes! And..."

"Depressing?"

"Somewhat. And..."

"Distant?"

"Yes! I loved the old you, but I adore the new you so much more."

"Thank you," I say with a playful smile before sipping from the mug.

"So, wedding date. Wedding date. Wed. Ding. Date. What's a good date?"

"Lizzy, I told you that we haven't even discussed it yet."

"Oh, you're so cute. Dear, you set the plans, and he follows. It's your day to be a princess. He's just lucky he gets to be there. It's completely your day."

"No. It's *our* wedding, like for the two of us, so it's our day."

She holds up her index finger, takes her phone from the coffee table, and manipulates the screen. "Hey, Fletcher. This is Lizzy."

"What! You called him?" I say in an exaggerated whisper while grabbing at the phone. Lizzy's arm reach is much greater than mine, so she's able to keep me at bay with her free hand. "No, hang up."

"Fletcher, Savannah's here, and I just heard the news! Congratulations! Now, will you answer a question? Your wedding, is it Savannah's show, or is it the both of yours to plan? ...What? You want it to be everything Savannah's ever dreamed of?" She holds her hand over the microphone. "See, he got the memo, and he's a dude." She removes her hand. "Yeah, so I'm talking to her about dates, and she's not sure what kind of timeline we're, I mean you're, dealing with." She pauses briefly. "You'd marry her tomorrow if she were up to it? You're a good man, Fletcher Reilly. I hear lots of good things about you, especially about your..."

I snatch the phone from Lizzy because I don't even want to know what she was going to say. It's a fifty-fifty chance it will be obscene, and those odds are too great for me. "Hi, Fletcher. Hey. I hope that my deranged friend didn't scare the hell out of you."

I hear him laughing. "I'm not scared in the least. Bring it on. I'm ready whenever you are."

"Be careful what you say. She'll have the entire wedding planned, and we'll be hitched by the end of the week."

"I fail to see the problem with that."

"Fletcher, we only just became engaged last night."

"Stop. Take a breath and quit comparing our lives to others. What do *you* want to do?"

"You're right. We both know that this is right, and this is exactly what we want. Fletcher, let's go get our marriage license right now. I want to be Mrs. Reilly by the weekend."

"You've got it. I'll meet you at the courthouse. I'm putting on my shoes right now."

"Are we really doing this?"

Lizzy's squealing and clapping her hands.

"We are. Let's get it all lined up. I'll see you in a little while."

"Okay. See you soon. I love you, Fletcher."

"I love you too, Savannah."

I end the call. "Lizzy, sorry to leave like this, but I'm meeting Fletcher at the courthouse."

She jumps up and down, hugging me tightly as I make my way to the door.

"Let me know if you want to use the lake house for the ceremony!" she yells as I'm turning the corner to leave the building. I throw her a quick wave.

I'm on the way to the courthouse to get a marriage license. Two months ago, I'd have laughed at the idea. Lizzy's right. I am a much different person than I used to be, and it's a great thing. I smile when I see Fletcher, arms crossed as he props against his bike. He wears a nicely fitted white shirt, blue jeans that hug his thick thighs, and aviator-style sunglasses. I notice that his tattoos just barely poke out from underneath the short sleeves, while his scruffy beard and disheveled hair make him simply irresistible to me.

I feel unbelievably lucky and special when he opens the door for me, takes my arm in his, and guides me up the steps of the courthouse. He stops at the Clerk of Court's door to give me a brief kiss. "Are you sure? There's no pressure. We can wait as long as you want before we do this," Fletcher says. "I've never been more sure of anything in my life. Let's do this."

twelve

We're at my apartment tonight; I curl in my favorite spot on the bed while pondering a few things. Fletcher snuggles up behind me.

"What's on your mind?" he asks, pulling me close to his body.

"Just thinking."

"About good things or bad things?"

"Both," I answer truthfully.

"Well, start with the bad, and we'll end with the good."

"Lizzy and I were talking earlier, and it made me realize that you don't know what happened to my parents."

"I figured you'd tell me when you were ready. I assumed a car accident. Am I right?"

I shake my head. "A car accident might have been easier to handle."

He sits up, and the sheet pools around his midsection. "What happened, Savannah?"

I roll to face him, but I don't sit up. "You pretty much know the history—dad was gone offshore a lot, mom was gone when he was gone, I was at Lizzy or Grampy's, but mostly home alone. Right?"

"Yes."

"I moved out to live with Paul as soon as we graduated high school. I didn't want to see my mother anymore, even if it was just random meetings every few weeks or so. Once I left, she started bringing her boyfriends to the house. Dad came home early from a hitch to surprise her, which was rare because he never left work early." I start to pick at my thumbnail. "Whenever Dad ended a hitch, he'd faithfully call me when he landed at the heliport to let me know his flight made it safely. A lot of helicopters crash out in the Gulf, and the weather turns on a dime. He knew I worried, so he'd always call.

" *'Hey, Savannah! I made it in a little early. Perfect flying weather. Come by for dinner tomorrow night, okay. There's something I want to tell you,'* " Dad said to me.

"I hated going over there, but seeing my dad countered having to deal with her. When I got there, all the lights were off, which I found strange, but essentially I shrugged it off. My first thought was that Dad had forgotten about the arrangements he'd made with me and that they'd gone out to dinner or something. I checked in the garage, and both cars were there. That's when I knew that something was wrong. I flipped on all the lights, searching the house for any trace of them. When I opened the bedroom door, and I was instantly sick. Three bloody bodies…"

"You don't have to go on," Fletcher says softly.

"I'm okay. You need to know. I called the police, and the house was buzzing with people for what felt like an eternity. I just sat in the corner, praying to be invisible. I didn't want to talk to anyone, I didn't want sympathy; I just wanted to be left the hell alone. But, it didn't happen. Interview after interview. They wanted to know if I had touched anything. If I knew what happened. If I knew why the third person was in the room with them. I answered what I could, and then I went off to mourn the loss of my father."

"I'm so sorry, sweetheart," Fletcher says.

"It's another reason I resent her. The third body was the guy she was screwing when my dad walked in on them. The loser had a gun in his pants and pulled it on my dad before he had a chance to fight back. After that, he shot my mom, and finally, himself. It was all over the news for a while, but the attention slowly diverted to other news stories."

"I see why you resent your mom. I can't say that I blame you."

I nod. "Lizzy had a fit when I told her that I've forgiven my mom. I tried explaining to her that there's a difference between forgiving and forgetting. I'll never forget, but if I don't let go of some of the hatred, it only hurts me, not her."

"Sounds like a good thing for you to do. Your mother robbed you of your peace for nearly your entire life. The best revenge is for you to be happy."

"I never really thought of it that way. My happiness has a dual purpose; it brings peace to my dad, and it shows my mom that she didn't ruin me."

Fletcher smiles while lying beside me again. "Exactly."

"Fletcher, do you believe in signs?"

"What kind of signs?" he asks, gently kissing my shoulders.

"Molly told me she believes that Brody gives her signs to let her know he's around and watching over her."

"She did?" Fletcher asks. "Like what?"

"Like she said when she cries really hard, sometimes a stuffed bear he gave her will fall from the shelf and land on top of her like it's giving her a hug. There were some other things she mentioned, too."

"Hmmm. Interesting," Fletcher says.

"So, do you believe?"

"Why do you ask?'

"Because I think my dad sent me a sign about you. If it weren't for that picture of you with the bike, our conversation would have ended at the Pole Co. console."

"My handsome looks and charming smile weren't enough to win me a date? I'm crushed."

"I'm sorry to hurt your ego, but you wouldn't have had a shot. However, I will admit that I found you very attractive. What was it about me? You couldn't see me, and I'm sure you've made hundreds of calls to customer service lines. What made you want to meet me?"

"You made me laugh."

"I made you laugh. What if I'd been a seventy year old woman with blue hair and ten grandkids?"

"Then I'd have treated you to a nice dinner as a thank you and sent you on your way."

I laugh. "I love you."

"You'd better. You're supposed to be marrying me soon. Speaking of, we have some things we need to figure out."

"Like what?"

"Like, whose apartment are we going to live

in? We really don't need two. And where is this wedding ceremony supposed to take place?"

"I already know that."

"You do?"

"Yep, where you proposed—the gazebo in the park. Since there won't be lots of guests, I think an early morning ceremony will be pretty. What do you think? Saturday? At eight? The ceremony should only be fifteen minutes or so, and then we're off to start our lives together."

"It sounds perfect." He kisses my forehead. "If it was your dad who encouraged this, he has my undying gratitude. That's kind of a nice way of looking at things. I wonder if Brody's been sending me signs, but I've been ignoring them."

"I don't know, but I can tell you that I've been a lot more open minded to the possibility since talking with Molly."

Fletcher smiles. "So, which one of us is doing the packing?"

"You are. My apartment's in a better location."

"I like being in the middle of nowhere. At least as middle of nowhere as I can get in the city."

"Why don't we look for something we both like? Maybe even a house?" I suggest.

"Yes, let's do it. Let's look for a house with lots of bedrooms that we can fill with babies."

I laugh. "Maybe I should finish school first?"

"Okay, school first, lots of babies after. Until then, we simply get to have fun practicing."

The good thing about Triceratops expanding is

that Fletcher's job expands with it. He's still able to work from home for the most part, but he's been much busier. He and Ben have a meeting to iron out the salary, and suffice to say, Fletcher goes from making okay money to really good money. This means that I'll be able to quit working and concentrate on school, and though I was excited to start before, I'm super excited to start now. But first, marriage.

Saturday arrives before I know it, and I smile broadly as I drive past the house that Fletcher and I will soon be buying. The offer has been accepted, but we're waiting to close. Our house. Ours. It's only a couple of blocks from Julia's, where Lizzy joins me to put on the finishing touches before heading out to the park for the wedding.

The rule is that no one is to go crazy for this wedding. I want everyone to wear something comfortable, and something they already own. Molly is wearing a super cute white dress dotted with yellow daisies and a black tulle underskirt, while Julia dons a beautiful pale pink pant suit. Lizzy opts for an ice blue A-line with a bateau neckline and a wide matching belt. I'm wearing a white, empire-waist chiffon dress that falls to the floor. My hair is swept up into messy, loose curls accented with white daisies. The girls all go on about how I need a touch of this, and a bit of that, and once they finish, I must say that I'm more than happy with my appearance. My makeup is soft, perfectly matching the flowing chiffon of my gown.

"Are you ready?" Lizzy asks with a squeal.

"I've never been more ready for anything in my life," I say. Lizzy takes the box that contains our flowers and searches the counter top to make sure we're not forgetting anything.

"I have the ring in my purse. Flowers are here. I think we're good to go."

Julia and Molly get into one car, while Lizzy and I get into the SUV her parents bought her. I make a comment about how nice it is, but she shrugs it off with an "ehn, it's okay."

We arrive at the park, and I'm even more excited when I spot Fletcher and Ben standing with the Justice of the Peace under the gazebo. Fletcher and Ben are wearing white button down shirts, jeans, and boots. I'm surprised to notice that Fletcher is clean shaven, and I can't wait to see his face up close. I practically run from the car, but Lizzy quickly catches up to me and stops me.

"Girl, you need to take it down a notch. Give Julia a chance to park before she misses the damn ceremony with your impatient self. Here, duck behind this tree so he can't see you." She starts to touch up my makeup with her fingers. Julia smiles at me, and Molly blows kisses as they walk past us to join Fletcher at the gazebo.

"Okay, you give me to the count of twenty to get down there so you can make your entrance, okay. And don't count as fast as you can either! Do the 'one-Mississippi, two-Mississippi' thing."

"Alright, just get moving. I want to see my man."

"Here, take your flowers. Remember, count slowly."

"I said I will," I tell her with a forced smile.

"I love you," Lizzy says. "You look beautiful."

"I love you too, Lizzy Lou. Thanks for being

my best friend."

"Thanks for being my best friend, too." She quickly fans her hand in front of her eyes. "Dang it. I said I wasn't going to cry." With that parting sentiment, she pageant walks toward the gazebo with her head held high.

By the time I mentally count to fifteen-Mississippi, I say, "Screw it," and begin the walk toward marriage. Lizzy turns once she arrives, and I see her gesturing her exasperation about my not listening to her. Her heart's in the right place, but every minute I waste hiding behind a tree is one minute I'm robbed of being Mrs. Fletcher Reilly.

His smile beams just as brightly as mine when I join the guests. I love Fletcher with a scruffy beard, but I LOVE Fletcher clean shaven. I can't wait to feel his lips on mine, his body... Okay, I need to stop and enjoy the present, but surely it can't be a bad thing to be so incredibly attracted to your husband, right?

"You take my breath away, Savannah," Fletcher says, cupping my cheek in his hand. His thumb softly strokes my cheek as his eyes intently search mine. "I love you."

"My handsome man, I love you, too. I can't wait to be your wife." Fletcher smiles and gestures to the Justice of the Peace that he should start the ceremony.

The Justice of the Peace has a little table set up behind him which has the marriage license on it, and he asks us to be sure everything is correct on the pages before he proceeds. It is, so next he asks, "The wedding party: bride, groom, matron of honor, and best man? Correct?"

"Actually, sir, there will be four best men,"

Fletcher says. "Ben Thibodaux." He points to Ben.

I give a confused look as I search the area for any friends or family I might have missed.

Ben hands him a small duffel bag, and after Fletcher unzips it, he pulls out a folded American flag and places it onto the table. "Brody Halsey."

I look to Julia, who is fighting back the tears. Molly, beaming with pride, grips her mother's hand.

"Matthew Mason." He pulls a well-worn oilfield hard hat from the bag and places it on the table.

"Daddy," I whisper as tears well in my eyes. "You?" I ask Lizzy. She smiles and nods.

The next thing he pulls from the bag is a tiny little baseball glove complete with a matching stuffed ball. "Lucas Calloway."

I recognize it as one of the few gifts I was able to give Lucas, and I keep it tucked away in a special box with the things I'd saved after his death. Red faced from all the crying, I grab Fletcher and hold him tightly. "Thank you for doing this. Thank you. Thank you. Thank you."

Lizzy passes around a box of tissues. The only dry eye is that of the Justice of the Peace, and that's because I caught him dabbing the tears with his collar before the tissue disbursement.

"Who's ready for a wedding?" the Justice of the Peace asks, sniffing hard.

I raise my hand, as does Fletcher. The remaining guests raise their hands, and the Justice of the Peace begins the ceremony. The service is short and to the point, and within a matter of minutes, I'm officially Mrs. Fletcher Reilly. Savannah Reilly. I say the name over and over in my head because I absolutely love the sound of it.

We go back to Julia's for a little bit of cake and mimosas, but that was all lagniappe for me. I craved alone time with my husband, and I secretly wondered if he craved the same. I got my answer when, after opening the last of our presents, he slings me over his shoulder and carries me to his truck. No big or elaborate honeymoon for us. A beautiful weekend in the French Quarter is our honeymoon, and we enjoy each and every second of it. I'm riding a cloud of euphoria, and I pray that I never, ever come down.

thirteen

Eighteen months pass since our wedding, and
I'm six months away from taking my board exams.
My days are jumbled between classes and clinicals,
and my nights are spent basking in the sweet bliss of
newlywed life. Fletcher assures me that he has little
time to miss me because business is booming for
Triceratops, and he spends nearly the entire day
working from our home office. Lizzy and Ben made
the move about a year ago, and since then, we've seen
them about once or twice a month, mostly when Ben
makes trips in to check on things at the local
restaurants.

I'm currently doing my pediatrics rotation, and
I think I've found my calling. However, after a
particularly taxing day, I need at least a five-minute
breather. The only empty room is a playroom that's
under renovation at the far end of the hall, so I sneak a
juice pack from the fridge, and head down to my
private sanctuary. My back's to the door and
disappointment swells in my belly when I hear the

hinges creak open. *Please don't be Darryl. Please don't be Darryl.* I'm about a hair away from getting a restraining order against the supposedly harmless janitor with a great big crush on me.

I'm not particularly fond or appreciative of the supposedly innocent joke started by some fellow students. My classmates told the middle aged man that I was hot for men who carried big brooms, so he went from carrying a standard sized corn husk broom on his cart to a push broom that can clear an entire hallway in one pass. It's so outrageously large that he regularly knocks the heck out of people, walls, objects resting on shelves, etc. Though I've tried everything from a sensible conversation to flat out letting him know I'm happily married and have no interest in him, he still chases me around the hospital like a lovesick teenager.

A normal person would announce himself or herself, right? Nothing. The person standing in the doorway is doing just that, standing and staring at me. "Darryl, please, for the love of God, they lied. It was a joke, and not one bit of it is true."

"Should I go?" a perplexed male voice calls.

I whip around to notice a tall blond man with beautiful blue eyes standing in the doorway. He's wearing a lab coat, and a pediatric stethoscope pokes out of his pocket. His name tag says that he's Dr. Robert Goodman, and I wish that the floor would swallow me up.

"I'm so sorry, sir," I say, jumping to my feet.

He shakes his hand in a gesture that says I should stay where I am. I slowly sit back in the tiny chair, and I'm suddenly very aware of how silly I must look sucking on a juice box while sitting in a chair three sizes too small for me. I'm not as self-conscious when Dr. Goodman pulls a chair next to mine and completely fails to sit down because of the length of his legs. "I guess I'll just take the bean bag over there," he says, sinking deeply into the bright orange ball.

"Should I..."

"Should you what? Should you introduce yourself? Absolutely."

I smile. "I'm Savannah Reilly, and I'm a nursing student doing my peds rotation."

"Nice to meet you, Savannah. Beautiful name, by the way. I'm Robert Goodman, and I'm an ER doc, but I've decided to change my specialty to pediatrics."

"That's quite a big change."

"It is, but it's long overdue. I was an Army doctor for several years, so combine that with the few years I've worked in the ER, and I'm burned out. I think taking care of kids will be a nice change of pace."

"I'm sure you've seen your fair share of tragedy."

"That's an understatement," he says. "So, you found the only quiet spot in the hospital. I must admit, I was a little sad when I realized I'd have to share, but you're alright, Savannah. I'll happily share my secret spot with you."

"Your secret spot, eh? Well, I'll have you know this has been my secret spot for three weeks now."

"Hate to burst your bubble, but it's been mine for six weeks. Guess we've been just missing each other for quite some time."

I laugh. "I guess so. Thanks for agreeing to share."

"Likewise," he says, stretching his arms high over his head. "I'm working a double, so I need to catch a few z's. They will give me a room in the lounge if I request it, but it's right in the middle of the busiest part of the hospital. There's no way to get rest in there."

"How do you get rest in here?" I ask.

He smiles as he wriggles himself from the beanbag chair then he gestures to me with his index finger. I join him at the back of the room where he moves a section of chairs away from the wall. Tucked behind the chairs are a pillow, sheet, and blanket. He opens the sheet and lays it on the floor behind the chairs, tosses down the pillow, removes his lab coat and shoes, then curls himself into the fetal position as he covers himself with the blanket.

"I'd be much obliged if you'd shut off the lights when you leave," he mentions.

"Of course, Doctor."

"Hey, if we share a secret hiding spot, we are on a first name basis, Savannah."

I smile. "Okay, Robert. Rest well."

"Thanks," he says, closing his eyes and moving his head around until he finds the sweet spot on his pillow. I shut off the lights and gently close the door behind me.

"How was your day?" Fletcher asks. He's still hard at work in front of the computer, so I drape my arms around his neck while kissing the top of his head.

"Busy. Looks like your day was pretty much the same."

"Yeah, but I'm about to call it quits for tonight."

"Okay, I'm going to jump in the shower. Have you had dinner?" I ask.

"No, but I picked up some stuff today."

"You did? Thank you so much. That deserves a kiss," I say, leaning forward. Instead of kissing me, he pulls me into his lap.

"If you're going to kiss me, you're going to do it right," he teases. I happily oblige by giving him a deep, sensual kiss.

"Wow," he says, blowing out a breath. I smile at his reaction. "So how was your day?"

"You already asked that, silly," I say, playfully pushing against his chest.

"Still leaning towards pediatrics?"

"Yep, sure am," I say, snuggling against him. "I fall more and more in love with the job each day."

"Not only are you going to be the best nurse they've ever had, but I'm certain you'll be the prettiest nurse they've ever had, too. I have to admit, I'm kind of lucky you're dealing with kids. Zero competition."

I laugh. "As if you'd have competition regardless. You are all the man I'll ever want or need, Fletcher Reilly. End of story."

"I love you," he says, softly stroking my cheek with his finger.

"I love you, too." I hug him tightly. "Now, I'm going to get in the shower," I whisper in his ear.

"Is that an invitation for me to join you?" he asks.

"Absolutely."

"I'll be there in just a second. Let me finish up."

"Okay, babe. Hey, Molly's been burning up my text messaging with requests to go to the water park. Do you want to take her this weekend?"

He sighs. "This weekend is not good for me. I have some reports that need to be finished by Monday, and I'm completely swamped. Don't let that stop you from going though. Maybe Julia can join you?"

"Julia. Your sister, Julia? At a water park? Did you seriously just say that?"

Fletcher laughs. "True."

"We'll just wait until next weekend."

"No, go this weekend. Have fun."

"Are you sure?"

"Positive."

I shrug my shoulders. "I'll let little Miss Molly know." I send the text then hop into the shower.

My thoughts immediately go to Fletcher. *He sure has been missing out on a lot lately. I'm glad that Ben's business is doing so well, but Fletcher's always on the computer or shuffling through paperwork. Weekdays aren't so bad since I'm in school all day and some nights, but I wish our weekends could be spent doing something besides hanging out at the house while Fletcher spends hours in the office. The next time Ben comes to town, I'm having a talk with him. I wonder if Fletcher has bothered to mention to him how time consuming the work is? Knowing Fletcher, no. He won't say anything because even though he's drawing a salary, Ben's still his best friend. If Fletcher's not going to mention it, I surely will.*

"You look in deep thought," Fletcher says, joining me in the steam-filled shower.

"I guess I was. Sorry."

"Whatcha thinking about?"

"Us, and the fact that we're both so busy that we never go out anymore."

"Staying in has its benefits." He pulls me closer and eagerly runs his hands down the length of my body.

"That's very true," I whisper, my body teeming with want. Fletcher is an amazing lover, and there's a certain way he touches me that sends all conscious thought out the window. It incites a deep primal urge for me to, for lack of a better phrase, screw his brains out. He's awakened so much passion in me, so much desire, that I'll do damn near anything to have him. The thing is, he knows it and regularly takes full advantage of it.

Two can play that game. I "accidentally" drop the bath sponge I'm holding, and as I'm on my way back up from retrieving it, his arm encircles my waist. He pulls me tightly against his chest, so that his lips fall beside my ear. "Do you want me?"

"You know I do." His strong hand grips my thigh, and I'm instantly lost in the throes of his skillful lovemaking.

"Tell me you love me," he whispers while thrusting deeply.

"I love you," I say in between gasps. "Always."

His lips trail kisses down my neck, and he lightly sinks his teeth into my shoulder. I can't fight it anymore, and for the next few seconds I relish the release of intense pleasure that has been building deep inside me. Fletcher holds me tightly, and I'm grateful because my legs feel as though they'll buckle under my weight.

He turns me to face him. "You are the best thing to ever happen to me. Don't ever doubt my love for you, okay?"

"I won't, baby. I feel the same about you. I love you more than you'll ever know. My life is with you."

He embraces me tightly, hugging me until the water runs cold and we're sent scrambling for the warmth of our bed. Even then, he wraps his arms around me until sleep finds the two of us.

I pick up Molly early the next morning in the hopes we'll beat some of the weekend's interstate traffic. An accident ruins that wish by putting us in gridlock for about an hour. We finally make it to the water park, and though we're having fun, it just isn't the same without Fletcher. Molly feels it, too.

"Aunt Savannah, I know I begged you to take me today, so please don't get mad when I say this, but do you think we can go shopping or something? It's so crowded here, and it's taking forever to slide…"

"Say no more. Let's get changed."

She smiles broadly. The first place I bring her is the mall where we window shop for hours. I notice her look longingly into the Victoria's Secret store.

"Do you want to go in?" I ask.

She looks down at her chest. "Do you think I'll ever get boobies?"

I make sure I don't laugh or smile, even

though I find her question amusing.

"It looks to me like you have boobies, Molly. Plus, you're still young. You know that they'll keep growing, right?"

"I'm thirteen and a half, and I'm stuck in an A."

"And your friends?" I ask, remembering those days vividly.

"Bs and Cs, at least."

"Come with me," I say, taking her hand while saying a quick prayer that Julia doesn't kill me for this. I divulge the secret of padded bras to Molly, and after she tries on a couple, she can't erase the smile from her face. I pull the tag off so she can wear the new bra, and take it and two more bras of a similar style to the register. I'm accepting the receipt from the cashier when Molly joins me at the checkout. I have to bite my lip to keep from laughing at her posture. She sure is proud of her new physique.

"Molls," I whisper, "Sweetie, just try to be natural. Let the padding do the work for you."

"Oh, okay," she says, exhaling the pent up breath she's been holding. As we walk through the mall, I catch her smiling at her reflection every time we pass a reflective surface. If I'd had known that a little bit of foam would've made her so happy, I'd have taken her shopping long ago.

As we sit in the food court drinking fresh-squeezed lemonade, Molly thanks me again for helping her with her problem. "I'm glad I could help. Mine didn't come in until I was about fifteen. I know your pain."

"Yeah, they say the teen years are rough, but they don't do much to prepare you for them." This time I can't fight the smile.

"Are there other issues that you're having?" I ask.

"Are you asking if I got my period?"

"Uh, no, not really. Not unless you have unanswered questions."

"My mom loves me, Aunt Savannah. I know she does, but let's just say she's not the best at forging open and honest conversations when it comes to things like sex and such."

I choke on my lemonade. "You're not having sex, are you?"

"Oh, goodness no! Ewww. That's gross."

"Keep that attitude until you're out of high school," I suggest.

"How old were you when you first had sex?"

Why does this kid feel so free to talk to me about these things? Okay, think this through. If you don't answer her questions, she's going to ask her friends and who knows what kinds of crazy things they'll tell her. It's best that the information comes from a knowledgeable and reliable source, right? Oh God, please don't let Julia kill me for this.

"Molly, you can't gauge the right time to have sex upon others and when they first did it. It has to be a personal decision, and one that shouldn't be made lightly. I know that there are a lot of shows and movies that make casual sex look fun and interesting and intriguing, but the honest truth is that sex with someone you love is the best it will ever be. It's worth it to wait until you're absolutely sure."

She looks in deep thought. "So you've had casual sex, and sex with someone you're in love with, and you're telling me that it's better to wait because love sex feels better than acquaintance sex."

"Pretty much," I answer.

"Okay, I want it to be good, so I'll wait."

"Wise choice," I say, fighting through the discomfort.

"What are your thoughts on contraception? Which methods work best?"

"Molly, that's a talk that's best left for another trip way in the distant future."

"Oh, okay," she says, slurping up the last of her lemonade. I rub my forehead with my fingers to ward off the headache that's threatening to surface. "You look like my mom," Molly says with a laugh.

"Huh? Oh," I say smiling while lowering my hand. "Anything else you want to look at while we're here?"

"Nah, I'm ready to go if you are."

I am, so we spend the drive back loudly singing along to the radio. Molly looks sad when I pull the car into Julia's driveway.

"I wish today didn't have to end. I always have so much fun when I'm with you, Aunt Savannah. I'm glad Uncle Fletcher found you." She bear hugs me when we reach the front door.

"Me, too," I say laughing. Julia's sitting at the kitchen counter when we come through the door, and her eyes squinch up from confusion when she spies Molly. I shake my head, hoping she gets the message to not say anything.

"Molly, why don't you show your mom what you got this afternoon?" I suggest.

"Mom, I got my boobies!" she says excitedly.

I smack my forehead with my palm then shake my head.

"I notice. What…"

"I took her bra shopping. I hope you don't mind. The bras only have a little padding in there, and I only got them because she was feeling insecure around her friends who've already blossomed."

"Molly, why don't you put your things in your room, okay?" Julia says.

"I'm a little conflicted about this," Julia admits once Molly leaves the room. "Don't get me wrong, I'm appreciative that you spent time with her, and that she feels comfortable enough with you to discuss such things, but do you think it's wise to let her wear that?"

"I understand your concern, but I didn't buy it to make her feel sexy, I bought it to boost her confidence and to make her spend less time worrying about catching up with the other girls. She's curious, but I know from talking with her that she's not ready for the other things that parents worry about with their teens. For Molly, it's all about keeping up with the Jones' in the looks department right now, Julia."

She breathes a sigh of relief. "Okay, I feel better now. Thanks for helping her through this. I try to be open and honest with her, but talking with your mom about these things…"

"Yeah, we had that conversation, too. Relax, you're doing a good job, Mom. She's so smart, and she's got a good head on her shoulders."

"I'm really glad Fletcher found you," Julia says, hugging me.

"You're the second person to tell me that today. I appreciate it, but I consider myself the lucky one. Speaking of Fletcher, I guess I should get home. I haven't heard from him all day. He's been so swamped with work, poor thing."

"Ask him if he'd like to barbecue tomorrow. I can throw some burgers on the grill, and we can swim."

"Sounds like fun. I'll text you once I get an answer."

"Thanks again, Savannah. Molly, Aunt Savannah's leaving," Julia calls down the hallway. Molly reappears in a flash.

"No problem," I say, smiling broadly when Molly tightly hugs me.

"Bye, Aunt Savannah. Thanks for today!"

"You're welcome, sweetie. See you soon."

After a quick wave goodbye, I drive the couple of blocks to my house, and I'm perplexed to find it absolutely silent inside. No television, no radio, none of the usual background noises that generally greet me. *Maybe Fletcher went out for a run?* No, his running shoes are still in their neat position next to the door.

"Fletcher," I call, but get no answer. I start going room to room in search of him. "Fletcher, I'm home!"

Room after room comes up empty. I turn on the bedroom light and everything looks just as I'd left it in the morning. I'm about to click off the light when a strange sound rattles from the walk-in closet. Fear slowly creeps into my throat making it difficult to breathe. My heart thuds in my chest as I'm turning the handle to slowly open the door. Once I peek inside, I throw it open completely.

"Fletcher? Oh, my God! Baby, what's wrong? Are you hurt?" I ask. He's curled tightly into the fetal position, his hands balled into fists covering his eyes.

"Make it stop. Make it stop," he repeats over and over. I lie on the floor beside him, carefully stroking his arm.

"Fletcher, it's Savannah. I'm home, baby. I'm home. I'm here."

He swats my arm away, and I'm in tears because my husband needs me, but I don't know what to do to help him. All of my medical training flies out the window when it comes to seeing him this way. I immediately call Julia and tell her to leave Molly at home, but to come as quickly as she can. She's at my house in about two minutes. I tell her as quickly as possible what's going on, and she follows me into the bedroom. She squats next to him.

"Fletcher, it's Julia. It's Sissy. We've gotten through this before, and we'll do it again. It's okay. You're home, and you're safe."

"Sissy?" he asks, slowly dropping his fist.

"Yes, it's Sissy."

"I killed Brody. I killed your husband. Molly's dad is gone because of me."

She slowly helps Fletcher to sit up, and she grips him while he trembles violently in her arms.

"You didn't kill Brody, Fletcher. The enemy did. He knew it was a risk when he signed up—we all knew the risk. Brody wouldn't want you to feel guilty because of his death, Fletcher."

"No, it was me. He only signed up because of me."

"No, he was a grown man, and he signed up because he wanted to sign up. He asked me if I wanted him to stay, and I told him to do what he felt was right in his heart. He wanted to serve his country, Fletcher, and there's nothing that you could have done to stop that."

"It was my idea."

"Shhhh." She kisses him on the forehead. "It might have been your idea, but it was his decision."

"The pain won't go away, Sissy. I fight and fight, but it won't stop."

"Why have you been hiding this from us, Fletcher? Why didn't you let us know that you've been having problems again?"

"Because I feel like a failure. Such a failure," he begins to cry, and my heart can't take it anymore. I turn away so he won't see my heartbreak on my face.

"You are not a failure, you're sick. You're having a relapse, and you need to go back to the treatment center."

"I don't want to go back. I want to stay here with my wife; I want to be normal again."

"You can be well again. You go back to the facility for a month or so, and you work hard, FINISH your treatment this time, and you come home and pick up things from there. Fletcher, you've been through a lot, and the doctors told you this might happen from time to time. They also told you that it's very important that you get help as soon as you start having issues again. How long has this been going on?"

"Since before I got married."

"Oh, Fletcher. Almost two years now, and you didn't tell anyone?"

"It's my fault," I finally speak up.

"Savannah? You're here?" Fletcher asks. "Go! Go now! I don't want you to see me like this."

"No, I'm not leaving," I say, kneeling in front of him. "I love you, and I want to help you. Baby, why didn't you tell me you were still having problems?"

"What do you mean by STILL having problems? What happened?" Julia asks. "What are you talking about?"

"There were fireworks the night of Ben and Lizzy's wedding, and Fletcher got very sick. Then there was this one other time, but nothing since…at least nothing I've witnessed."

"Fletcher, tell us the truth, how bad is it?" Julia questions.

He hangs his head in defeat. "I can't leave the house without panicking."

Julia rises. "I'm calling the facility to get you a bed."

He tightly grips her wrist. "No, I can work through this. I just need some time. Savannah will help me. Won't you, sweetie?"

"Yes, of course, baby. I'll do anything to help you."

"See, no need for all the other stuff." He slowly rises to his feet. "I'm feeling much better already."

"Why don't you lie down for a little while," I suggest. He agrees, so I pull back the covers then tuck him in once he's settled. "I love you."

"I love you, too," he weakly answers. He looks absolutely exhausted and defeated. I kiss him softly on the lips then turn out the lights. Julia and I retreat to the kitchen.

"You're not going to be able to do this, Savannah," Julia warns. "You weren't there to witness how bad it got before. Call Ben and talk to him about it. He needs treatment from trained professionals. I know you love him, and you want to be with him, but believe me when I tell you that the hospital in Colorado is the best thing for him."

"I hear what you're saying, but Julia, I have to take his feelings into consideration, too. Maybe we can try to work on it together, just for a week or two, and see if his condition improves. I'll do lots of research, and maybe we can get him to see a local therapist…"

Julia sighs. "I can't tell you what to do; I can only offer my advice, which I've done. I'm here if you need me. Stay strong." And with those parting words, she leaves.

Fletcher sleeps the rest of the afternoon and all through the night, but my night is spent trying to figure out the right decision for Fletcher and me. I don't fall asleep until close to four in the morning. Later that morning, I awaken to find he's fixed me breakfast in bed. "I'm sorry about yesterday," he says, placing a tray filled with pancakes, bacon, and eggs in front of me.

"Sorry for what? You didn't do anything wrong," I say, smiling as I take in all of the goodies he's fixed for me.

"I know it was probably scary to see me like that, but I want you to know it doesn't happen often. Also, I know that I haven't been leaving that house to run errands and such, and that is unacceptable. I want to work on that immediately, and to prove to you that I'm doing better, we'll go anywhere you desire."

"Well, we were invited to Julia's for barbecue today."

He nods. "Barbecue at Julia's. Okay. No problem. Sounds fun."

"You might want to text her and let her know

that we're coming," I suggest before biting into a crispy piece of bacon.

"On it," he says, practically bounding from the bed to get his cell phone from the living room.

"You're certainly in a good mood today," I yell from the bed.

He lies next to me. "Yep! It's a whole new day, a better day. The first day that I finally get my life back on track and back to normal."

"I like your attitude," I say, accepting the kiss he's leaning forward to give me.

"Julia says to be there around eleven and to bring our swimsuits."

"Sounds like fun. I had a really good day with Molly yesterday."

"I was going to ask you about that."

"We didn't stay at the water park very long. It was so crowded, and we weren't having much fun, so we went shopping instead."

"Did you buy anything nice?" he asks.

"Not for me."

"Why not?"

"I was too busy helping to cure some of Molly's teenage angst."

"Oh, boy. I can only imagine."

"It wasn't so bad. Well, it wasn't until she asked me my preferred choice of contraception and why."

"She what! Please tell me that she's not having sex."

I laugh. "She's not, and she's not interested."

"Okay, I can breathe again."

"She had boob envy, but the problem is now resolved."

"How? Did you buy her a box of tissues?"

"No, I didn't have to. We women have our secret ways of handling such things."

"Secret, huh? Have you been holding out on me?" He removes the breakfast tray and sets it on the dresser. "See, I've always thought that your exquisite breasts were all natural, but now you have me wondering. I'm going to have to closely inspect them to make sure you're not hiding something from me." He slowly pulls down the sheet that is tucked under my arms.

"Fletcher," I fuss, yanking it back up, but failing miserably. Though I start off laughing at Fletcher's extensive list of "tests" to prove whether or not my breasts are up to par, I end up enjoying the lovemaking that follows, and we stay in bed until just before we're due at Julia's.

RHONDA R. DENNIS

fourteen

We have an incredible time at Julia's, and I really feel as though Fletcher's on the mend. Maybe he just needed to let his secret out of the bag before making forward progress? A day of laughter, delicious food, and swimming is just what the doctor ordered. He's refreshed, relaxed, and anxious to start a new day. At least that's what he tells me as I'm leaving for the hospital the next day.

A huge smile is plastered on my face when I finish my clinical shift, and I can't wait to get home to Fletcher. My optimism quickly dissolves when I find the house looking like a herd of water buffalo have crossed through. Everything is always neat and in its place. That's just how Fletcher lives, but this? Something is wrong. Fletcher's fast asleep on the sofa, and I need answers.

"Fletcher," I softly whisper as I try coaxing him awake. Nothing.

"Fletcher, honey, wake up," I say a little

louder this time while shaking him.

He flies from the sofa and pins me to the floor before I can scream. One hand covers my mouth while his forearm presses into the soft flesh of my throat.

"What do you want from me?" he demands in a low gravelly growl.

I gasp, desperate to draw air into my lungs, but I can't. I try hitting him, pushing against his face, but nothing is working. His eyes are black with anger, and his face is contorted into a snarling grimace. Instinct takes over, and I knee him in his groin as hard as I can. He rolls off me, and I eagerly suck in a lungful of sweet, precious air. My energy is zapped from the struggle, so I'm unable to stand, but I do manage to roll onto my knees and crawl away from him. He snatches my ankle and pulls me to him.

"No, Fletcher, no more. Please! It's me," I croak.

He's back on top of me and about to lower his fist when reality crashes back to him. His eyes soften, his face goes pale and slack, and as I lie there sobbing, he props against the sofa and puts his head in his hands.

"Tell Julia to make the call. Also, please ask her if you can stay with her until I leave," he says, deep sadness in his voice.

I crawl to him, and I try pulling his hands from his face. "I'm okay. Look at me. I'm okay. I don't want to leave you, Fletcher. I'm not going to Julia's or anywhere else for that matter. I'm going to stay here with you, my husband, and we're going to get through this together. If you think the treatment center is best, that's fine. We'll make that call, but

I'm not going anywhere, Fletcher. I love you too much. I can't desert you when you need me most."

His eyes are red from the tears he's shedding. "I almost killed you, Savannah. Twice. Oh, my sweet girl, look at your throat," he says in nearly a whisper.

"I'm fine. Fletcher, I shouldn't have startled you like that. I should've known better. You were in a deep sleep, but the house is trashed... Anyway, it's my fault."

"No," he says, reaching for my face, "it's not, baby. This is my problem. I'm broken again. I can't believe that I hurt you." He cries harder, and I pull him tight.

"The only pain I'm feeling is the hurt in my heart because of what you're going through. I want to take away all of your pain, all of your terrible memories. I want to help you get better."

"But you can't take it away. No one can. It's deep seated in me, Savannah. It's a part of me now."

"I know it is, but with some work, you'll be able to control it again. It won't consume you. I'll call Julia right now. Why don't you take a shower? Okay, sweetie?"

He nods then drags himself to his feet. "You're my everything, Savannah. Please tell me that you know I'd never hurt you on purpose."

"I know, Fletcher. I know that with all my heart and all my soul."

He nods again before trudging off to the bathroom.

I give Julia a brief rundown of what has happened, and she insists on coming over right away to see for herself that everything is okay. I let her in, and she gasps when she sees my neck.

"It's just red from the pressure. It'll go away soon," I tell her.

"Where is he?"

"In the shower," I answer.

She pulls a sheet of paper from her pocket and hands it to me. "This is some information on the facility and the contact info for the doctor who treated him the last time. You can keep this copy for yourself. I'm going to call right now."

She paces up and down the living room as she explains to the nurse what has happened, how long it's been going on, and all of the other information the nurse requests. The nurse tells Julia that the earliest they can accept him is Tuesday of next week, but if we feel he could be a danger to himself or others, we should have him admitted to a local facility until then. I vehemently shake my head.

"He only hurt me because I startled him. I'm not going to have him committed for that."

"I understand, but think about it long and hard before you say no, Savannah. Are you supposed to walk on eggshells the next week or so?"

"I won't have to. He'll be fine. We'll be fine. Thanks for coming over, but I'm sure I have it from here."

Julia looks hesitant at first, but she finally rises to leave. "Of course. Call if you need, okay?"

"I will. I promise," I say before showing her out. My next call is to Ben. I explain the situation, and once he realizes how intense it is, he tells me to expect him and Lizzy the next day. They'll spend the days with him while I'm in school, and the evenings, they'll spend at his lake house. I thank him profusely for the help, and then I go to check on Fletcher.

He's in the bed, nervously twiddling his thumbs. "Julia's arranged for your stay. We'll fly to Colorado on Monday, and you'll check into the facility on Tuesday morning. Ben and Lizzy are coming into town. They'll be here tomorrow. Ben says he's going to spend the days with you so I won't have to miss much school. Plus, he's excited to see you. It's been a while since you two have just relaxed and had a good time."

"So I get a babysitter until I leave, huh?"

"No, you get a wife who loves you and wants to spend as much time with you as possible before you leave. You also have a dear friend who wants to do the same."

He sighs. "This isn't fair to you, Savannah. You didn't sign up for this when you agreed to marry me. Are you sure you don't want a divorce? I won't contest it."

"Why would you even ask something like that?" I straddle him so I can look him in the eye. "Fletcher, I love every ounce of you. This is just a setback. Every couple has them. This is ours. I'm going to be there when you walk into that facility, and I'm going to be there the day you're released. Let's promise that we're going to spend the next week looking for the positive in this and that we'll try to have fun. Going to the facility is a good thing."

He gives a half smile. "Okay. If you say it's a good thing, then it must be. I'll try my best to stay positive through this."

"You're going to be fine. Who knows, maybe you'll be even better than you were before once you complete the entire course of treatment. You WILL complete the entire course of treatment this time, won't you?"

He nods. "I will."

"Okay," I say, kissing his forehead before lying next to him and situating myself in the bed. Once the light is off and I'm still, he drapes his arm over my hip.

"Savannah, I'm so sorry for all of this."

"Stop apologizing, Fletcher."

"You know I'd never hurt you on purpose, right?"

I roll to face him. "You've already asked that. I assure you, if I didn't, I wouldn't be here." Kissing him softly, I take his face in my hands. "I know the real you. I know your heart. You're a good man, Fletcher Reilly, and despite everything, you have to know that you're my savior. You freed me from my personal hell, and you showed me how to live life the right way. Don't forget all the good because of what's happening now. This is only temporary."

"I love you so much."

"I love you, too." One last kiss and we sleep for the night.

I call in sick to class the next morning, partly because I don't want to leave Fletcher alone, and partly because the redness on my neck didn't go away as quickly as I'd hoped. Fletcher has moments of obvious anxiety, but he only seems to get lost in that terrible dark place when he is left alone.

Ben and Lizzy arrive around lunch time, arms laden with Triceratops bags. "Someone call for delivery?" Ben asks.

"Get in here, silly!" I say, taking some of the

bags from him and Lizzy then giving them both a welcoming kiss on the cheek.

"Fletcher," Ben says, hugging him tightly and giving him a few slaps on the back, "I see you're just as fugly as ever."

"You'd know all about fugly wouldn't you? Lizzy, you should've seen some of the girls he dated before you." He lets out a howl, and Ben laughs.

"It's good to see you, man," Ben says.

"Thanks for coming." Fletcher kisses Lizzy on the cheek. "And thank you for coming, too."

"It's our pleasure, plus I've been dying to spend some time with Savannah. I've missed you so much, and I have tons to tell you. But first, who's ready to eat?" she asks with a huge smile.

We dive into our oversized combos, and after one bite, I remember why Ben is so successful with his business.

"Best burger ever," I say, taking as big of a bite as my mouth will allow.

"Others seem to think so, as well. We're expanding again! Four new stores coming to Houston and three in San Antonio!"

"That's wonderful news! Congratulations!" I exclaim.

"And you, don't you worry about anything. You'll still get full salary while you're in treatment. It's company policy, so don't think I'm giving you preferential treatment or anything."

"That just took a huge weight off my shoulders," Fletcher admits. "Thanks, Ben."

"Savannah, you're so close to graduating! I'm so proud of you," Lizzy says.

"Well, I still have about five months to go, but

I know I've made the right choice. I love it, and I hope to find work in the nursery or somewhere else that involves pediatrics."

"I can't believe how far you've come. How far we've come! So much has changed since our Pole Co. days."

"Absolutely."

"Well, sorry to cut this visit short, but we're going to get a little shopping done to restock the lake house. Fletch, if you're feeling up to it, how about we play a round at the golf course tomorrow?"

"That sounds good."

"I'll come by about eight, and we'll get some breakfast before we hit the course."

"See you then."

After Lizzy and Ben leave, Fletcher and I spend the rest of the day lazing around the house and working on projects. I curl up in a chair to study while he works from his laptop on some things for Triceratops. Things are nice and quiet until he slams down the lid of his laptop.

"What's wrong?" I ask with concern.

"I'm just feeling a little… it's hard to explain. I feel like I'm letting you down."

"Fletcher, stop. We've talked about this. Beating yourself up over something you have limited control over isn't going to help you. You have an illness, and you're going to a facility to get treatment for that illness. You haven't let me down."

"There's so much that I want to do with you."

"And we'll do it, but it's going to be later. We couldn't do much anyway with me being in school," I say, kneeling on the floor and resting my head in his lap. He softly strokes my hair.

"I don't deserve you."

"I don't deserve YOU."

"I love you, Savannah."

I smile at him. "Ready for bed?"

"Shower first?"

"You read my mind."

The patient load is minimal during my hospital shift which gives me plenty of time to think about Fletcher. I try my best to be upbeat, stoic, and compassionate around him, but the truth is I'm terrified. What if the treatment doesn't help him? What if he has another violent outburst and I'm unable to stop him? What if he decides to leave treatment early again? So many doubts and uncertainties plague my thoughts, so I slip away to my special hiding place in the hospital's deserted playroom before going home. I need a good cry to relieve the negative thoughts, and I can't do it at home. I'm in my tiny chair, my face in my hands, sobbing when the door opens.

"Aww, you beat me... Savannah? What's wrong?" Dr. Goodman asks, squatting next to me.

I try drying my tears as best as I can with my fingers while shaking my head. "It's nothing. I'm just having some personal issues."

He digs around in his pockets and produces a few two by two squares of gauze. "I'm sorry it's not tissue, but it's all I have."

"Thank you," I say, accepting his offering.

He tries sitting in one of the tiny chairs, but once again, he fails miserably. Instead, he sits on top of one of the play tables. "I've been told by many people that one of my best qualities is my ability to listen to problems and offer sound advice. Why don't you tell me what's going on?"

"You're a doctor, not a therapist. I don't expect you to listen to my problems."

"I offered and that's a far cry from expecting it."

"I don't even know where to begin," I say.

"A good starting place would probably be the marks on your neck. How did you get them?"

I draw my hands to my throat. "I didn't know they still showed."

"They're not overly obvious, but to someone who is trained to spot things like that, it shows."

"It's not what you think."

"It never is," he says, slowly shaking his head.

"No, seriously. My husband, he's a war veteran experiencing PTSD. He'd been hiding the severity of his condition from me for a long time, but recently, it came to light. He was sleeping on the sofa, and I woke him suddenly, and…"

"He attacked you."

"Yes, but it wasn't him. I mean it was his physical body, but I could see it in his eyes, my husband was gone."

Robert nods. "Is it the first time he's gotten physical?"

I shake my head. "Once, before we were married, but it was tame compared to this recent one. I love my husband dearly, and I know that he'd never do anything to intentionally hurt me. He's a wonderful man, full of charm and charisma…"

"Hey, no one's saying he's a bad guy. Remember, I started as an army doc. I've seen PTSD. I'm sure your husband is a great man, but I do hope he seeks treatment."

"He has. I guess that's one of the main reasons I was crying. He'll be gone for at least a month. The facility he'll be going to is in Colorado, and we've never been apart for that long. Plus, I worry that the treatment might not work this time. What's his life going to be like then?"

"If he's going to the place I'm thinking of then you can rest assured that he'll get the best care available. They work wonders with vets, and I'm sure you'll see that many of your fears are unfounded."

"Really?"

"Really," he says in a self-assured tone.

"Thank you for listening."

"Of course. Look, here's all my contact information, including my cell number." He scribbles a number on the back of a business card. "If you or your husband wants someone to talk to, needs some advice or questions answered, just call. Anytime. Day or night."

"Thank you so much, Robert. This means a lot to me."

"I'm happy to do it. You've had your crying session, a quick counseling session, and now I'm going to shoo you out so I can catch a nap before my next rotation." He gives me a playful wink.

"Seriously? I pour my heart out to you, and you're going to make me leave?" I chide.

"Yep. Hit the lights when you go, please."

"Fine," I say, opening the door slightly then pausing. "Has anyone ever told you that you look like Eric the vampire from the TV show *True Blood*?"

"I get that all the time," he says with a smile. "I guess I should watch an episode to see just how much I resemble this guy."

"I'm glad to hear that it's not just me who thinks so." With that parting comment, I switch off the light and head home.

The house is dark when I arrive, and nerves make my stomach clench into a tight ball. *Maybe Ben and Fletcher are having such a great time together that they decided to get some supper?* I open the door, click on the light, and I'm greeted with a chorus of "surprise!"

"What's going on?" I ask, completely perplexed. Molly, Julia, and Lizzy, all wearing tiaras and fluffy ball gowns, smile radiantly.

"It's your princess party! Uncle Fletcher said you never had one growing up, but that you really wanted one. Look, we have a gown for you, and a tiara, and presents, and cake, and..."

"Molly, leave a little for her to discover on her own, please."

"Sorry, Mom," she says. "This is going to be so much fun!"

"Your gown, your highness," Lizzy says, passing me a gorgeous solid white ball gown.

"I don't know what to say," I stammer.

"You don't have to say anything. Go put on your gown."

After dumping an armload of books onto the counter, I take the dress from Lizzy and head to the bedroom. When I come out, I admit to the girls that I'm feeling a little silly.

"I think it's incredibly sweet and romantic that your husband came up with this plan. I have to admit that I'm a little jealous," Lizzy says. "Fletcher called me up and said he wanted you to experience a memory you were robbed of during your childhood. He had no idea what went into putting together a princess party, so he left it all to me. I'm so glad these stinking pageant gowns are finally being put to a good use."

"So what does happen at a princess party?" I ask.

"Well, if I remember right, we'd giggle a lot. Talk about our future Prince Charmings. Get mad at each other at least once. Eat candy non-stop, top it off with a hunk of cake and ice cream, then go home and drive our parents mad because of the sugar rush. After that came the sugar coma and the inevitable sugar crash," Lizzy answers.

"Yeah, that sounds about right, except you left out the part about the cheesy games we'd play," Julia adds.

"Oh, my gosh! The stupid games where we used to scare ourselves silly at slumber parties! Do you remember those? Light as a Feather and Bloody Mary! I still feel apprehensive when I look into a mirror when the room's dark," Lizzy excitedly conveys. Julia nods.

"Light as a Feather? What?" I ask.

"They're sleepover games, Aunt Savannah. You never played them?"

I shrug while shaking my head. "Should I have?"

"Nah, it's just one of those things that kids do to scare the heck out of each other. You didn't miss out on much," Julia says.

"Or did she? I think she should play Bloody

Mary at least once," Lizzy teases.

"I don't think so," I say. "What does Bloody Mary have to do with a princess party?"

"It's a childhood game, one you missed out on. Come on!" Lizzy pleads.

"Okay, how does it work?"

"You have to go into the dark bathroom, stare into the mirror, and say 'Bloody Mary' three times, and you have to say it loud enough for us to hear you," Lizzy explains.

"And what's supposed to happen?" I ask.

"She shows up, covered in the blood of her victims, and she reaches through the mirror to scratch off your face!" Lizzy makes a clawing motion with her hand for added effect.

"That's it? That's all I have to do?" I inquire, not impressed.

"Yep," Lizzy says.

"All of your faces are intact." I remark.

"I never made it to the third repetition," Lizzy answers.

"Me either," Julia seconds.

"I got scared as soon as they closed the door. I never said it once," Molly admits, wide-eyed.

"Really? You sure are a bunch of chickens," I tease.

The group giggles from behind as I make my way into the bathroom. I turn out the lights, and Lizzy closes the door.

"What did you do that for?" I ask.

"Remember, it has to be super dark," she yells through the door.

"Whatever. Okay, here I go. Bloody Mary. Bloody Mary. Bloody Mar...," I scream loudly as I throw open the door, and they scream, too. The looks on their faces are absolutely priceless! Lizzy's gripping her chest, Julia looks confused, and Molly, well, she is a mix between the two.

"Did you see something?" Lizzy excitedly asks. "What was it?"

"It was just as you told me. There was this woman in a long white dress, but it wasn't covered in blood or anything…," I start to explain.

Lizzy's face goes from terrified to not amused. "You're talking about yourself, right?"

I smile broadly. "Uh huh."

"You scared the hell out of me!" Julia exclaims, plopping onto the sofa.

"Y'all were trying to scare the hell out of me!" I say with a laugh.

"Okay. Moving on. Who wants to talk about boys?" Lizzy asks.

"My talk would be boring because our lives are pretty much open books," I explain.

"Mine, too," Lizzy says.

"But not Julia. What's going on in the man department, huh?" I prompt.

"Not much," she answers, wriggling uncomfortably in her seat.

"She went on three dates with Mr. Henry," Molly chimes in. Julia sends her a look that says "shut it," but it's too late.

"Mr. Henry? Who's Mr. Henry? Why haven't I heard of him?" I tease.

"Because, there's no guarantee that it will go anywhere, and I don't have to tell you every bit of my business. Okay?" she says with a huff.

"I saw them kissing in the driveway," Molly

says with a giggle. Julia looks embarrassed. "And I'm pretty sure they used tongue."

"Molly!" Julia fusses while Lizzy and I roar with laughter.

"Did you, Julia? Was there tongue?" Lizzy asks.

"Wait, I still want to hear who this Henry guy is," I chime in.

"He's my teacher!" Molly says with a giggle.

"What! No way! You're not dating him to boost her grades, right?" Lizzy teases.

"Of course I'm not!" Julia snaps after shooting Molly another dirty look. "We just happen to share a common interest in history."

"Sounds like you share more than that!" I say with a laugh.

"Okay, that's enough. Here's the deal. We met the night of the school carnival; the same night I met you, Savannah. He gave me his number, but I never called him. I wasn't ready to see anyone yet. We'd run into each other occasionally when I'd visit the school, and each time he'd tell me he was still interested. Though I appreciated it, the timing still wasn't right. Fast forward to a month ago, and Princess Molly here conveniently forgets her history book in my car. I run inside to drop it off at the front office, but I run into Henry in the hall. Literally. Like I bowled him over, and we fell into a heap on the floor. He helps me up and apologizes profusely the entire time, even though we both know the fault was all mine."

"Awww, I'm loving this story so much!" Lizzy exclaims.

"Well, it's as I'm dusting myself off that I

notice blood coming through the knee of my pant leg, and when Henry bends over to check it out, that's when I notice the big lump forming on the back of his head. We're sitting in the school nurse's office…"

She's interrupted by laughter from me and Lizzy.

"You both wound up in the school nurse's office! This is priceless!" Lizzy squeals.

Julia continues her story, "Well, while we're waiting for the school nurse to arrive, we start talking about Molly, about current events, about our pasts. He tells me that he lost his wife four years ago in a car accident, so we both know what it's like to lose a spouse to a tragic circumstance. After the nurse patched up our injuries, he asked me if I'd like to meet for a cup of coffee. I accepted, and now you know everything."

"Well, not everything. You still haven't told us if there was tongue," Lizzy says with a giggle.

"Maybe a little," Julia says, blushing. We all laugh loudly, while throwing her an encouraging comment here and there. "Who wants cake?" she asks, desperate to change the subject.

Everyone excitedly sits around the kitchen table, and partakes in some light-hearted conversation while devouring the scrumptious princess cake. Lizzy went all out for this party. There are princess plates, cups, napkins—even the forks had crowns adorning the handles.

As the chatter begins to wind down, I take advantage of the lull to thank everyone for helping me to fulfill a childhood dream.

"Most of the thanks goes to your husband," Lizzy says. "He was very insistent that you get your princess party."

"It amazes me what that man remembers. I say some things in passing, yet he seems to commit them to memory."

"He's always been that way," Julia remarks. "He's incredibly thoughtful, and he loves to surprise people."

"Yeah, he does," I say with a content sigh.

"Speaking of, I see headlights in the driveway. I guess the guys are back," Lizzy informs.

"Perfect timing. This one has school tomorrow," Julia says, scooting her chair under the table.

"Don't feel bad, Molly. So does this one," I say with a grimace.

"Yeah, but you're almost done, Aunt Savannah. Do you know how many years I have left?"

"Don't rush those years; enjoy them," I advise.

"Mom tells me the same thing."

"She's right. They both are," Lizzy offers.

"If you say so," Molly says with a shrug.

Ben and Fletcher come through the door, and I know right away that Fletcher isn't feeling well. His face in incredibly pale and sweat glistens on his forehead. I don't want to draw unnecessary attention to his situation, so I give him a quick kiss before taking his hand and leading him in the direction of the bedroom.

"We'll be right back," I inform. "Please, if any of you want to bring some cake home, feel free to take as much as you want."

"Actually, I have to get Molly home, so no cake for us. We'll catch up with you later."

"Okay, goodnight. Thanks for everything," I say.

"Why don't you take a shower?" I softly whisper to Fletcher. He nods, and in a slow gait, he meanders into the bathroom. It's not until I hear the water running that I finally seek answers from Ben.

"What happened?" I ask, my voice laden with concern.

Ben sighs. "We were alone, sitting on the patio of a bar and grill, just talking and trying to relax after a good day of golfing. Suddenly, this obnoxious jerk decides to bring his group of equally obnoxious friends outside. I could see that Fletcher was getting agitated, and I told him we could leave, but he wanted to stay. I think things would've been okay, but the dude kept going on about how he was some kind of war hero, and that he had served as a combat veteran. This guy had the crowd eating out of his hand, but Fletcher openly called bullshit because he knew the guy was lying. It only took three questions for Fletcher to blow the guy's validity out of the water, and the jerk wasn't very happy about it. You know, with Fletcher actually being a combat veteran, having people like this douche going around falsely seeking glory is the ultimate insult. Fletcher started talking about the true heroes, the fallen, he even mentioned Brody. The crowd swayed their attention to Fletcher, and they began ostracizing the loser. He got so mad that he took a swing at Fletcher, and Fletch put him out. I mean like lights out, unconscious, flat out on his back, with one punch. The crowd cheered, Fletcher ran, and I caught up with him at the truck. We waited around for the police, but they never came, so we rode around for a little while before coming here. He's mad at himself for losing his temper, but Savannah, the guy totally deserved it. If Fletcher wouldn't have done it, I would have."

I nod. "Thanks for letting me know."

"Sure. Lizzy, you ready to go?"

"Yeah," she says, the shock from hearing the story still in her voice.

"I'll be here at eight, okay?" Ben asks.

"Perfect. Thank you."

I show them out then I sit on the edge of the bed until Fletcher comes out of the bathroom. He's running a towel through his wet hair, and when he looks up to see me, he asks, "So, Ben filled you in?"

I nod. "He says the guy deserved it."

"It's still no excuse for what I did. What if I had killed him?"

"You didn't. Hopefully, you taught him a lesson about lying to get attention."

"But I could've."

"Fletcher, we all have the potential to kill. Every last one of us. It depends on the situation, the circumstances, and the motive. Fortunately, most people don't kill, but we all can."

"Is this supposed to make me feel better?"

"The point I'm trying to make, and failing miserably at, is that you did what a lot of people would've done. Ben told me that if you hadn't hit that guy, he would've."

"I don't think it's the fact that I hit him that bothers me. Ben's right; he totally deserved it, and probably a few more, but the sucker was out cold in one punch. What bothers me is the fact that when it happened, I blacked out. Completely. I remember talking to the crowd, then the next thing I remember after that is seeing him sprawled out on the ground and feeling my fist throbbing. It scared me so badly that I took off. I've zoned out before, but blacking out? That's something different. I hate to bring this up, but the times I attacked you...," he hangs his head, "I was aware of what I was doing, but I wasn't aware of who I was doing it to. This time, I wasn't even aware of what I was doing. Does this mean I'm getting worse?"

"I don't know, baby," I say, lightly rubbing his shoulders. "But I do know someone we can call, if you'd like. He's one of the new doctors at the hospital, Robert Goodman. He used to be an army doctor, and then he worked as an ER doc. He's switching specialties to pediatrics, but he's very knowledgeable about PTSD, and he's easy to talk to."

"You've been talking to a co-worker about my problem?"

"No! It's not like that, Fletcher. He found me sitting in one of the empty rooms, and he said he could tell that something was on my mind. I wasn't going to tell him anything, but he eventually got me to open up, and I felt much better after talking to him." The fact that Dr. Goodman found me bawling in the waiting room was a detail Fletcher didn't need to know. "He gave me a card with all his contact information, and he said we could call him day or night."

Fletcher shakes his head. "I don't think it's a good idea."

"The only reason I bring it up is because I think he can relate. You both saw and experienced terrible things, and while Ben, Lizzy, Julia, and I try to sympathize, we can't relate to it on the same level as someone who has actually been there."

He sighs. "Okay. Will you see if he's available, just so I can determine if I need to be locked up these last few days before leaving for Colorado?"

"Of course." I dig through my purse for the card, and Robert picks up on the second ring. I apologize for disturbing him, but he insists that I'm doing no such thing. I give him a brief rundown of the night's events, and he agrees to come to the house. He arrives in less than fifteen minutes.

"I was just down the road at the gym...," he's silent for a few seconds once I fully open the door to allow him inside, "so I apologize for being underdressed."

It takes me a second to realize I'm still wearing Lizzy's ball gown and tiara. "I'm so embarrassed," I say, yanking the tiara from my head. "My friends threw me a princess party because I never had one growing up, and then Fletcher came home, well... I don't usually walk around my house in a tiara and gown."

He laughs. "Good. I was going to ask if I should go home and change into my tux."

"No, you're dressed just fine." Fletcher comes out the bedroom wearing gym shorts and a t-shirt. "See, we're casual here. Fletcher, this is Dr. Robert Goodman. Dr. Goodman, this is my husband, Fletcher Reilly."

Dr. Goodman extends his hand in Fletcher's direction. "It's nice to meet you, Fletcher. Please call me Robert."

"Nice to meet you, too. Thank you for agreeing to come over."

"I'm happy to do it. So, tell me a little bit

about your time in the military," he says, jumping straight to the point as soon as they're sitting at the kitchen table.

I interrupt them. "I'm going to excuse myself so you two can talk and I can study. There's plenty of cake on the counter if you'd like some, and there's still half a pot of recently brewed coffee, too. Good night, Dr. Goodman. Fletcher," I say, kissing him lightly on the top of his head, "I'm right in the bedroom if you need anything." He takes hold of my hand, and kisses it before I leave.

"Good night, sweetheart," he says, with a smile.

I spend about two hours studying before I can't manage to keep my eyes open. I turn out the light, and it's not until about one in the morning when I feel Fletcher crawl into the bed. I roll to face him and sleepily ask how the meeting went.

He tells me it went well then lightly kisses the tip of my nose. "We'll talk about it more in the morning."

"Okay," I agree, snuggling closer to him. "I love you, Fletcher."

"Do you know what I'd love?"

"What's that?" I ask, feeling more awake.

"For you to show me. Show me how much you love me, Savannah."

I'm fully awake now, and once I slide free from my nightshirt, I show Fletcher Reilly just deep my devotion is to him.

 fifteen

I see Dr. Goodman briefly the day before
Fletcher and I are due to fly to Colorado. He tells me
that he was glad to meet Fletcher and that he hopes he
was of some help. I assure him that he most certainly
was. Even so, Fletcher still continues to have panic
attacks and black out sessions, although very few
happen when I'm home with him. Ben is the person
having to handle the episodes. He does it with
patience and is diligent in trying to keep the intensity
of the attacks to a minimum. Sometimes it works;
sometimes it doesn't. My heart hurts for my husband.
I see the toll the seemingly endless barrage is taking
on him, and I'd give anything to be able to take that
pain and struggle away from him.

My last night at home with Fletcher isn't as
quiet and uneventful as I'd hoped. Normally, once we
go to bed, things are fine. This particular night is
plagued with restlessness and frustration brought on
by the terrifying nightmares that haunt his psyche. He
jerks awake twice and bolts upright in bed, his body
drenched in sweat as he gasps for breath. The first
time it happens, I manage to calm him with soothing
talk and tender touches. The second time, he thrashes

and flails about, and as I try to quiet him, I take an elbow to the cheek. Fletcher is so upset that he's hurt me again that he spends a full hour profusely apologizing even though I assure him I'm fine. It was a dreadful night for the both of us, and we give up on the notion of actually getting sleep.

I go to the kitchen to cook breakfast while Fletcher retreats to the office to finish up some last minute paperwork for Triceratops. It's obvious that something is weighing heavily on his mind when he sits down to eat.

"I've made a decision, and I want you to hear me out," he proclaims.

"Of course. What is this decision?" I ask, taking a sip of my coffee.

"I don't want you to fly with me to Colorado."

"What? Why?" I ask, sitting a little straighter in my chair.

"I've really thought this through. First of all, if you go with me, you'll miss at least two more days of school in addition to what you've already missed. I don't want you to do that. You're going to miss even more days when it's time for me to come home, and you've worked way too hard to get docked on attendance. Plus, think about how much nicer it will be for you to greet me in person AFTER I finish with my therapy."

"But.."

Fletcher holds up his hand. "There's more. Second reason. Do you really think we'll get to spend any quality time together on this trip? Checking bags, flights filled with strangers who hear our every word, an overnight hotel stay where all we'll do is fall into bed only to get up extra early the next morning to get

me checked in. Then after all of that, you're going to
have to fly back home all alone. That's going to keep
me from putting a hundred percent into trying to heal
because I'll be so worried about your safety that I
won't be able to focus on my treatment. Not to
mention, it's a whole lot of unnecessary hassle."

"I don't see it that way," I argue.

"If you give it some thought, you'll agree.
I've already cancelled your ticket, and we're being
issued a reimbursement."

"Fletcher!" I fuss.

He pulls his chair closer to mine, props his
elbow on the table, and lightly tips my chin with his
finger. "I'm right about this one."

"You cancelled my ticket," I say, still fuming.
He brushes his lips against mine, but I don't respond
to his kiss.

"Savannah, this is for the best. Everything I
do is because I believe in my heart that it's for the
best. Please don't be mad. Please." He gives me
puppy dog eyes and a pouty lower lip.

I sigh. "I'll concede, but only because you say
it'll interfere with your treatment. Am I at least
allowed to bring you to the airport?"

He smiles. "Of course. I want you to give me
a send off that will leave the masses blushing."

I laugh. "You sure about that?"

"Oh yeah, baby," he says, raising his
eyebrows.

We arrive at the airport about an hour before
his flight. I'm with him while he checks his bags,
checks the flight info to make sure everything is still

on schedule, and makes his way to the security gate. I'm suddenly filled with yearning for him, and he hasn't even left yet. It's the anxious anticipation of knowing that we'll be apart from each other longer than any time since we've met. The thought of it tugs at my heart, but I work hard to hide it from Fletcher. I see in his face that he's battling with his emotions, too, but I don't call attention to it.

We find a quiet little corner to huddle in, and I'm the first to speak. "It's pointless to pretend that we aren't going to miss each other. My thoughts are going to be on you day in and day out, but it's going to be okay. I'm going to be eagerly counting down the days until you come back to me. I love you, and I'm so proud of you for reaching out for help. Finding you was the best thing that ever happened to me, and I'm so grateful that you saw something in me that no one else did. You're my heart, Fletcher Reilly. I hope you have a good flight, and please call me when you get settled in at the hotel tonight."

"Ah, my sweet Savannah, everything I do is for you. You make my life so much better. Thank you for standing by me through all of this. There are a lot of women who would have bolted after the first incident, but you... Well, please remember that my love for you is immeasurable, and that I'm so incredibly sorry for ever hurting you. I'm grateful for your confidence and devotion. It's what gets me through."

"Fletcher, you never hurt me on purpose. You're a good man. Please, quit punishing yourself for something you had no control over."

He shakes his head. "None of that matters. I'm supposed to protect you... to keep you safe. It crushes my soul to know everything you've been through in your life and to know that I added to that pain."

"That's not how I see it at all, Fletcher. You rescued me from that life. Your love saved me from the nothingness that consumed me. Please, baby, please quit being so hard on yourself. You're sick right now, but you're going to get better, and the day you come home to me is going to be a new and better beginning for us."

He's holding back tears, but I'm not able to contain mine anymore. They gently fall down my face. "Don't mistake these tears as a sign that I'm not going to be okay while you're gone. I am. I'm going to be just fine, so don't worry about me. All these tears mean is that I'm going to miss you like mad because I love you so much."

"That's exactly what I want to hear," Fletcher says, scooping me off my feet so he can kiss me. After one final parting kiss, he sets me down and picks up his bag. Hand in hand, we walk to the end of the security line. I stay with him all the way until it's his turn to be processed, and I put on a brave face as he waves to me through the glass window that now separates us. I blow him a kiss, wave a final goodbye, and then quickly turn away so he won't see the fresh tears falling.

Once I'm home, I immediately start cleaning in an effort to preoccupy my thoughts. I start with light house work, but then I move onto the heavier stuff. Even getting down on my hands and knees to viciously scrub the floors doesn't work at keeping my thoughts from drifting to Fletcher. Eventually, I give up on the cleaning altogether and expend my nervous energy elsewhere. I'm constantly checking his flight status, flipping on the news to be sure there weren't any emergency landings or crashes, and in between, I'm simply wearing a hole in the floor with all my pacing. Hopefully, this severe anxiety will end once I know he's safely arrived at the treatment facility. He's still somewhat of a loose cannon, and I pray that he doesn't have any triggers to set him off on the way. I should've insisted on going with him, but damn Fletcher and his smooth talking ways! He didn't want me to go, his reasons for not wanting me to go were actually pretty valid, and no matter, it's too late to do anything about it now.

I check the flight status, and it shows that Fletcher's plane landed in Colorado three minutes ago, so I breathe a sigh of relief. Now I just wait for him to check into the hotel and give me a call, then the first step will be complete. I'm sitting with my hand on the phone when the doorbell rings. So excited about Fletcher's phone call, it doesn't even register to me that someone's at the door, and I answer the phone instead. Realizing my silly mistake, I hang up the phone and head to the front door. Not thinking twice about it, I tell the sheriff's deputy that he must have the wrong address because I didn't call in a complaint. The door is almost closed when he pushes his hand against it to keep it open.

"Is this the Reilly residence?" My stomach flips. *The guy Fletcher hit is pressing charges, and Fletcher's out of state. What does this mean? Are they going to have to cut his treatment short? Can they wait until he finishes treatment before they do something? Maybe I can talk to the guy, explain the situation, and he'll drop the charges?*

"Yes sir, it is, but Fletcher's not here right now. He's in Colorado."

"May I come inside?" he asks.

"Of course," I say, holding the door open for him. "Can I offer you something to drink?"

"No, ma'am. Thank you anyway." His hand rests on the pistol on his gun belt, and he's quiet for a beat as he takes in his surroundings. Once he's made a full sweep around the place with his eyes, he asks, "Are you here alone, Mrs. Reilly? I presume that you're Mrs. Reilly, Savannah Reilly."

"Yes, I'm Savannah, and yes, I'm alone. As I mentioned before, Fletcher is out of town."

"This truly is the worst part of my job," he says, moving to cross his arms in front of himself while shifting his gaze to look down at his feet.

"I don't understand. What do you mean?"

"May we sit down?"

I hold out my hand to gesture that the sofa is available. Once we're seated, he looks at me, a sympathetic sadness shows in his eyes. It suddenly clicks.

"This isn't about the other night, is it?"

"No, ma'am. I'm not sure what you're referring to, but this is unrelated."

"No," I say with disbelief.

"It's with great regret that I have to inform you..."

"NO! Don't say it. I dropped him off at the airport. I saw him go through security."

"Mr. Reilly never boarded the plane."

"He had to have! It's some kind of mistake. A terrible mistake."

The deputy uncomfortably picks at his thumb nail while disclosing the information he has, "Mr. Reilly walked out of the airport and rented a car from one of the nearby agencies. He then drove himself to a secluded area not far from I-10 where I'm sorry to say, he appears to have intentionally overdosed on sleeping pills. He was found by a deputy patrolling the area and pronounced dead at the scene by the coroner. There was a note. The original is in evidence right now, but it will be released to you at the close of the investigation. However, I have a copy of it for you. You have my deepest condolences, Mrs. Reilly."

I sit, my mouth agape, shaking my head. The deputy places the letter in my hands, but I refuse to look at it. *It's a joke. A terrible joke. Fletcher isn't a quitter. He loves me, and he'd never leave me, not on purpose anyway. No. He's not gone. He's not!*

"Were you the deputy who found him?" I ask.

"No, ma'am. It wasn't me."

"Because it might not have been Fletcher in that car. I was going to show you a picture, and then you could tell me…" He knows I'm grasping at straws, and he interrupts me.

"Mrs. Reilly, it was Fletcher in that car. There's no doubt about it. Is there someone I can call to come be with you?"

I lurch from my seat. "Julia. I guess you can call Julia," I say, tossing him my phone as I hurriedly pace the floor. I run my hands through my hair as the full weight of what he's told me sinks in. Fletcher has left me forever, and there's not a damn thing I can do to get him back.

I drop to my knees, collapse to the ground, and

beat my fists against the floor. "NOOOOOOOO!"

The deputy helps me stand, and I turn my anger onto him. "He gave up. He gave up on us. How could he do this to us? Why? Why wasn't my love enough to save him? Why didn't he give the treatment a chance?"

Julia comes through the door just as the patient deputy is helping me to the sofa. Her blotchy red face is streaked with tears as she grips me tightly. I squeeze her back, unable to talk because of the sobs that rack my body.

"Is there anything else I can do? Anyone else I can call for you?" the deputy asks.

"No, thank you very much, sir. We'll take care of each other," Julia says, taking control of the situation.

"Here's my card. Please don't hesitate to call if you need anything. We'll be in touch as more information becomes available. Again, I'm very sorry for your loss."

Julia nods and offers the deputy a little wave as he leaves the house. I desperately cling to her as I wail in agony.

"Shhhhh. It's okay. Savannah, it's okay. Cry. Get it out." She gently strokes my hair. After a few minutes, the tears refuse to come, and I pull away from her shoulder.

"How can you be so calm through all of this?" I ask in between shaky breaths. "Is it all just a joke? Is this some kind of cruel joke that you guys cooked up so I'd be relieved when Fletcher surprises me by walking through the door? Please tell me that's it. Please!"

"No, sweetheart. It's not a joke, though I wish

like hell that it was." She pulls her hand to her mouth, and her eyes brim with fresh tears. "I'm not cool and calm. Inside I'm falling apart, but only one of us can fall apart at a time. One of us has to be strong."

"I need to call Ben and Lizzy," I say, suddenly swallowing a huge hunk of emotion so I can semi-function on autopilot. They are in their car on their way back to Dallas, so I ask Ben to pull to the side of the road before breaking the news to him. He's as devastated as the rest of us and promises to be back in Lafayette as soon as possible.

Julia's still sobbing when I decide to return the favor from earlier and hold her. She calls out for her brother asking the same question I did—"Why?"

"There's a letter," I tell her. "I don't know if I want to read it, though. Once I do, it's over. This letter is the last communication that I'll ever have from him. That will be it. He'll never have anything new to share with me."

She nods. "I understand what you're saying, Savannah, but reading it is the only way we're going to know what happened. We have to know."

I slowly open the envelope, and my heart grips when I recognize Fletcher's handwriting. I slowly peruse the letter my love has left for me.

My Dearest Savannah,

If you're reading this, then I've been found and you know what I've done. Please let me start by saying I'm so incredibly sorry for the hurt I'm putting you through right now.

Understand that I'm doing this for a very good reason, and that it's the only way. I've thought this through very extensively, and no matter which avenue I explored, this always came back as the best option. I'm broken. More broken than anyone knows. I got really good at hiding it, but towards the end, it surfaced more and more. And then I physically hurt you, not once but three times. Savannah, a piece of me died each time I realized what I had done. You told me that it wasn't my fault, and that you forgave me each time I laid hands on you, but regardless of whether or not it was intentional, I HURT YOU. You deserve so much better than me, and I know for a fact that you would never leave me, so I had to leave you.

Maybe treatment would've made me better, but I can't depend on a maybe. What if I'd accidently killed you or someone else? Who's to say that it won't happen sometime down the line? When I was home alone, I was able to do a lot of soul searching, and I believe my life's purpose was to connect with you in a way that no one else could. We'd both been through terrible tragedies, but where you were able to work past your trauma, I bathed in mine daily. The faces, the smells, the sounds, the pain, I couldn't make them disappear, not even for one stupid day. I'm sorry that I hid that from you, but you blossomed so much while we were together, and seeing that is what got me through the last couple of years.

I always knew in my heart that though

we were meant to be together, it would only be temporary. I was the guy who awakened you, but there will be another who will complete you. You thought it was me, and so did I, at first, but that's not the case. I could barely take care of myself. It was getting harder and harder to function every day. Ben was nice enough to keep me on salary, but what he didn't tell you is that I was messing everything up. I wasn't working on stuff for the business all those days, I was writing in a journal, keeping track of my thoughts. I desperately hoped that writing about the demons would make them disappear. It didn't. It intensified their power, but I couldn't stop. I was once again trapped in their darkness, and the only light around was the one that came from you. But what happens when something drains the power from a light source? It doesn't matter if that source shines as brightly as the sun, it will eventually dim if it's taxed enough. That's what I was doing to you. I helped you to find your light, but then I started to drain it. No way am I going to be responsible for your light going out.

You promised me that you'd continue with school. I expect you to do that. Please, mourn me, but don't be consumed by it. I'm free now. My shackles have been removed and my demons slain. I hope that it's not too far off before you're able to smile when you remember me, instead of shedding the tears that I know are falling from your eyes right now. Imagine me there, wiping them from your face.

I promise that if I'm able, I'll look for Lucas, your dad, and Grampy. I'll give your baby the hug you've been longing for, and if that sort of thing is allowed where I'm going, I'll adopt him as my own. We'll be waiting for you when it's your time to join us, but don't rush it. You now know how to live a beautiful life, so go out and live it. Do all the things we weren't able to do. Look for the signs. If Molly was right, I'll try to give you some from time to time to let you know that things are fine.

I adore you. I cherish you. I love you. Live for me! Live the life I could never have.
Yours Always,
Fletcher

The last page is a copy of a photograph from our wedding. Me, with my glowing smile, and Fletcher with his handsome face... My falling tears smudge the ink.

I hand the letter to Julia so she can read it, and then I immediately scour the office for the journal he referred to in the letter. I find it in the top right drawer underneath a life insurance policy, a list of final wishes, and a wilted daisy. Julia enters the room.

"He had this planned, Julia. He knew. He knew when we went to bed last night. He knew when we had breakfast this morning. He knew when I kissed him goodbye. He fucking knew the entire

255

time! How could he do this to me? How could he leave me? How did I not see it coming?"

She softly rubs my back. "I don't have the answers. I wish I did, but I'm just like you. I'm feeling the same anger. I'm feeling the same guilt. I'm feeling the same sadness." She sighs heavily. "Don't blame yourself. None of us knew. None of us noticed how bad it was."

There is a sticky note on the plastic sheath covering the insurance policy. On it he's laid out where he'd like the money to go: funeral costs, paying off the house, taking the trip we were going to take (I'm to bring Julia and Molly with me), and then I'm to save the rest for a rainy day.

"What does he say about funeral arrangements?" Julia asks.

"He wants to be buried in a plot next to Brody. He feels that he should've died that day, and even though he physically survived, he considers that day his true date of death. He wants to be laid to rest next to his brother." I swallow hard because all of this is steadily ripping my heart to shreds. "He says that he didn't die a hero's death, but if possible, he'd like 'Taps' played at his funeral. Oh my God, this is so hard to read." I put the note down until I can better compose myself.

"Savannah! Savannah! Where are you?" Ben calls from the front room. I'm suddenly filled with so much rage that I run through the house and charge at Ben full force. The collision not only startles him but knocks him off his feet. I take advantage of his confusion and pummel the hell out of him while he's on the ground. Lizzy screams at me to stop, but I can't. I hit him over and over until I'm exhausted, and Ben just steadily takes it. When I collapse onto his chest from fatigue, I start to sob. "Why didn't you tell me? Why did you hide the fact that he wasn't doing his job right? I could've gotten him help. He'd still be here if it weren't for you. You have to know that. It's your fault he's gone."

"Savannah!" Julia fusses, trying to lift me off Ben.

"She's not saying anything I haven't already told myself. She's right. Savannah, this probably won't provide you with much comfort, and it doesn't excuse anything, but you have to know that I only did what I thought was best. He was helpful, and he did do a lot of work for me, but eventually it got to be too much for him. I thought I was being a good friend by cutting his workload. I was only trying to help. You have to believe that, Savannah. I'd give anything to do it all differently, but I can't. If you want to spend the rest of your life blaming me, go ahead, but please don't think that I did any of this on purpose."

I'm too tired and emotionally drained to stand, so I carefully crawl my way over to the sofa, prop my face in my hands, and lean back against the cushions. "I'm sorry, Ben," I softly say. "I'm so sorry. Of course you did what you thought was right, and I'm grateful for what you did. I'm just so hurt and so angry. So unbelievably angry." I sigh loudly. "Will you please forgive me?"

"There's nothing to forgive, Savannah," Ben says, picking himself up from the floor. "Will someone please tell us what happened? How did he...," Ben forlornly hangs his head.

"I'll make some coffee. Maybe it would be better for us to sit around the table to discuss the situation," Julia suggests.

I nod. We all follow her into the kitchen, and once we've situated our mugs, I begin to tell the story, "You know I was supposed to fly with him to Colorado, but instead, I dropped him off at the airport because he cancelled my ticket the night before. He told me that he didn't want me to miss more school than necessary, and he also had a whole list of reasons why it would be better for me not to fly with him. I never once suspected anything out of the ordinary. We said our goodbyes, and I left him after he'd passed through security."

"There was nothing he said that seemed odd? His demeanor wasn't off?" Lizzy asks.

I shake my head. "The only thing that makes better sense now than it did before is that he kept telling me everything he does, he does for me. I thought he was talking about getting treatment, or cancelling my flight, or something along those lines. I now know that he was talking about leaving me."

"So, he never got on the plane?" Ben asks.

"No. A deputy showed up at my door earlier today and said that Fletcher left the airport and rented a car. He drove it to some isolated spot not far from I-10, and a patrolman who was making his rounds found him. They believe he took an overdose of sleeping pills, but they won't know for sure until the toxicology results come back. He left this note. It's not the original, but they said I'll get the original as soon as they wrap up the case." I gently place the envelope I'd been fiddling with on the table and push it towards Ben.

"Are you sure?" he quietly asks. I nod. He takes the envelope and excuses himself to read it.

The front door opens and just as quickly, slams shut. "Mom! I got your note saying I should meet you at Aunt Savannah's... Whoa, who died?" Molly jokes. After studying the looks on our faces, anxiety shows on hers. "Mom, did someone die?"

I turn my face away from her.

"Oh, Mom. It wasn't... was it? Did something happen to Uncle Fletcher?"

"Yes, I'm afraid so, sweetheart," Julia answers.

Hearing the distraught wails coming from young Molly kills me. I manage to quickly kiss the top of her head before dashing into our bedroom. My bedroom. There is no more "our." Fletcher left me. He abandoned me. He abandoned all of us, and now he's gone forever while we're left behind to tread water in a sea of sorrow and regret.

After about half an hour of being alone, Lizzy cracks the bedroom door. She tiptoes through the dark room and slips in the bed next to me.

"The pillows smell like him," I whisper. Lizzy doesn't respond. Instead, she lightly strokes my hair. "Are Julia and Molly still here?"

"No," she quietly answers, "they left about ten minutes ago. Julia said she'll come by tomorrow morning to help you with the arrangements."

I nod. "I'm sorry I attacked Ben."

"Don't. We both understand. I'm so sorry that you have to go through this pain again."

"You'd think it would quit hurting so much by now, right? I've been dealing with pain and loss my entire life, yet it still manages to crush me." A single tear rolls from the corner of my eye.

"I don't think it'll ever not hurt to lose

someone you love, Savannah."

"Fletcher wants me to finish school, and he wants me to find someone new to love, and he wants me to go on like none of this has even fazed me. How in the hell am I supposed to do that?"

"You just take it one step at a time. Each day will get easier," Lizzy answers.

"I'm pregnant."

Lizzy sits up in the bed. "What?" she exclaims.

"I didn't want to tell him until he got back because I wanted him to focus on the treatment instead of me. He died without knowing he's going to be a father."

"Oh, Savannah," Lizzy gasps. "Why didn't you say anything before? Are you feeling okay? The stress. The…"

I shake my head. "I'm okay, at least as far as that is concerned. I'm not cramping or bleeding. I promise that I'll try to rest more and to be more careful with how I handle things. If I lose this baby, then I lose everything. I lose my last connection to Fletcher, and I can't let that happen."

"You'll just have to lean on us more. Ben can stay down here for a couple of weeks before he has to go back to Texas. I can stay as long as you need."

"Thank you for being such a great friend. I always wished that you were my sister," I admit.

"What are you talking about?" Lizzy asks. "I AM your sister."

I manage to give her a slight smile before rolling away from her. She moves in close so she can wrap her arm around me, and it's then, with me holding Fletcher's pillow and knowing that Lizzy is at my back, that I'm finally able to sleep.

 sixteen

Fletcher's farewell is very small and intimate. Since it's just Julia, Henry, Molly, Ben, Lizzy, and I, we decide to have a graveside service only. The funeral home arranged for a military burial, and knowing that Fletcher is being honored as the hero he was brings me comfort. I'm dazed throughout the service; I'm startled at the twenty-one gun salute, and tears fall freely during "Taps." I graciously accept the folded flag from the white gloved honor guard member and clutch it to my chest as they lower the man I'd intended to grow old with into his final resting place.

It's not until we're walking away, and I hear Molly tearfully pleading to her father to please take care of her Uncle Fletcher that I can't go anymore. I fall to my knees.

"Savannah, come on. Let's get you home,"

Lizzy says, while Ben helps me to stand.

"Does she need to go to the hospital?" Ben asks with concern.

"She's exhausted," Lizzy explains. "She needs food and rest."

Their voices seem so distant. I look across the cemetery for Lucas' grave, and I easily spot it thanks to the blue teddy bear I keep out there. Standing beside it, I swear that I see Fletcher dressed in his military uniform. He waves to me, reaches his hand to the side, and a little blond boy runs through the headstones to join him. Fletcher points in my direction, and waves again. The little boy looks to see what Fletcher is pointing at, and when he sees me, he smiles and waves frantically.

"Please tell me that you see them. Please," I desperately whisper to Ben and Lizzy.

"See who? Where?" Lizzy asks, looking in the same direction.

"Over there. Do you see them? No, they're leaving. Don't go. Don't go without me."

Fletcher and Lucas blow me kisses then gradually disappear as they walk away hand in hand. I try calling to them, but they don't stop.

I wake up in a cold sweat and gasping for breath. It's the same dream I've had every single night since Fletcher's funeral two weeks before. My first instinct is to touch his side of the bed. It's still empty. I slide out of bed because I know by now that sleep is futile after having "the dream." Clicking on the light in the office, I find Fletcher's journal. It's right where I left it the day I found out he'd died. I hadn't had the heart to open it, but it's time. The first page I turn to happens to be a bookmarked page dedicated to the day we found each other.

I met a girl today, and there is something very different about her. We've never met in person, but I'm drawn to her. Today is supposed to be the day that I end it all—the memories, the pain, the suffering. I called to find out my electric bill balance because I wanted to make sure that I left enough money behind for Julia to pay my outstanding bills. This woman, she intrigued me so much that I've asked her to find me. Maybe she'll do it. I hope she finds me. I don't know what it is about her, but she's special.

I flip to another section.

They were gone for awhile, but now they're back. Why do I get no reprieve? I served my country. I live a good life. Why can't I shake them once and for all? It's like I'm destined to relive the torture, hear their laughter ringing in my ears, smell their briny stench for the rest of my life. I can't live like that. I won't live like that.

I find another entry.

I'm trying so hard to find balance. Savannah is the woman of my dreams, and I know we can have an amazing life together—if I can just be normal. I'm going to keep doing my best to keep the demons at bay. I wish I ruled my life, not them.

I'm so grateful that Savannah's in school now. It's been so exhausting trying to keep the secret day in and day out.

I woke up early this morning, like around three in the morning, and it wasn't until I was fully awake that I realized I was in the kitchen with a steak knife in my hand. What was I going to do with it? Go back in time and kill my captors? Kill myself? Kill Savannah? It's getting bad, much too bad for me to risk hurting her any worse than I already have. She says I gave her life. How tragic would it be if I were the one to accidentally take it from her? I can't let that happen. I won't let that happen. I know what I have to do.

I turn to the last entry.

Everything is set. It's so much harder keeping this from Savannah than I thought it would be, but I know it has to be done. The demons have taken over completely. I used to be able to control them somewhat, but I'm no longer able to fight them. The nightmares are unbearable. The constant fear and paranoia rob me of my every happiness. The blackouts are getting more frequent, and violence comes too easily. I wish I knew for sure that the center could help me, but I feel in my gut that it will only be a temporary fix to a permanent problem. I'm too broken, and the pieces shattered into such tiny pieces that even if I were able to be "fixed," I'd never be right. There are too many scars. Too many regrets. Too many evil memories seared into my brain. Savannah deserves so much more. I love her more than my life, and that's why I feel compelled to sacrifice myself for her happiness. She'll hurt because I know without a doubt that her love for me is

*real and pure, but it's important that she heal from my
passing the same way she healed from the other
tragedies in her life. I envy her strength, I admire her
courage, and I adore her passion. Savannah, if
you're reading this, please promise me that you won't
mourn for too long. Pick up the pieces, stay positive,
continue your schooling, and know that I'm finally at
peace. I'm so tired, Savannah. So incredibly tired
that I can't bear the thought of having to live in my
hell for one more day. Forgive me for being selfish,
my love. I'm not asking you to understand; I'm
asking you to trust that I'm doing what I believe to be
in our best interest. Your love has saved me so many
times, you've been so incredibly patient with me, and I
fear that one day you'll grow resentful. You'd swear
to me that you won't, but sweetheart, I feel it will be
inevitable. It might have been five years down the
road, ten years down the road, maybe even twenty or
more. How are you going to feel when you look back
on your life and realize I'm what held you back?
Savannah, please find happiness, because it's only
through your joy that I will live on. I love you so
much, and I'm so sorry for this. I wish I could've
been the man you thought I was-- the man I wanted to
be for you. Thank you for giving me the best years of
my life. I'm yours always. Fletcher*

    I close the journal and toss it on the desk. I
can't understand why I didn't see it. Why didn't I
pick up on the warning signs? Maybe I should've had
him committed until the bed at the facility came
available? Fletcher would be alive if I had. I feel
laden with guilt and uncertainty. Fletcher begged me
not to feel this way, but it's impossible not to wonder

what might have been. What if I had told him about the baby? Would that have been enough to make him change his mind? My heart aches for him, and my body longs for his touch. My ears crave the sound of his voice, and my eyes would give anything to see him walk through the door. The only concrete sense that I have available to me is his smell. It's still all around me, so I close my eyes and breathe in deeply. *Why did you have to leave me, Fletcher? Why did you have to die?*

Though I'm physically and emotionally exhausted, I resolve to follow Fletcher's final wishes to the best of my ability. It might not be today, tomorrow, or even months from now, but one day my heart will heal. It has to for Fletcher's sake and for the sake of our unborn child.

seventeen

Fletcher wasn't there the day I graduated nursing school, but Julia, Henry, and Molly were. He wasn't there the day that I got my letter stating I'd passed the state boards, but Julia made sure we celebrated with a nice dinner and a small party. Fletcher wasn't there the day I welcomed his son into the world, but Julia was my coach. He also missed it when his daughter arrived twelve minutes later. I think the day the twins were born was the first day that I truly began to heal. It's also the first time I got a sign from Fletcher.

Not long after the twins were born, an elderly gentleman entered the suite. He wore dress blues, and said that he was passing out American flags to the veterans when something drew him to my room. I explained to him that my deceased husband was a war veteran, and he made sure that both of the babies had one of the little flags for their baby books. Though Fletcher wasn't there physically when the children were born, I felt him in my heart. The older gentleman confirmed it for me.

Fletcher Matthew Reilly is every bit the spitting image of his father. Amelia Rose Reilly has some of his features, but the majority of her characteristics are mine. It's difficult being a single mother of newborn twins, so I decide to take a year off before I consider finding a job. Julia and Molly pitch in as much as they can, with Molly going as far as spending the night or entire weekends with me when she's free. We grow incredibly close, and I enjoy watching her grow into a beautiful young woman.

Julia and Henry marry the day the twins turn nine months. The fussy duo makes an appearance with the wedding party by fussing so much that I have to hold them, one on each hip, while standing on the altar with the bride and the groom. Luckily, the guests laugh when the little ones begin a chorus of "dah" and "muh muh muh" back and forth to each other. They also draw laughter when they vigorously shake their heads back and forth in the "no" fashion, then stop long enough to laugh and point at each other before doing it again.

Mortified, I continually whisper to Julia that I'm sorry, even going so far as offering to leave with the babies, but she insists that we all stay right where we are. That's how our family works now. It isn't just me and the babies in one family, and Julia, Henry, and Molly in another, we are one big cohesive unit that works well together. It's hard to believe that Julia is the same woman who gave me the cold shoulder the first day I met her. She was simply sister-in-law once upon a time, but now I consider her a sister in every sense of the word.

Lizzy and I still talk on a regular basis, but she and Ben are so busy with the restaurants that I hardly see her anymore. Additional stores opened in five more states, so most of our conversations happen while she's on the road. She and Ben are incredibly happy even though their life is hectic, and I'm glad that Lizzy has finally found the acceptance she's always craved. Her parents have come around somewhat since learning of Ben's success, but she's still very cautious around them, and in her words, she sees them in "very small doses."

As time goes by, I receive more signs. Most are small; some are huge: a daisy on my doorstep, the babies staring off in a direction where there is nothing to be seen, very vivid dreams. Those signs are my favorite, yet I despised them at the same time. I love how real they feel. I can touch him, smell him, hear him, talk to him. They also make me incredibly sad afterwards when the realization hits that he's not with me anymore. I continue to miss him terribly.

A windfall of signs comes when I take the kids in for their two year old checkups. The children happily play while we wait to be called to the back. They're generally good in the doctor's office, and the fact that Dr. Gettis is also a young single mother makes her all the more understanding on the days when the twins are cranky or in overdrive.

We're finally called to the back and waiting in the exam room, when I start fussing at little Fletcher for digging in the drawers. I'm also asking Amelia to please get up off the floor, and neither one of them wants to listen. I scoop them up and place them on the exam table then make a temporary barricade with my arms. They quiet down as I tell the story of *The Three Little Pigs* in as animated a voice as possible.

"...and I'll huff, and I'll puff, and I'll blooooooooow the house in," I roar. "Not by the hair of my…"

The door opens, and I'm startled to see Dr. Goodman entering the room. "Chinny chin chin?" he asks since I remain silent.

"Yes. Hi," I say dumbfounded.

"Hi, Savannah. Who have we here?" he asks, giving each of the toddlers a tummy tickle. They go nuts.

"Fletcher and Amelia," I answer.

"They're precious. I know that you and Fletcher must be very proud. Congratulations."

Thankfully enough time has passed that I'm much better at answering Fletcher questions.

"Fletcher passed away not long after we last saw you."

I can see the shock on Robert's face. "I'm so sorry. I had no idea. What was it?"

"Suicide," I answer. That word is still just as hard to say, and most of the time, I have to force it out.

"I'm so sorry to hear that. Honestly, I'm at a loss for words."

"Please, don't be. It's been a very long and bumpy road, but we're doing okay. These little munchkins keep me pretty busy." I make a funny face at them, and they burst into another round of giggles. "What are you doing here? It's like you dropped off of the face of the earth, and now you're suddenly back."

"I was offered a job in North Carolina, but it didn't work out. After my two year contract was up, I came back here. I recently bought into this practice, so I don't have a lot of established patients yet. Karen, Dr. Gettis, caught some kind of stomach bug and had to go home early, so I'm taking over her patient list for today."

"Are you still enjoying pediatrics?" I ask.

"Absolutely. It's the best decision I've ever made. What about you?"

"I'm embarrassed to say that I'm still not working. I was going to once the kids turned one, but I couldn't do it. Plus, I was fortunate enough to be able to stay home with them thanks to the life insurance policy Fletcher had taken out. I'll be looking soon, though. I need to become self-sufficient before the money runs out."

"Are you going to work in a hospital or in a doctor's office?" he asks.

"Originally, I wanted to work at a hospital, but now that I have the kids, an office job will offer much better hours."

"Hmmmm." He scratches his forehead. "I hope I'm not being presumptuous, but I need to hire a nurse for my patients. I was going to take out an ad in the paper, but since you're here… would you consider taking the job? I'll offer a competitive salary, benefits, free on-site childcare, and maybe a few other perks."

"Free on-site daycare? Are you kidding me?"

"Not at all. Most of the staff here are young, and a few are nursing mothers who need to be accessible for their children's feeding schedules. There's an area in the back with a small kitchen, a snack area, playroom, and a sitter."

"This can't be happening," I say with surprise.

"It is. Let me finish giving these cuties their checkups, and then you can bring them to the sitter while we discuss it more. Is that okay?"

"Yes! Absolutely," I say, excitement growing by the minute.

They're given an excellent bill of health, growing and progressing right on schedule. Afterwards, Robert introduces me to the sitter, who is a lovely middle aged woman with one of the kindest faces I've ever seen. I instantly like her, and the twins take a liking to her, as well. Once the twins are playing with the other children, Robert and I leave and go to his office. I take a seat while he shuts the door. The first thing I notice on his bookshelf is a scuffed up hard hat.

"I didn't realize being a pediatrician warrants protective equipment," I joke while pointing to the shelf.

He smiles. "There are days I could probably use it, but no, it was my dad's. He was an offshore man for a lot of years, but now he's living the retired life in Costa Rica with his fifth wife."

I draw my fingers to my mouth. "Fifth?"

"Yeah, fifth. This one's only five years younger than I am."

"Wait, what?"

"Wife number four was thirteen years younger."

"Wow."

"He's always the life of the party," Robert says in a mildly reproachful tone while shuffling some papers on his desk. "Anyway, let's talk about the job. The hours would be from seven to four on Monday through Thursday, half day on Fridays. Paid holidays. The in-house daycare. Medical and life insurance are provided for you and your family, spouse included if you…"

"No, it's just me and the kids," I answer. He

nods.

"I'm thinking we'll start you off with an hourly wage, and we'll have a yearly meeting to discuss increases. Sound fair?"

"Yes. Absolutely," I stammer, still in shock over how easily this is all falling into my lap.

"When can you start?" he asks.

"Now wait, I never officially accepted the job," I tease.

"You're going to accept it, and you know it, so admit it," he teases back.

"You don't know that. Maybe I'm entertaining other offers."

"Is that why your face is so lit up right now? Hmmm? You're pondering all the lucrative offers trying to figure out which one is right for you?"

"Maybe," I say with a smile.

"Well, why don't you think about it overnight and get back to me?" He walks around his desk so he can take a seat on the corner closest to me. In doing so, he knocks over a picture of a beautiful Golden Retriever wearing a collar embellished with a faux gem-centered daisy.

"Awww, you accessorize your dog?"

"It's only fitting since her name is Daisy."

"How old is she?"

"She's knocking on eight. I got her as a puppy when I was discharged from the army."

I lean forward in my chair to pick up a picture frame that faces away from me. A beautiful blonde haired girl with huge blue eyes smiles at me. "Is this your daughter? She's so precious."

"No, unfortunately I'm not able to have children of my own. Long story. Anyway, she's my niece, Elizabeth, but we call her Lizzy." His face lights up. "Hey, I hope it's not too much of a faux pas for me to bring this up, but the last time I saw you, you were wearing some sort of princess stuff…"

I'm confused, yet curious as to why he's bringing it up. I give a long, drawn out "yes."

"Maybe you can help me? Her birthday party is coming up this weekend, and it's a princess themed party. I have no clue what to get her. Can you give me some advice?"

"Sure. Where are you planning to shop?"

"Can't I find princess stuff anywhere?"

I laugh. "You're such a boy."

"Thanks for noticing. If it were a soldier party, she'd be set for life." He's quiet for a few seconds, and I can tell he's pondering something heavily. "I have no idea if this is appropriate, inappropriate, or just downright creepy, but do you think maybe you could come with me to pick out some things. I'd be happy to pay you for your time."

I laugh. "It's fine. I'll be happy to help you out, free of charge."

"If you won't accept cash, maybe I could repay you with dinner?"

I freeze for a second. *Am I ready to take this step?* Robert is incredibly handsome and charming, yet I'm uncertain. *Is it a date? Is it just a couple of friends picking up where they left off?*

"Okay, it's obvious that I messed up. Is it too soon to ask for a dinner date? We can cancel dinner if you wish, but will you please still help me with the gift? I seriously have no clue about princess parties. If you do, my undying gratitude will be yours always."

Those last two words seal the deal. I hear you loud and clear, Fletcher Reilly. I look at Robert, a huge grin on my face. "Dinner sounds wonderful," I say with a smile. "It's a date."

RHONDA R. DENNIS

epilogue

Fletcher was right about some things; others I'm forced to figure out on my own. I discover that a person can have more than one true love. Fletcher will always be my first true love, whereas Robert is my here and now. Fletcher flew into my life like a tornado, turning upside down everything I'd ever thought I'd known about living. I needed that jolt—that proverbial kick in the pants. He was the shock to my system that got everything flowing, working, and moving forward. He showed me how to truly live all the way until the day he abandoned his own life because of the incessant pain he kept hidden from us.

I miss him every single day. I'm absolutely convinced that if he hadn't died, we'd still be happily married and raising our sweet little family together. There would have probably been set backs, but we would have dealt with them as they came along, and we would have overcome them—of that I have no doubt. I wish Fletcher would have had the same confidence. We worked so well together because where one slacked, the other was strong.

279

I don't feel that we got a fair shot. We were both damaged goods when we entered our relationship, and we needed to confront our pasts before we could move forward. I found relief by releasing my inner demons. Unfortunately, Fletcher's consumed him. Regardless, I can't go back and rewrite history, though I wish every single day that I could.

Robert is such a good man: patient, kind, caring, loving... I can't even begin to list all of his admirable qualities. I love him dearly. It's not the way I loved Fletcher, but still the love is pure, true, and powerful. I call it mature, or grown-up love. It's the anti-Fletcher, and by that I mean it's not spontaneous and raw, but it's right for me at this point in my life. For instance, Robert and I started our relationship slowly. We spent time truly getting to know each other. I told him all my history in one fell swoop. I wanted to get it all over and done with before progressing past the whole friend/boss-employee situation. He shared his history with me, though his was considerably less tragic, and once that was out of the way, we determined that we were interested in more. It wasn't until our pasts were shared and resolved that we finally decided to begin a romantic relationship. I'm doing things conscientiously, contemplating decisions thoroughly before moving forward, and it's all because of the children. I have them to consider with every decision I make because they are my everything.

It was six months into my new job before Robert and I had our serious conversation about our pasts. Another six months passed before we made the decision to move our relationship from friends who occasionally have dinner together to formally dating. A year later we were engaged, and a year after that, we were married. Having my five-year-old sweethearts beside me when I pledged my love to Robert was one of the most special moments of my life. Three months after that, when Robert officially adopted my children, we became even stronger as a family. Don't misunderstand me; Fletcher still plays a large role in the children's lives even with Robert raising them. Fletcher will always be "Daddy," whereas Robert is "Poppa" to the Reilly-Goodman children. Robert always wanted children of his own, but since he couldn't, he throws every bit of paternal love into helping me raise a couple of wonderful children, and he's absolutely amazing at it.

My once empty heart is filled. I love my life, and I do my best to live each day to the fullest. Happiness has found me, and it's not fleeting; it's forever. What I have with Robert is the real deal. I've finally found my way, but it never would've happened without that random phone call from a stranger who turned out to need me just as much as I needed him. Old Maebelle was right. Marriage sucks, but only because one day it will come to an end. Fletcher, our ending came far too soon. Thank you for sending me the signs. May you rest in peace, my love. Until we meet again, a special piece of my heart belongs to you, and will remain yours always.

the end.

Romantic Suspense by
Rhonda R. Dennis

<u>The Green Bayou Series</u>

Going Home: A Green Bayou Novel Book One

Awakenings: A Green Bayou Novel Book Two

Déjà Vu: A Green Bayou Novel Book Three

Unforeseen: A Green Bayou Novel Book Four

Between Four and Five: A Green Bayou Extra
(Short Story)

Deceived: A Green Bayou Novel Book Five

Green Bayou After Five: Connie's Wild Night
(Short Story)

Between Five and Six: A Green Bayou Extra
(Short Story)

Vengeance: A Green Bayou Novel Book Six

Romantic Comedy by

Rhonda R. Dennis

MAGNOLIA

BLOSSOMS

ABOUT THE AUTHOR

Rhonda Dennis lives in South Louisiana with her husband, Doyle and her son, Sean. She would love to hear from you. Visit her website for more information. www.rhondadennis.net.

Or write to her at:

Rhonda Dennis
P.O. Box 2148
Patterson, LA 70392

To like me, follow me, or leave a review:

Facebook: The Green Bayou Novels
RhondaDennisWrites
Twitter: @RhondaRDennis
Goodreads Author

Made in the USA
Charleston, SC
08 February 2016